THE TENANT

ANGELA LESTER

INKUBATOR
BOOKS

Published by Inkubator Books
www.inkubatorbooks.com

ISBN (eBook): 978-1-915275-48-6
ISBN (Paperback): 978-1-915275-49-3
ISBN (Hardback): 978-1-915275-50-9

THE TENANT is a work of fiction. People, places, events, and situations are the product of the author's imagination. Any resemblance to actual persons, living or dead is entirely coincidental.

PROLOGUE

Through a gap in the curtains she can see the blue light flashing. Darkness is gathering outside. A car door is slammed shut and someone opens the screeching gate. When she hears the doorbell she hauls herself up.

She ignores the second ring. On her way to the stairs, she opens the living room door. The half-light makes everything look black and white, like in an old photo, she thinks. She hasn't been in there for weeks. Everything still seems the same, as if frozen in time: the overflowing ashtray on the table, the pile of magazines on the floor. Her glance falls on the dark stain on the carpet, the bloody handprints on the wall. A movement in the shadows makes her jump. Something scurries over the carpet. The house is infested with mice.

A man is shouting outside, but she slowly makes her way upstairs. The sickly-sweet stench is far stronger here. Now people can smell it outside. The next-door neighbour asked about it the other day. She kicks away the towel rolled against the bottom of the door.

Holding her breath, she presses the handle down. The window is open, the curtain billowing in the cold breeze. The fair hair looks like a halo against the darker pillow. The colour has drained from her face; the white lips are cracked. A skinny arm dangles over the edge. She touches it lightly – it feels ice cold.

There is a crash downstairs as they break the front door open. She walks over to the bedside cabinet where the old alarm clock is still ticking. Next to it is the white plastic bottle with the tranquillisers. She opens the screw top, pops a few pills into her mouth and forces them down.

1

The terraced houses on Chapel Road were all similar, with bay windows on the ground floor and two rooms above. Some looked like student houses to me, with piles of bin bags in the front gardens, while others appeared more respectable with doors and window frames newly painted. Maybe the road had been more upmarket once. I was in a cul-de-sac leading to a railway bridge. No. 112 was right at the end, a pebble-dashed house with dirty lace curtains downstairs. It looked shabby and uncared for. The small front garden was concreted over, but weeds were growing through the cracks and the white paint-work around the windows had turned grey with dirt and age. The low stone wall at the front was bowed with some bricks missing.

I hesitated a moment, then walked up to the front door. I could hear a hoover inside. I rang the bell. When nothing happened, I rang again and then knocked. Suddenly the door was opened.

"Hi." A plump middle-aged woman looked out. She wore

a loose chequered shirt over ill-fitting jeans. Her eyes were a light hazel brown behind square metal glasses.

"I'm here for the room."

"I'm expecting someone in an hour."

"That would be me. We talked on the phone." I had immediately recognised her high-pitched voice, yet it didn't match her matronly appearance.

"Are you Kate, the music student?"

"Yes. Sorry I'm so early. The enrolment was over in no time and there was no point in hanging about..." I trailed off, feeling a bit uncomfortable under her unwavering gaze. "I could come later if that's more convenient."

"No need. I'm Amy." Her podgy hand touched my shoulder. "Sorry for the inconvenience; I haven't finished the cleaning yet."

I followed her into a dimly lit hall. The air was damp and musty, a strange smell mingling with the sharp odour of cleaning fluids. I nearly slipped on the wet tiled floor.

"The bedrooms are upstairs and we can share the rest," she said, leading me through a glass panelled door into a stuffy room. There was an electric fire, a sofa and a couple of upholstered chairs facing a silver television set that could have easily been twenty-five years old. A tall glass-fronted cabinet contained dusty plates and glasses. Here too was the musty smell. I noticed that the wallpaper, an imitation wood grain, was peeling at the window.

"It's a bit damp," I said.

"I'm going to renovate downstairs." She held my gaze. "There was no time for that before. My mother was not well; I looked after her." She sighed. "She was poorly for years. I haven't changed anything since she passed."

"Of course, I understand," I said, quickly doing the maths. She looked middle-aged. There was a lot of grey in her frizzy hair. Her face was pale, the skin oily without any noticeable lines. Her mother could have been in her seventies or eighties for all I knew. No wonder she hadn't decorated yet. It must have been a difficult time for her. She was probably still grieving.

"My mother loved this room. She used to spend a lot of time in here."

"There are some nice old pieces." I glanced at the ugly glass-fronted cabinet. "The house must mean a lot to you."

"Yes, I've always lived here." Without another word she turned around. I followed her into the middle room. She switched on the ceiling light. The small room had only one window to the back and was cluttered with a random assortment of chairs, a rectangular table and dusty shelves. All I saw was the upright piano. It stood against the back wall, a beautiful instrument with intricate designs and candle-holders on either side.

"You can use it if you like," she said. "It would be lovely to hear someone play on it. Didn't you say on the phone you were a pianist?"

"It's beautiful." I stroked my fingers across the dark polished wood. "Is it tuned?"

"No idea." She gave me a sideways glance. "How come you're starting college at your age?"

"I suppose it was something I always wanted to do."

"What did you do before?"

"I was a librarian in Carlisle."

"I suppose you must be good at playing."

"Not as good as I would like to be." I swallowed. "But it's important to me and I need a new start."

"Running away from something, are you?"

"I wouldn't say that." I could feel the blood rushing to my face.

Seeing my embarrassment, she chuckled. "How silly of me. I was only joking. It's good to follow your dreams. Come on." She gently pulled my arm. "I'll show you the rest of the house."

The door to the kitchen was open. She'd been scrubbing the floor. It smelled of bleach. Faux marble laminated kitchen units ran along two sides with a big metal sink in the corner. There were cobwebs near the window and at the corners of the ceiling. But I had been too early and could hardly blame her for not finishing the cleaning.

I followed her up the stairs to the landing. Walking past what seemed to be her room, she quickly closed the door, but not before I had caught a glimpse of the chaos inside: papers and books strewn all over the floor. The bathroom was next to it and another bedroom a bit further down on the other side.

"I've just been sorting out some stuff." She shoved a full bin bag out of the way. "I thought I'd get rid of the pictures for you."

It was a decent-sized room overlooking the back garden. Along the left-hand wall was a pink quilted bed with a matching pink upholstered headboard. Behind the door was a wooden wardrobe. On the other side near the window stood an old-style bureau dresser. The red velvet curtains were half-drawn, leaving the room in a dusky light. It struck me that this would have been her mother's room. There were still marks on the wall, hooks and nails where pictures had hung.

"I would probably paint the walls," I said hesitantly. "If that's OK with you."

"Of course. You can do what you like with it."

I went to the window, my footsteps noisy on the wooden floor and I wondered if there had been a carpet before.

It was a small garden, completely overgrown with trees and shrubs. There was a broken concrete garden cherub half-covered by weeds. I could hear the low rumble of a train going past.

"You hardly hear it when you close the window," she said. "Only a few freight trains go past at night."

"It could be a nice little garden," I said politely. "Do you sometimes get the sun out there?" I turned around. She was still standing in the doorway, as if reluctant to come inside.

"I don't have a lot of time for lying in the sun."

"Of course. You said you were busy. What is it you do?" I asked, remembering the papers in her room.

"I'm writing a book."

"How interesting. What is it about?"

"The past." She hesitated, opened her mouth as if to say more and then closed it again. "That's why I'm renting out the room. I haven't got much time for anything else. It's a lot of work if you take it seriously."

"I bet. I wish I could write."

"Really?" Her eyes held mine. "When are you moving in? Will you drive up to get your stuff?" There was something hasty in her tone of voice, an urgency that made me turn away and look out of the window again.

"It would be nice to have a garden," I said to win time. "Have you had other people interested?" My glance fell on an apple tree among the shrubs. It had some sort of fungal disease, the branches covered with mould. It had produced some apples, but they were all deformed with brown, unhealthy-looking spots. I shivered in spite of my coat.

"No, no one so far. But someone else is coming later on."

"I'll let you know."

"Could you move in straight away?"

"Yes. I've got the necessary things with me. My suitcase is still in the hotel. The other stuff can stay in storage in Carlisle."

"It would save you paying for another night." There was that urgent edge to her voice again.

"That would be good," I agreed, following her downstairs. "I have to watch it, now that I'm not working. Life's expensive with no money coming in."

"You won't get it cheaper anywhere else."

She was right. I'd had a look around the hall of residence. The rooms were as tiny as prison cells: nothing but four walls, a bed, a desk and a wardrobe. It was the only place I could afford, but I hadn't liked it a bit. I also knew that I'd feel out of place, so much older than everyone else.

"Don't leave it too long," she said. "Someone is coming at four o'clock. I have to know by then."

"I'll give you a ring." I shook her hand. "It's a nice house and the piano is a real plus. Thanks for showing me round."

"No problem. Let me know what you've decided," she said and closed the door behind me as I left.

The drizzle that had been coming down all day was beginning to turn into heavy rain. The sky was dark with clouds, a leaden unbroken grey, obscuring the sun. I made my way over to Albany Road and took shelter in Coffee #1.

A waitress brought the tea in a white china pot. I took a sip, trying to calm my unease. "Running away from something." It hadn't been far from the truth. An image of Jeremy surged through my mind, a look of anger on his face. Our last chat had been in a café like this.

I shook my head to shoo away the thought. The brooding only made it worse. It would do me good to have some company, I reasoned, turning my attention back to Amy and the house. She was in her late forties, I guessed, about ten years older than me. She had seemed quite keen. Perhaps she was lonely? Her mother had probably died in that room. But so what? Countless people must have lived and died in these old houses.

I thought of the ceiling rose in the living room. There was definitely potential, the rooms just needed painting and even the garden could be trimmed and tidied up. The position was ideal – so near the college – and it was cheap. My financial situation was beginning to worry me a bit. I didn't have an income now, and the course fees had all but exhausted my savings.

AT HALF PAST three I was standing in front of the house again. I had fetched my suitcase from the hotel and stopped to get some groceries and wine on my way back. I rang the bell. Without the whining of the hoover the old-fashioned chime was clearly audible. It took a few moments until she came to the door.

"Oh hi," she said, as if surprised to see me again. She glanced at my suitcase. "I was beginning to get a bit worried: you didn't phone."

"But here I am, ready to move in," I said cheerfully. "If that's still OK with you. Is the other person from the agency still coming?"

"I cancelled the viewing," she said. "Of course, the room is still yours if you want it. You know where it is, so I'll let you get on with it. I haven't finished the hoovering yet."

"I've bought a bottle of wine and cheese." I handed her the shopping bag. "Maybe we can have a glass later on."

She peered into the bag. "Thanks, but you shouldn't have."

"What time shall I come down?"

"Any time you like. Whenever it suits you."

I could hear the TV in the living room, some sort of game show she was watching. She was probably having a break from her cleaning. I stepped over the hoover and carried my heavy suitcase upstairs.

I opened it on the bed and got out my new paisley-printed scarf. I had wondered what would be suitable for wearing at college and on my last day in Carlisle I'd gone into town and bought some bits and pieces in Gap: a leather bag, a few new blouses and the beautiful boho-style scarf.

I glanced across the room. As before, my attention was drawn to the hooks and discoloured patches on the wall. The wallpaper, with its pattern of lilac roses, looked dark and gloomy in the fading light. Perhaps I should hang up some photos. I had to make the best of my new place. Realising that I was still clutching the scarf, I unclenched my fingers and dropped it on the bed. This was a new start, and I had to leave the past behind – it really didn't matter anymore.

I changed out of my damp slacks into a more comfortable pair of jeans and unpacked quickly, putting dresses on hangers, tossing the underwear onto the top shelf of the wardrobe, stacking my books on the table. I would need some sort of carpet to dampen the sound. The echo of my footsteps was beginning to unsettle me.

I crossed the room and fully opened the curtains, but the afternoon light that seeped through the dirty windows was murky and grey. It was still raining. Raindrops splattered across the window, blurring my view. I thought of Amy's relieved expression and wondered if I should have given her a ring. She had cancelled the other viewing because of me.

I stood for a long while looking out. The future was uncertain. No wonder I felt a bit edgy. For once I had changed the course of my life and made a decision. I had to make a success of it. There was nothing much left for me in Carlisle. It would be impossible to go back to the library now and work with Jeremy again. Not after what had happened in the summer.

I caught sight of the bulging bin bag outside. It was the one I had seen on the landing earlier on. A wooden picture frame was sticking out.

"I was wondering about the rent," Amy startled me out of my thoughts. I swung around, surprised to see her in the doorway. I hadn't heard her coming in.

"I'm a bit out of pocket with all the bills I had to pay," she said in her high-pitched voice. "I'm really sorry, but I was wondering if you could give me the money now."

"No problem." I picked up my purse. Luckily I had been to the bank.

"Thanks." She took the three hundred pounds. "Have you eaten? I'm starving. The miserable weather always makes me hungry. I could order a pizza for us." Her eyes darted around the room as if to see whether I had made any changes.

"Yes, fine." I wondered about the bread and cheese but didn't want to ask. Shortly after I heard the delivery man at the door.

When I made my way downstairs I found her in the living room, the pizza still in its box, two plates and wine glasses on the low wooden table in front of her. It was warmer than upstairs. She had turned the fire on – an old-fashioned gas fireplace with artificial coals and bright blue flames.

She opened the box, cut the pizza and handed over the plate with my half: pepperoni and tomato, not exactly what I would have chosen. I poured the wine. The glasses were beautiful with pale green bowls and amber stems.

"Lovely glasses. Were they your mother's?"

"Yes, I think so." She shrugged. "But she never drank out of them. She didn't care much for pretty things." We started eating.

"It can't have been easy for you," I said, interrupting the awkward silence. "Looking after her..."

"No, it wasn't." She licked her fingers, smeared with tomato sauce. "She was in a bad way."

"I'm sorry." I took a sip of my wine. "What was wrong with her?"

"She had a problem," she said, gazing at me. "She drank herself to death. It started when I was still at school. She wrote me sick notes when she needed me at home. She'd work for a couple of weeks and everything would seem OK – until something happened again and bang! She'd buy a bottle of gin and go on another bender. The sober periods grew shorter every time. In the end she gave up working altogether. Over the last few years she didn't even get out of bed anymore."

Lost for words, I took another bite of my greasy pizza. I had to force myself to eat. Thick slices of pepperoni sat in pools of melted cheese.

She refilled our glasses.

"It must have been so terrible for you," I said eventually.

"Why are you whispering?" She chuckled. "Don't worry, she's gone – she won't come back."

"Of course not." I managed a smile.

"What about you?" she asked. "I'm sure you had a better time. Your parents must have been proud of your piano playing. Did they expect you to become a celebrated pianist?"

"I don't think so." The word celebrated made me laugh. "My dad wanted me to have a secure career." I told her about my father and the tobacconist's shop he had managed.

"And what about your mother?" she asked. "I bet she wanted you to go to music college."

"Not at all. Playing the organ in church would have been more up her street. She thought that artists and musicians were expendable. Or maybe she thought that I wouldn't get in anyway."

"And then you did what they expected? How boring is that?" She shook her head in mock-dismay.

"Yes." I laughed. "I suppose that's what I'm like. But I didn't mind being a librarian. It wasn't a bad decision. I quite liked my job."

"But what about your playing? I hope you didn't give it up." She looked disappointed.

"Not really, though I stopped practising for quite some time when my sister died. It was a sad time, but in the end I took it up again. I was never good enough to be a concert pianist, but I still could be a teacher. I just have to do it now, before I'm too old." I leaned back, relaxing into the sofa. I had never talked about it like that before. Amy's directness was strangely liberating.

She wore her frizzy hair tied back. Her face was a bit flushed from the wine and her light eyes seemed to have more colour and life. She looked almost pretty in the warm glow of the standard lamp. I remembered how I had worried about making friends, how shy and awkward I always felt in social situations, and yet here I was, drinking wine with Amy, opening up to her and talking about the past.

"Here's to the future," I said, raising my glass. "I'll help you with the decorating. It'll be fun. The house will scrub up nicely, you'll see. We're going to make a good team."

2

Dr Jack Turner was my personal tutor. He was in his mid-forties, tall with greying hair and square Ray-Ban glasses. I had met him during freshers' week. With my sweaty hands clasped tightly I had sat in the armchair opposite his desk as he talked me through the assignments. There were essays to be delivered on time, oral and written exams and of course performances, including a big concert at the end of term. Sensing my unease, he looked at me with concern and asked if there was anything bothering me. I explained to him that it wasn't the academic work but the performing I was a bit worried about. I told him that I had never played for a bigger audience before and that I wasn't very confident.

"It'll get better with experience," Dr Turner had said, smiling. "You'll get used to it soon enough. I saw in the entry audition that you can play." There was no hint of condescension in his voice, but I could tell that he was just being kind. Performing in front of the lecturers had been nerve-racking. I had just about struggled through the repertoire of grade eight pieces with stiff, cold hands.

Glancing around the foyer now, I could still not quite believe that I was actually part of this. It felt as if they had turned a blind eye. I was determined to prove that Dr Turner's kindness had not been wasted on me, that I was worthy of the chance he'd given me. The students stood around in groups, chatting. I recognised faces from the introductory tutorial, but no one seemed to notice me as I made my way to the stairs. Term was starting slowly; there was only one lecture today, an introduction to music history focused on the eighteenth century.

I was about fifteen minutes early, and the big lecture theatre on the second floor was still empty. I sat down in the last but one row of wooden seats, got out my pen and paper and had another look at my lecture timetable. From the corner of my eye, I saw Dr Turner enter, carrying a big pile of books. He left them on the desk at the front.

"Hello there," he said, stopping on his way out. "I was wondering if I could ask you a favour. The choir needs an accompanist. We're doing Mozart's Requiem. Our pianist is on leave until December." He paused a moment, his intelligent eyes expectantly fixed on me. "Let me know. You'd be really helping us out and it would be a good opportunity for you to get used to it." And then he hurried out of the door, maybe to fetch more books.

A few students were coming in through the side door, amongst them Gemma Adams, a chubby girl with fuzzy blonde hair and butterfly glasses. I knew her from the introductory meeting. Gemma was from Carlisle, like me. We'd even been to the same school, a chaotic comprehensive on the outskirts of town – she of course twenty years later than me.

"Hi," she said, sitting down next to me. "Were we supposed to read something to prepare for this?" She glanced at the pile of books on Dr Turner's desk and let out a sigh. "I haven't even looked at the reading list yet."

More and more students were coming in now and the theatre was filling up. A red-haired girl in front of us turned around.

"We shouldn't have had that last drink," she said to Gemma with an exaggerated grimace. "Or maybe I should have stayed in bed. Nothing happens in the first week anyway. My head is killing me."

"Your own fault, you wanted it." Gemma laughed. "You still owe me the money for the taxi."

Dr Turner came back in and closed the door. The noisy chatter gradually died down as he went to the front and set up his PowerPoint.

"Good morning, everyone," he began. "Who can tell me about the eighteenth century? Who were the most influential composers?"

A girl in my row raised her hand.

The lecture went by in a daze. I still could not believe he had asked me to do the accompaniment for his choir. He obviously had faith in me – certainly more than I had in myself. I made a lot of longhand notes, scribbling into my new notebook, only now and then looking up at the Power-Point so as to avoid his gaze. It had been a kind offer, but I needed more time to think about it. It would be best to leave straight afterwards before he had the chance to mention it again.

Towards the end he talked about the coursework we had to hand in by the end of November. The essay had to explore how baroque music bridged the gap between Renaissance and early music. Everything was done electronically these days, of course, and we could log into a website for all the information we needed.

"Not much time, with everything else we've got to do."
Gemma moaned as we got up.

"You'd have more time if you stopped going on about it."
The red-haired girl had caught up with us at the door.

"Yeah, right." Gemma pulled a face. "You can't copy the
stuff from the Internet here. They'll find out straight away."

They obviously knew each other well. Everyone was
leaving now. I briefly lost sight of them in the crowd, but they
waited for me in the foyer.

"Coming along?" Gemma asked. "We're having something
to eat in Aberdare Hall."

"Not today." Looking up, I saw Dr Turner on the stairs.
"I've got to be somewhere." They both stared at me, startled
by the note of panic in my voice. "Maybe another time." I
quickly walked off, through a swing door and then into the
library.

A few students were sitting at the tables, reading and
writing. For a moment I just stood there, taking it in: fingers
tapping at a keyboard, the whir of a copy machine, the
hushed voices. The windowless room with its rows of book-
shelves and humming light was so much like the library in
Carlisle. I inhaled the familiar smell. It would be so much
easier, so much safer to order books, conduct searches – do
what I had done successfully for all those years.

I found Mozart's Requiem at the back among the other
vocal and orchestral scores and the librarian, a friendly
middle-aged woman, checked it out. The corridor was empty,
but there was music coming from most of the practice rooms.
I wondered if I should find an empty room to have a go at the
Mozart, but then decided to go home. I needed time and
space to think.

The sun had come out and it was noticeably warmer now
as I stepped out of the red-brick building. There were
students sitting on the grass, chatting in little groups of threes

and fours or eating their sandwiches. I kept my gaze straight ahead as I walked past, hoping that Gemma and her red-haired friend weren't amongst them.

AMY HAD GIVEN me a spare set of keys and I let myself in through the front door. The house felt empty: the breakfast dishes were still on the kitchen table, the heating was off and the kitchen had a depressing feel. As in the other rooms the wallpaper was stained with damp. The windows were so dirty they didn't let in much light. I switched on the ceiling lamp, but the naked 40-watt bulb only added to the cheerlessness.

There was not much in the fridge – just a bottle of Diet Coke and the piece of cheddar I had bought the other day, still unopened in its plastic wrapping. Not quite sure what to do, I put the kettle on and, waiting for it to boil, opened the door to the garden to let in some air.

My glance fell on the bin bag outside. It was the stuff Amy had discarded from her mother's room. The bag was undone. I took out the wooden picture frame and put it right side up. It was the portrait of a woman. There were the bookshelves and I straight away recognised the piano. The photo had been taken some time ago when the house had been in a much better state. She was sitting at the piano, her hands on the keys. She was beautiful in a pre-Raphaelite way: the fair complexion, her long red hair, those slender pale hands. There was a faraway expression in her eyes. Could that be Amy's mother, I wondered. Who else would it be? She looked nothing like Amy, and she certainly didn't look sick – there were no tell-tale signs of her drinking. Had the picture been in her room? How depressing for her to look at her younger, more beautiful self when she'd been in such a terrible state later on.

There was other stuff: a portrait of the young Beethoven

with short dark hair and piercing dark eyes and, digging deeper, I found a couple of porcelain cherubs and vases. What else had Amy thrown out? There had been no clothes in the wardrobe, no personal things at all.

I shivered in my thin jumper. The sky had clouded over, and it looked like rain. A sudden gust of wind made the apple tree rustle and rattled the open windows upstairs. I looked up and, for a fleeting moment, thought I saw a movement up there in my room. I kept on looking, but there was nothing, just the curtains billowing slightly in the breeze.

I laughed at myself. No one was watching me. I had probably just imagined it because I felt guilty for snooping around. I quickly put the pictures back into the bag, taking care to leave them in the position they had been before.

The water had boiled. I made myself a cup of tea and took it with me into the middle room. The tall piano with its polished wood glowed darkly. I opened the stool and saw some sheet music inside. I glanced through it: mainly Beethoven, Schubert and Bach. Sitting down, I tried a few chords. The sound was amazing. I blew against my cold hands and ran my fingers through the first movement of a Schubert Impromptu.

I hadn't been playing very long when I sensed again that someone was watching. Looking up, I saw Amy in the open doorway, peering in from the dark hall.

"I didn't want to interrupt," she said.

"I thought I was on my own." I closed the lid.

"I was in my room."

"I found the scores in the piano stool. Were they your mother's? It's quite demanding stuff."

"I don't know anything about it." For a moment her face grew distant and sullen. "Maybe she played it when she was younger. I told you that she stayed in bed most days."

She brightened a bit then as she came nearer and glanced

at the score. "It sounded really good. You told me everyone else was better than you. I thought you were just a beginner."

"I didn't say that. I just..." My voice was shaky and, to my embarrassment, I felt a prickle behind my eyes. The tension I had felt all day suddenly got on top of me. I swivelled round on the piano stool, so that she wouldn't see. "I just don't like performing."

"Why is that?"

"I don't know. It's stressful." I got up, wiping away the tears. "I think about the mistakes I can make and then everything goes wrong..." One arm around my shoulders, she led me into the living room, like a mother would lead a sick child. She sat next to me on the sofa.

"What's brought this on?" she asked.

I told her about the choir.

"But you don't have to do it." She gave me a paper handkerchief. "Why don't you tell him to ask someone else? It's not fair to put so much pressure on you."

"No. I think he wants to help me." I blew my nose. "I told him that I'm not comfortable with performing. He wants me to get used to it and lose my fear."

"But you don't really need to perform a lot, right?" She frowned. "You only want to be a teacher. Why all that extra stress with the choir? You'll just have to get through the stuff for your degree."

I took a deep breath. "But I don't want to let him down. He's been so kind to me..." I trailed off.

"'He's been so kind to me,'" she chuckled. "It almost sounds as if you fancy him."

"He's a very nice man," I said stiffly. For a moment I felt like walking out on her and that grimy old house. If only I had not given her the rent... My glance fell on the unsightly damp patch beneath the window.

"Why don't we make a start on the decorating?" Her tone

had softened. "Sorry for winding you up. I was only joking. The house is really getting me down. Let's go and buy the paint."

"Why not?" I nodded. She was right, of course. We really had to make start. The wallpaper in my bedroom gave me the creeps. It was the pattern Amy's mother had looked at for all those years from her bed. I had been awake for hours in the night, lying on my side, my eyes fixed on the opposite wall, just able to make out those eerie roses in the dark, sensing her spirit was still in there. No wonder I was feeling a bit edgy.

"And I'm starving," Amy said, getting up. "Maybe we can get something to eat on Newport Road. You're hungry too?"

"What sort of food are you thinking of?" I said, still a bit miffed. "I'll have to get some money from the machine."

"Nothing too expensive." She rubbed her chubby hands. "So what's the plan? Are we going? I could do with a burger. I know where we can get the paint."

HALF AN HOUR later we were at the McDonald's on Newport Road. We sat down at a table near the window with our tray of chicken burgers and chips. The table was dirty with crumbs and ketchup smudges. A girl in uniform who'd been mopping the floor came over and wiped it clean. There was a group of teenagers at the table next to us, shouting and laughing.

"We should get in some food," I said over the noise. "We need to eat something healthy – like vegetables and fruit."

"Maybe we can buy a microwave." She grabbed a couple of chips and popped them into her mouth.

"Did you cook for your mother?"

"She didn't care much for food. She had a lot of stomach

trouble. She wouldn't have eaten vegetables anyway. Sometimes she didn't eat for days."

"But it can't have always been like that."

Amy didn't answer and for a minute or two we focused on our food. She was eating fast. Her face was glistening with perspiration. When had she had her last proper meal, I wondered. There never seemed anything else but crisps in the house. She was wearing the blue and white chequered shirt again, which looked a bit grey at the sleeves. It struck me that she probably didn't have the money to buy herself new clothes.

"When did your mum buy the house?"

"I don't know," she answered, chewing. "Before I was born."

"That would have been in the sixties?"

"Yes, around that time," she said vaguely. She looked across to the teenagers. "Kids! Why do they always make so much noise?"

"It must have been a nice house back then."

"Why?"

"I was wondering about your mum. When did she start drinking so much?"

"When I was little. What does it matter?" She wiped her mouth with a paper napkin. "The house has always been a dump. Anyway, it's all in the book I'm writing."

"Are you writing about your childhood?"

"Yes." She sat back, her big arms folded. "I've written the first chapter. There's a lot about my mother. I don't want to talk about it now. It only gets me down. Maybe you can read it when it's finished."

AFTERWARDS WE WENT TO B&Q a little further down the road. We asked for directions and a thin young man in a suit came with us down the aisle and showed us around. We chose the paint he recommended, a light magnolia for my room, blue for the bathroom and pale yellow for downstairs. Adding paintbrushes, rollers and scrapers, we rolled our rattling trolley to the till.

WHEN WE CAME HOME it was already getting dark. I felt like starting straight away. I filled a bucket in the bathroom and with a brush started wetting the wallpaper near the door; it was the section you saw from the bed. The soft wet paper was quite easy to scrape off.

It was all about being in charge and changing the things that held me back. Seeing the shreds of that horrible paper come off in big pieces was a relief. The darkness in me was beginning to lift. With every stripped sheet, I was feeling more energised and positive.

A fleeting image of Jeremy bubbled up. Taking off the sodden old paper felt like ripping those memories out of my mind: the lonely evenings waiting for him. "You're a liability," he'd said in the café. "You're crazy, phoning me up in the middle of the night. And now you can't even remember shouting at me. You should see someone about your drinking."

All the time I could hear Amy downstairs – the TV was blaring again – there were voices and music. After a couple of hours, my fingers and knuckles began to hurt from the peeling. It was getting late. The top layer was gone. But there was another layer underneath: an egg white under paper, which was softer and much more tricky to scrape off.

When I went downstairs to fetch a couple of bin bags, I found Amy in the front room, watching *Casualty*.

"It took longer than I thought. I'll do the painting tomorrow," I said.

"I'm surprised you can see in that dim light." She chuckled. "You must be determined."

It was nearly eleven when the final strip came off. I called Amy to show her what I had done.

"Wow," she said, stepping into the soggy mess. "I'm so glad you got rid of it. You really deserve a reward." She reached into the pocket of her jeans and got out a packet of pills. "I had them in my drawer – they're still OK. Diazepam." She smiled. "It's just what you need. My GP prescribed them when I couldn't sleep, after my mother had died. It really got to me. It says in the instruction leaflet that they're also for anxiety. They'll calm you down a bit and help with the performing. You can take them when you have to play for that choir."

"I'm not sure." I reluctantly turned the red-white packet in my hand. "I can't just take tablets that are meant for someone else."

"Don't worry. You can check them on the Internet. Lots of people take them. They're not dangerous." She cocked her head to one side. "Unless you take them all at once." She chuckled. "No, honestly, they really make a difference. It's up to you. Anyway..." She glanced at my bare walls. "Now you've made a start I suppose I'll have to do downstairs as well."

But she didn't of course. She soon lost interest – and as I was busy and not prepared to do all the work on my own, the room remained unchanged for all those months I lived with her. At first, we joked about it, but when things became more difficult, it was never mentioned again.

3

The following week was busy. I went to more classes, met new lecturers and saw the same students again. Gemma Adams was in most of my courses and we sometimes had coffee or lunch together in Aberdare Hall. The sister of her red-haired friend had been to the Music Department before. Gemma knew a lot of gossip through her.

"He was going through a messy divorce a couple of years ago," she said when she was sitting next to me in History again. Dr Turner had turned his back to us as he was setting up his PowerPoint. "He was suspended for months."

"Why? What happened?" I whispered back.

"Affairs," she answered, her eyes shining. "Couldn't keep it in his pants. He had a thing with a first-year student. Or was it sexual harassment? I can't remember. Anyway, it was the reason he got divorced. His wife had probably had enough." She dramatically rolled her eyes. "Sandra's sister said he nearly lost his job because of it."

Throughout the fifty minutes lecture I kept surreptitiously glancing at him, only half-concentrating on his slide show of eighteenth-century instruments. With his open face and jovial manner he seemed like a family man to me rather than someone who would go off the rails and cheat on his wife. Was his easy charm just a front, a part of his public persona, I wondered. The expression of his mouth, the way it now and then curled into an ironic smile, when an answer was not to his liking, suggested that there was a different side to him.

He appeared to be popular with the students. I had heard that he had a daughter who was still at school. Someone else had told me that he had composed several pieces and was quite well known in the Welsh music scene. He had apparently been friends with Simon Rattle in Birmingham, where he earned his first degree.

When the lecture was over, I made my way downstairs to find an empty practice room. I had still not made up my mind about the choir, quietly hoping that he would ask someone else. But I had started practising the Mozart anyway. Playing relaxed me between classes. I liked the anonymity of the practice rooms, the musty smell, and that it was always half dark in there because of the narrow windows. I had just started playing when someone knocked. I expected a student and was a bit startled to see Dr Turner's face in the door.

"I thought it might be you," he said. "Sorry to interrupt your Mozart, but could you come to my office later to talk about the accompaniment? I need to give you the rehearsal schedule." He gave me a broad, pleasant smile. "Sounds excellent," he said. "Keep up the good work."

My heart was beating faster as I carried on playing. How could I get out of it now?

Eventually I made my way upstairs.

"Come on in," he said, opening the door. He was talking on his mobile. "I won't be long," he mouthed in my direction and motioned to me to sit down.

"The train gets in at six," he said in a low voice. "I'll pick you up at the station."

I took a seat, pretending not to listen. There were a couple of framed pictures on his desk, family photos by the look of it. One showed him together with a happy looking woman and a slightly chubby girl. It was a holiday photo somewhere by the sea. The woman was pretty with big sunglasses and a white canvas hat. I thought about what Gemma had told me about his divorce. Were they still getting on well, I wondered. The photo made me sad – it reminded me of Jeremy again, of the holiday in Rome we'd had together.

Dr Turner ended his call and sat down at his desk. "Sorry for making you wait. How is college treating you?" He picked up a paper. "Let me give you that rehearsal schedule first."

I took a deep breath. "Maybe it would be better to ask someone else."

"But I just heard you practising it." He gave me a vaguely puzzled look, and I felt the same embarrassment I had experienced at our first meeting. It was flattering that he wouldn't take no for an answer, but it also made me tense. He'd obviously made up his mind to get me out of my comfort zone.

"I understand that you're a bit nervous," he said, "but I think you worry too much. No one will judge you. It will be just for the first couple of months. Our usual accompanist will be back in December, and we'll have an orchestra for the performance." He glanced at his watch. "In fact, you could join the altos later on. We're all struggling through at the moment." He got up, the hearty smile still on his face. "I would be very grateful indeed. Why don't you just give it a go?"

I heard his mobile go off again in the pocket of his grey jacket. "Sorry – I'm a bit pressed for time," he said. "But there will be tutorials soon. I hope we can talk a bit longer then. Will I see you at rehearsal?"

The hand he held out was cold, the fingers long, white and slender. I shook it, though I was still unsure, and left the office with a feeling of unease.

In the foyer downstairs I ran into Gemma. We decided to have lunch and made our way to Aberdare Hall. She was surprised when I told her the news as we stood in the queue for our chicken curry and chips.

"When did he ask you?" She playfully pinched my arm. "You're a dark horse. Why didn't you tell me before?"

"I don't know if I can pull it off."

"Of course you will. He must think you're up to it."

When we had got our food she steered me towards a table near the window.

Her eyes wandered about, looking who else was there.

"Look," she said, glancing at the table next to us. "They don't come here often."

I followed her eyes. There was a couple, a newspaper spread out in front of them. They looked older than the other students, in their late thirties perhaps. The man was tall and thin in a slightly crumpled light suit. His lank hair fell over his forehead as he was reading, and there was something effeminate in the way he kept pushing it back. The woman was striking with short blonde hair.

"Isn't she beautiful?" Gemma said.

"Yes, quite unusual." I tried not to stare too obviously. She wore her hair in cropped layers. It framed her face and lay close on the sides and back of the head. She reminded me of Twiggy or other actresses from the sixties like Mia Farrow in *Rosemary's Baby*. The style was perfect for her delicate features and large grey eyes. The expression on her face was a mix of boredom and distaste. It made me wonder what he was reading to her.

"Do you know them?" I had lowered my voice, but the cacophony of chatter was so noisy I had to ask again.

"That's Clara. She teaches singing at college. Sandra had a lesson with her. She said that she's a bit aloof, not very chatty anyway. Doesn't give much away. I guess she's not a people person. I heard she was a member of the Welsh National Opera. She had been in the chorus. I don't know why she left. Perhaps she didn't get on with them – no idea... But she has a really beautiful voice. You'll meet her at choir. She's singing the soprano solo." She shrugged. "They're in a world of their own."

"Are they together?"

"No, he's gay – but they share a house. Philip teaches composition. He's a composer himself. His mother is German. Someone said he's got a lot of money from her side. Dr Turner is friends with them. Sandra's sister went to a party at their house. She was in Philip's composition class. It was quite extravagant apparently; they made music together, jazz, that kind of thing, and it went on until the early hours. She said that people were taking cocaine... There were a lot of excellent musicians. She was flattered to be invited."

"Where do they live?"

"In a beautiful old house in Pontcanna."

I glanced over again. They'd finished their coffee. The man folded the paper and got up. Clara said something that made him laugh and then they walked away, he ahead, not quite as tall as I had thought at first. She followed in his wake, slow and straight-backed like a dancer, illuminated by the bright light that came through the overhead window. Neither of them had noticed that we'd been watching them.

THE REHEARSAL WAS on Friday evening, six to eight, in the big concert hall. I had been determined not to take Amy's tranquillisers, but as the day came nearer my resolve began to waver. Amy showed me a reassuring report on the Internet. It said that Diazepam was quite safe – as long as you only had one now and then when needed. You had to take them regularly for weeks to become addicted. I was so desperate that it didn't take much for me to change my mind.

I took a couple half an hour in advance, as advised in the instruction leaflet, but my stomach was in knots. Entering the foyer through the main entrance, I had to force myself to go through the double-door of the hall and not turn around and walk away in the other direction.

There was the same commotion that precedes any kind of choir rehearsal: someone at the entrance giving out scores, people standing together in groups chatting while others rearranged the rows of chairs. Dr Turner was standing at the piano, talking to Clara. She was wearing a simple knee-length skirt with a crisp white blouse, an outfit that might have looked dowdy on someone else, but really suited her.

I hesitantly made my way towards them. They looked at ease with each other. Of course: Gemma had told me that they were friends.

"Thank God, there she is," Dr Turner said, smiling. "Excellent! We've got the soloist, the pianist..." He glanced around the room, waiting for the noise to die down, and for a moment I wondered if there was still a chance to make my excuses. With a giddy feeling I sat down and adjusted my stool.

"I can turn the pages," I heard Clara volunteering to Dr Turner. She had a rather deep voice, unusual for a soprano, I thought. She was standing next to me now, but didn't bother to introduce herself or address me directly.

"Thanks." I didn't look up.

"Kate will take over on the piano for the time being," Dr Turner announced. There was a short burst of applause. "Let's take it from the beginning. The Introitus!" He raised his hands.

I started a bit fast, but carried on. My fingers flew over the keyboard, running through the familiar patterns. Determined to get through it, my eyes were fixed on the music, hardly paying attention to Dr Turner's conducting. I played mechanically – without much expression or what my former teacher would have called "the sacredness" of it. But my hands were doing the job and my knees weren't shaking. It had to be down to the pills. Only when Clara turned the page halfway through the first movement, I suddenly came to a halt.

"Good place to stop." Dr Turner let out a congenial laugh. "So far, so good, but let's take it from the Exaudi again – and if the tenors could sing up a bit this time; I could hardly hear you."

There was a moment of silence, but I could hear Clara behind me, her quiet breathing and the shuffling of her feet.

"Or rather let's begin with the soprano solo – Clara, would you please do your bit?"

I raised my eyes when Clara stepped forward and started to sing: "Te decet hymnus..." Her voice was sweet-toned and serene, ideally matched to Mozart. I watched her over the piano as I tried to blend in. She was standing slightly in front of me now. For a moment I felt at one with her in the magic harmony of Mozart's music, dazzled by the effortless flow of her singing. I almost knew that part of the score by heart. But it didn't last. When I looked at the music again, I had suddenly lost where I was. Clara turned around, her eyebrows raised.

Dr Turner made us go through it a few more times but we didn't achieve that harmony again – in fact my playing seemed to become more self-conscious and wooden with every repeat. I was relieved when the rehearsal was finally over.

There were some general announcements: the concert

would be on the last Saturday before Christmas at St David's Hall. There would be a full orchestra and an all-day rehearsal the weekend before.

I allowed myself to look around the room and made out some faces I knew: Gemma, her friend, Sandra, and several others I remembered from the lectures. Clara didn't talk to me; she didn't smile.

"Well done." Dr Turner came over. "Can we rely on you until November? I hope you can join the choir later and sing with us in the concert. Will you come along for a drink in the Mackintosh? We always go there after rehearsal."

"Of course, why not?" I replied, taken by surprise. I waited for Gemma. She was chatting with one of the basses, a bearded student with straggly hair. By the time she had finished everyone else had left.

"Well done," she said. "See, I told you that you'd be all right." But I had a feeling that she was just being kind.

THE PUB WAS HEAVING with young people when we arrived. The music students had pushed two tables together. They were already cluttered with glasses and bags of crisps. We fetched a couple of low stools from the bar and somehow managed to squeeze in. Everyone was talking in raised voices, shouting over the noise.

Gemma went to the bar to get the drinks. My eyes followed her as she wound her way around the tables. There was a queue and it took a while until she got served. I let my glance wander around the place and saw that Clara hadn't turned up – nor had Dr Turner. Why had he asked me to come, I wondered, when he hadn't intended to come himself?

"Thought you could do with a large one." Gemma handed over a glass of red wine. "It really wasn't so bad," she said with a smile. "You were just a bit tense – that's all." She patted my shoulder. "It'll be better next time."

"Clara was really good." I took a big sip of my wine. "What an amazing voice she has."

"Yes, I told you, didn't I?" she shouted back. "Look, there she is."

Clara had just come through the door. She hardly looked in our direction and straight away made her way to the bar.

Gemma downed her pint of Stella.

"I told you she keeps herself to herself," she kept on shouting. "I bet she will stay there all evening. She's probably waiting for Dr Turner. He's the only one she bothers with. She never sits with us."

"How could she sit at our table? There's no space," I said into her ear. She didn't seem to mind my sharp tone; maybe she hadn't even noticed it.

She told me about a night out dancing with her friends at a club in town. I couldn't hear her very well through the chatter, but I nodded now and then, pretending to be interested. Once, I cast a furtive glance at the bar where Clara sat drinking on her own with her back to us. I still felt the look she'd given me earlier on and wasn't keen to talk to her, but Gemma had finished her drink, and I could hardly leave without buying my round.

Several people were waiting to be served. Clara was at the end of the bar, nursing a cocktail. There were a couple of girls between us. I hoped that she wouldn't notice me but she did. Before I could turn away she raised her hand and beckoned me over. I caught a glimpse of myself in the mirror behind the liquor bottles: startled and flushed, my eyes wide open.

"Hi," she said. "What was the problem earlier on?"

"I don't know."

She leaned slightly forward, her large grey eyes fixed on me. "Was I too slow for you? I think we were out of sync."

"Sorry, I know. I'm only covering and I wasn't well prepared. I told Dr Turner that I wouldn't be very good."

"He must have thought that you were good enough." She half-smiled. "Are you a postgrad?"

"No, it's my first term. I was a librarian before."

"And then you suddenly decided to do music?"

"No, not suddenly." I faltered. "I suppose I always wanted it."

"But you became a librarian instead." She gave me an intense, evaluating look. My face was burning up – I was far too warm in my turtleneck jumper.

"Sorry," I said. "I'm just not used to playing in public."

"Well, maybe he'll find someone else... if you're not even enjoying it." She turned away.

"My sister died when I was ten," I said abruptly. "It was difficult for me. I didn't play for years... I nearly gave up altogether."

"I'm sorry you had a difficult time." She glanced at me, more cordially now. "Those early years are crucial for playing." She hesitated. "Maybe we can practise together if that would help – just to get the timing right... you could come to my place..."

"Yes, maybe," I mumbled. A student was edging his way between us and I thought our chat was over when she suddenly tapped my arm, trying to get my attention again.

"Why don't you come to the concert tomorrow? Eight o'clock in St David's Hall." She gave me a smile. "The late Beethoven sonatas. One of Jack's gifted friends, Ellen James, a former student, is playing. She's excellent. You can get a ticket on the door. It'll be worth it. There'll be drinks at our place afterwards."

"Thanks for telling me," I shouted back and finally ordered the drinks.

"You took your time," Gemma said, a bit peeved. "What were you talking with Clara about?"

"Nothing much, just the rehearsal." For a moment I wondered if I should mention the concert, but then decided not to. Maybe it wasn't what Clara wanted. Gemma would probably tell everyone. Why had Clara invited me of all people, I wondered. Was it because she felt sorry for me? Why didn't she ask Dr Turner to find someone more suitable to play – he was her friend after all? Instead she wanted to practise with me.

I drank my second glass of wine, and the rest of the evening seemed to float by in a daze. The background music, the heat from the bodies, the noisy laughter – none of it mattered now.

Later on, Dr Turner came into the pub and joined Clara at the bar. I saw them chatting and wondered if they were talking about the rehearsal. But I didn't worry anymore.

I was a bit tipsy as I walked home. There was a nip in the air. I breathed in the autumnal smell of wood fire – thinking about what had happened. Gemma was a nice girl. But there were nearly twenty years between us and all she did was pub-crawling and clubbing. Clara and Philip seemed so much more interesting. Maybe I would get to know Clara better now. Maybe she could be a friend. My steps felt lighter – there suddenly seemed a lot to look forward to.

4

The house looked empty; all the windows were dark. I let myself in and switched on the light in the hall. I noticed a smell of burning which became worse as I opened the kitchen door. There was a frying pan on the stove on low heat with two charred pieces of meat, which could once have been steaks.

I switched off the oven and took out a tray of hard, inedible chips. They looked as if they'd been in there for hours. Where was Amy? What on earth was going on? Had she gone out and forgotten about her cooking? The pan was glowing with heat – it could have gone up in flames. The kitchen table was laid with plates, cutlery and glasses. There was a bowl of green salad too and an open bottle of wine.

Shouting her name, I crossed the hall. The door to the living room stood ajar; she was lying on the sofa.

"Amy!" I turned on the light.

"What's the matter?" She sat up. "What time is it?"

"You left the food on. It's all burnt."

"Oh dear, I must have dozed off." She stared at me. "Why didn't you ring? I thought we were going to celebrate. I only had a glass of wine whilst I was waiting. Christ, I was fast asleep."

"Celebrate what?" I stared at her unevenly flushed face. The gas fire was on and the room felt stuffy. Next to her on the sofa table was a half empty glass of wine.

"How did it go?" She looked at me blankly. "How was your playing? Did the tablets help?"

I nodded. "Not brilliant, but it could have been worse. We went to the pub afterwards. I had no idea that you were cooking."

"But I told you this morning." She sighed. "Never mind. What a silly idea. I should have known that I would ruin it."

"No, not at all," I said, beginning to feel a bit guilty now. "It's just because you fell asleep. It probably would have been OK if I'd come home in time. Sorry, but I really don't remember you saying anything about it – or maybe I wasn't listening."

"It doesn't matter." She let herself sink back again and closed her eyes. "Did you have a nice time?"

"We just had a couple of drinks. I'm really sorry I forgot. Let me at least help you clear up." It was only natural that she'd expected me back. I hadn't been out that long before.

I went back into the kitchen and threw away the ruined food. The steaks had been expensive – nearly ten pounds. The price was on the plastic packaging in the bin. I started the washing up.

"Who was in the pub?" Amy was standing in the open kitchen door, leaning against the frame.

"The students from choir," I said lightly. "It was a bit too noisy for a proper chat, but in the end, I talked to the woman who is singing the solo for us."

"Sounds lovely. What did you talk about?"

"Just the rehearsal. And she invited me to a concert tomorrow."

"You must be very pleased." She turned her face away. "I think I'll have an early night." She sighed. "Sleeping on that sofa was a bad idea. No wonder I have a sore head. Truth be told, I can't stand waiting. It makes me nervous. When I was little, I used to wait up hours for my mum, worrying that she wouldn't come home. The state she was in sometimes!" She shook her head. "Oh my word, I thought that was all in the past. Anyway, we'll have to put the rubbish out. There's a collection tomorrow." I heard her heavy steps as she went upstairs and closed her bedroom door.

I finished the washing up. Glancing out of the window into the back garden, I saw that the bin bag was still there. The kitchen light illuminated the small patio whereas the tree and overgrown shrubs towards the back were engulfed by darkness. I stared out, suddenly afraid that someone was hiding out there. It was that eerie fear of being watched again. What was the matter with me? Why the constant feeling of unease? Had it something to do with Amy's mother – with the picture I had found? Could there be an echo of the past? Maybe it was Amy's fault for writing about it. A sudden draft came through the window and made me shudder with cold. Maybe the spirit of her mother was somehow surfacing through her.

I shook my head. What a ridiculous thought! I'd never been superstitious and I wouldn't start now. There was nothing out there – just the old tree with its mildewed apples swaying in the wind. Amy was a bit down: writing about the past was obviously upsetting her. No wonder she could be moody sometimes. She should go out there and meet new people. Someone had to pull her out of it and get her back into the here and now.

.   .   .

I WAS TOO wound up to sleep. It was a cloudless night, and the full moon lit up the room. I arose to close the heavy velvet curtains, then returned to bed. I heard the rumble of a heavy freight train going past, a sound Amy's mother would have known well. I thought about her music scores – the annotations I had seen in them. Her writing looked neat and tidy. Had her hands been shaky later on – had they been too unsteady to play. Or had she just lost interest in her music altogether? Amy had said that she'd spent most of her time in bed. How awful to watch someone so close fall apart without being able to help.

After what seemed like hours, I eventually fell asleep. At half past three I was woken up again. There was a dull banging downstairs. I switched on the light and sat up, holding my breath. Someone was at the front door. Then I heard a creaking sound and footsteps on the stairs. Eventually it was quiet again. For a long while I just lay there, listening with every nerve, my heart still racing.

When I dozed off in the early hours, I had a terrifying dream: Amy had taken her own life. Coming home, I found her in the living room, collapsed and bleeding from her wrists. The blood had formed a big pool, so deep that I couldn't cross the room. I watched from a distance, tears running down my face.

I WOKE with a terrible feeling of dread. The sunlight seeping through the curtains dazzled me, and it took me a while to realise that it had just been a dream. It was nearly eleven, but I felt as if I hadn't slept at all.

As I made my way downstairs, I heard a babble of squeaky voices coming from the living room. Putting my head around the door, I half-expected to find Amy lying in a pool of her blood, but she was very much alive, sitting on the sofa, her legs stretched out on the table, watching *The Simpsons*.

"Coffee?"

"No, thank you."

"Do you mind if I join you?"

She didn't respond.

When I came back with my coffee and sat next to her she was still staring at the screen.

"I'm sorry about yesterday," I said.

"Why? What happened?" Her eyes were fixed on Homer Simpson arguing with his wife.

"I would have been back for the meal if I had known."

"So what?" She shrugged. "I thought you'd be home as usual, but then you weren't. What's the big deal?"

"Sorry. My mind was probably on something else."

"Or you forgot. Like you forgot to put the rubbish out last night." She gave me a weary smile.

I took a sip of my coffee. Was that what the banging had been about? Amy had folded her arms in front of her; her jaw was tight. I had hurt her even more than I had thought.

"Sorry, I should have remembered," I said. "I've been a bit stressed out with everything. Maybe we could go out? Spend the afternoon in town and have a look around the shops? I'm going to a concert later on."

"What sort of music?"

"Classical. It's a university thing. A few people from college are going."

"Do you have to go?"

"No, but it would be quite rude if I didn't. A former student of Dr Turner's is playing Beethoven sonatas. You wouldn't like it." I stared into my empty cup. "We could have something to eat. My treat..." I trailed off.

"OK. Why not? A meal would be nice." She gave me a

sideways glance. "And why wouldn't I want to go to the concert with you?"

THE AFTERNOON WAS grey with a light drizzle falling from low clouds. We had a look around Cardiff market, bought a new electric kettle and finally went upstairs to have a drink in one of the cafés. Amy sat down at a table outside, and I went to get the coffee, which was served in old-fashioned mugs. Ordering at the counter, I caught my reflection in the large silver coffee maker: my pale face with the round glasses, my sensible beige mackintosh.

"What's the matter?" Amy said when I was back. "You look upset."

"I don't like the coat I'm wearing."

"Why not?" She stared at me, bewildered. "It's just a coat. What's wrong with it?" I should have known. Fashion was not something she cared about. I'd never seen her in anything but her jeans and the chequered shirt.

"I've had it for years." I glanced over to the scruffy-looking vintage stall next door. There were boxes with vinyl records and racks with clothes outside. As Amy was reading a tattered copy of the *Echo*, I went and browsed through fair-isle jumpers and seventies velvet jackets. I picked a purple one with pretty golden buttons, took off my coat and tried it on – it was the right size.

"Looks shabby," Amy said, looking up from her paper. "I bet it smells musty."

"Of course, it's vintage." I looked at myself in the mirror. The velvet was a bit thin at the collar. Maybe Amy was right. It was too expensive, and I didn't really need it anyway.

"Let's go for a meal," I said quickly. "Nothing fancy, I'm afraid. I'm a bit short of money now, but there's a Wetherspoon's nearby."

A bit short of money was putting it mildly. The house I'd inherited from my parents just wouldn't sell and I still had to pay the council tax and basic bills. In fact, I had overdrawn my account so much I couldn't pay my credit card bill.

"They do sandwiches here," Amy said, glancing at the greasy menu on the table.

"Don't be silly." I got up. "The Wetherspoon's will just fine. I may be out of the woods soon anyway. I'm going for a part-time job in the college library. The librarian said there is a good chance that I'll get it if I try."

IT WAS a Saturday afternoon and the Wetherspoon's was very busy. When we arrived the tables were strewn with crockery, cutlery and food. We cleared a table near the large arched window and sat down. It was a good place to look down on the busy street outside. The building had been a theatre in a former life, and many of its features had been kept in place: the stalls, some private boxes and large red velvet drapes.

"Let's have the merlot," Amy said, studying the drinks menu. "Not much more expensive than in Tesco's. What are you having to eat?"

We both decided on chicken tikka masala and I went to the bar to order. When I came back, Amy was looking out of the window, her gaze absent-minded as if deep in thought.

"Won't that library job take up too much of your time?" she asked, returning to the conversation from before.

"Hope not." I shrugged. "Anyway, I have no choice."

"I know. I need money too. Maybe I can make some with my writing. I'll be sorted if they make a film of it."

"Yes, that'd be good," I said lamely. "Hope it works out." She didn't seem to have any doubts about the success of her book. "Have you ever considered selling the house?" I asked, pouring the wine. "I was just wondering..."

"Why?" She frowned. "Do you think I should?"

"I just thought you might be happier somewhere else. A new start could be just what you need."

"But you've only just moved in."

I looked up as a waitress finally cleared the table next to us.

"A new place might be good for you to get over those sad memories."

"Don't you like the house?" She gave me a hurt look. "I thought you were happier with your room, now that old paper is gone. We'll have to make a start downstairs as well."

There was a long awkward silence, only interrupted by the clinking of the crockery the waitress amassed on her tray.

"You're the one with the new start," Amy said eventually. "Why did you really want to leave Carlisle? Why did you say you couldn't go back?"

Had I really said that to her? I couldn't remember.

"Well," I said, clutching the stem of my glass. "I had a difficult time."

"What was difficult?"

"Work."

"What happened?"

"A colleague..." I took a sip of my wine. "There were problems. I couldn't work with him."

"Couldn't he have left instead?"

"No, it was my fault. There were tensions." I could feel the heat rising to my face and was glad when the waitress arrived with our food. We started to eat. It was a good choice. The chicken was not over microwaved, the poppadoms crisp and there was more naan bread than we could possibly eat.

"You're just too nice, taking the blame for everything," Amy said, chewing. "What happened?"

"I suppose it was a bit of unrequited love."

"What a silly man. Couldn't he see what was good?" She laid her chubby hand lightly on mine. "What was he like?"

"Not handsome, if that's what you're asking." I looked out of the window. There was a couple with suitcases – the man dashing ahead, the woman trying to keep up. Her face was red with the exertion. "Everything about him was quite ordinary – but he was kind and honest, or at least I thought he was. He was a good librarian, thorough and reliable, people respected him..."

"Did he tell you that he wasn't interested?"

"No, that was the trouble. I thought he liked me too. We even had a holiday in Rome together – he couldn't get enough of the sights." I laughed, surprised what a relief it brought to talk about it. "Churches, art museums, the Vatican..."

"So, why did he pretend?"

"He didn't. He never said that he loved me. His wife had left him, and he was still not over her. But I thought it would come with time." I concentrated on my curry. An image of Jeremy came to my mind: the silver framed glasses, his short greying hair.

"What happened after Rome?"

"I saw him with someone else." I lowered my voice. "He had his arm around her. She was younger than me, pretty, with long straight hair. I'd never seen him that happy before."

"And that's why you left Carlisle?" Amy said in a soft voice. "It must have been really bad. Couldn't you sort it out?"

"I don't know. I might have got used to it and stayed on if he hadn't been so annoyed with me."

"What reason did he have to be annoyed?" She poured the rest of the wine, sharing it evenly between our glasses. "I thought you were the one who was upset."

I took a long swig.

"He said that I had phoned him."

"What's wrong with that?"

"...in the middle of the night. That I'd shouted at him and made a scene. He said that I had woken him up."

"And did you?"

"That's exactly it. I can't remember making a scene. I'd had some wine – more than usual perhaps. No wonder he was angry with me. He said that I'd phoned him several times."

"Do you think he made it up?"

"No, I don't think so." I took a deep breath. "He wouldn't have lied to me. I know I phoned him once or twice. It must have been the wine. I was really upset about it. It was so embarrassing that I couldn't remember what I had said. It had never happened to me before. I had a spell of sleep-walking after my sister died, but that was different."

"Oh dear! He didn't deserve you." Amy smiled. "You're well shot of him. I'm glad you had a go at him. I wonder what you said." She chuckled, glancing at the menu again. "Why don't we have another bottle? It'll do you good."

"No, not for me. I don't want to be half-cut at the concert."

"Do you really have to go? Who will be there?"

"Lots of students."

"Maybe you'll find a new boyfriend. Are there nice students in your course?"

"They're bit young for me."

"What about your lecturer, that Dr Turner. Will he be there?"

"Yes, probably. The pianist used to be his student."

"What's he like?"

"Who?"

"Dr Turner."

"What do you want to know?"

"Does he like you too?"

"Don't be silly." I laughed. "What makes you think he

would be interested in me? I'm probably the least glamorous woman he knows."

"Is that why you wanted to buy that velvet jacket?" She put an elbow on the table and rested the side of her head in her palm. "I was just wondering because you talk so fondly of him. You said that he's very nice, that he's about your age and that you were on really good terms."

I was startled. Had I really talked so much about him? I had wondered about being friends with Clara, but Dr Turner had never really crossed my mind.

"You said that you really liked him." She smiled. "Don't worry. Your secret is safe with me. I won't tell anyone. But I bet you could be in there if you tried."

I glanced at my watch. "I think I'd better make a move. I don't want to be late."

"Maybe I'll come along after all," Amy said, getting up. "I don't feel like going home." She laughed again in her quiet way. "And someone has to have an eye on you."

5

The foyer was thronged with people, standing together in groups, talking and laughing. I recognised a couple of faces from college. A tall, thin girl from Dr Turner's course was handing out programmes, and I was beginning to wonder if this was mainly a college event.

"Let's go inside," I said, leading the way through the crowd. It smelled of filter coffee and perfume. I regretted now having had the wine. It was uncomfortably warm and I was feeling slightly nauseous. The crowd parted just enough to let us through. As we passed the bar I suddenly saw Clara. She was with Philip and Dr Turner. The sight of them sitting around a table, holding their drinks and chatting, startled me. I turned to steer Amy away, but Clara had seen me and lifted her hand to catch my attention.

"Good to see you," she said as we approached. "It should be very good. You won't regret coming." She glanced at her watch. "I suppose we'd better go in soon. Let's have a drink in the break."

"Good idea," I said. Heat crept into my cheeks. Feeling Dr Turner's eyes on me, I had the sudden urge to turn around and leave. I knew I wouldn't be able to engage in small talk. His glance moved from me to Amy and back again.

"This is my friend, Amy," I said quickly, pushing lightly against her back to move her on. "See you all later."

Our seats were quite high up.

"Was that your Dr Turner?" Amy said as we were entering the auditorium. "I could see that you like him. You were a bit flustered." She smiled. "But don't worry. I don't think that he noticed."

"You're making it all up," I said, turning my face away. "I just can't bear the heat in here."

People were bustling in now, taking their seats. A few minutes later I saw them in the second row, making their way past seated members of the audience. I was relieved that they didn't sit anywhere near us. Dr Turner was next to Clara, his bald patch with the dark fringe shining under the lights.

At the centre left of the stage – majestic, shiny and black – stood the grand piano. We had been lucky to get tickets; the hall was packed. Gradually the general hum of voices died down; there were last muffled coughs and clearings of throats. Then the pianist made her entrance. She smiled and didn't seem at all fazed by the enthusiastic applause that greeted her. Her posture was graceful and poised – everything about her oozed self-confidence. She looked young and beautiful with her radiant eyes and long dark hair. I would have guessed her to be in her late twenties or early thirties at most.

With precise movements, she sat down, placed her foot on the pedal and looked at her hands. There was a long moment of absolute silence – and then she started to play.

I watched in awe as she raced through the dramatic cadences of the beginning. The *Waldstein* was one of the most difficult of Beethoven's sonatas. The music soared. She played with real passion, and yet it seemed effortless, her fingers hitting the keys with precision and force.

Dr Turner was leaning forward in his seat. Once or twice he tilted his profile in my direction, bending his head to whisper something into Clara's ear. I couldn't make out his expression, but there was no doubt that he was very proud – hardly surprising – she had been a student of his!

As the music flowed and swirled in my brain, some childhood memories surged up. My first piano teacher who had been so encouraging... all the hours I'd practised and the excitement and hope I'd had for the future. I had performed a lot in those days: for my parents, for Father O'Leary and my mother's friends from church. I had been sure that I would be a pianist one day. Maybe I'd have been good as well if I had carried on.

I gazed at the girl, at her fingers flying over the keyboard throughout the amazing second movement. She made the piano sing. Out of the corner of my eye, I saw Amy fidgeting on her seat, shifting her heavy body from one side to the other, once even looking at her mobile phone.

Other images came into my mind: Father O'Leary again, his attempts to make me play after my sister had died, his long, dark figure behind the grille as I confessed to all sorts of minor sins but never talked about what really bothered me.

The last dramatic movement brought me back to the present moment – and then the first half was over. There was an eruption of applause.

"I'll buy the drinks," Amy said, getting up. "You can introduce me to your friends."

I WAITED for her near the bar.

"Are you enjoying it?" Dr Turner asked in passing on his

way to join the queue. Clara and Philip were not with him. He stopped to wait for my answer.

"Of course. She's wonderful." I stared at him like a deer caught in the headlights.

He looked at me, slightly amused and probably wondering what was the matter with me.

"She was a student of mine. I always thought she had a bright future. But not all talented students make it as professionals. It's very competitive."

Turning my head, I was relieved to see Amy arriving with the wine.

"Oh hello again," she said, glancing at Dr Turner. She handed me a large glass of red. I took a big sip.

"You'll get me drunk at this rate," I said in a joking way, but neither of them laughed. Dr Turner looked a bit puzzled – and Amy was probably gloating because she thought I fancied him. Or was I reading too much into it again? Her broad face had resumed its usual placid expression.

"I'd better go and get my drink before it's too late," he said. "Will I see you at the party?"

"I'm not sure." I stared at Amy. "I'm here with my friend."

"Well, why don't you bring her along?" There was the ironic tone to his voice again. "Clara said she had invited you."

"Yes, I'd like to," Amy said, smiling at him.

"Well, that's settled then. There's always too much food, and Philip bought enough wine to get us all drunk." He winked at me. "He never does things by halves."

SHE PLAYED the *Appassionata* in the second half. I tried to listen to the music, but my thoughts were not with it. Clara looked beautiful in a forties style dress. She was sitting between Philip and Dr Turner again, attentive, bolt upright with her hands on her lap. I wondered where she had been in the break.

Dr Turner was only being kind. I had to tell them that I wasn't feeling well. Maybe Amy and I could leave through one of the side doors before the others came out. I felt a sudden rush of adrenaline – a surge of panic rising in me. I tried to focus on the pianist attacking the last movement: a volley of chords building up – and then there was the final sequence of arpeggios and it was over. The audience got up; there was a standing ovation.

"Do you know where Clara lives?" Amy asked as we were leaving. "Maybe someone can give us a lift."

"I'm not sure that's a good idea."

"Why not?"

"We can't just turn up. Clara doesn't even know who you are."

To my surprise, she was waiting for us in the foyer. "You can come with me. There's enough space. Philip is going with Jack. I need to be there in time to get things ready," she said, leading the way to the exit.

CLARA DROVE AN OLD VOLVO. Amy sat next to her in the front. She asked a few intrusive questions, but Clara didn't seem to mind. Her voice was quiet and matter of fact. I learned that the house they lived in belonged to Philip's mother who spent most of the year in New York, running an agency for free-lance musicians. She came back twice a year, over the Christmas holidays and then in the summer for a few weeks. But living together was apparently not that easy: they got in each other's way and it often ended with Clara and Philip fleeing the house, either going on an extended holiday in Europe or spending time in his mother's empty flat in New York.

Apparently Clara and Philip were even closer than I had thought. Looking out of the window, I thought about what Gemma had told me: what a talented composer Philip was – and that he was gay.

It was a beautiful large Victorian house. Clara left our coats in a room near the front door. Following her along the corridor, I could hear piano music. Glancing into the first room, I saw a man sitting at the piano improvising a jazzy tune. Around him was a semicircle of blue velvet chairs – as if put there for an audience.

"Help yourselves to food and drink: whisky, gin, vodka, whatever you like. We'll have the champagne later on." Clara led the way into a spacious room. There was chatter coming from the adjacent kitchen. I lagged behind, stunned by the beauty of the room. A chandelier hung from the ceiling; there was a wood fire burning in the Victorian tiled fireplace and bookshelves lining the high walls. Books and papers were strewn about, and music scores piled-up on the oak dining table. A standard lamp with a yellow-fringed shade spread a warm light.

Other people were arriving now – the pianist, radiant, her cheeks red and the long hair blown all over from the wind outside. Dr Turner put his head around the kitchen door and gave her a smile.

Amy, who had brought a plate with quiche from the kitchen, inspected the bottles lined up on the table.

"What about you?" she asked. "Don't you want to line your stomach?"

"I'm not hungry," I said. It was uncomfortably warm and I was feeling a bit queasy.

"G and T?"

I nodded. She poured me a generous slug of gin and filled the glass with tonic water.

Some people were sitting on the sofa now. Philip was in a corner, talking to a middle-aged woman in a leather skirt with short spiky hair. There was something dishevelled in the way he looked, maybe his slightly greasy hair or the shadows around his eyes. Cole Porter drifted from the stereo.

"His agent managed to find him a publisher," said Clara, following my glance. She poured herself a straight whisky. "They're talking about it now."

"What is his book about?" Amy asked.

"Which book?" said Dr Turner, who had joined the conversation.

"Amy is writing a novel," I explained.

"I see," he said, a mocking glint in his eyes. "No, it's not a book. He's written a piece of music, a symphonic poem based on *Death in Venice* by Thomas Mann. A lot of passion and romantic obsession... One of the greatest stories of the twentieth century. We'll have to celebrate."

"Sounds very interesting," I said, clenching my glass.

Luckily, the pretty pianist came in again, demanding his attention. I got myself a second slug of gin and sat down on the sofa next to a serious looking man in his mid-twenties with shaven hair and horn-rimmed glasses. Tall and thin, I had seen him in the library before. His name was Jonathan.

He was a little shy, and I asked a few questions to make him talk. He had graduated in Swansea and was now in Philip's composition course to do a PhD. His thesis was about music therapy. He told me all about it, but the gin was making me woozy and I couldn't concentrate. For the next half hour I kept staring at his moving mouth as he explained the impact of music on children with behavioural problems.

He was telling me why he preferred Cardiff University to

Swansea when I suddenly felt sick. I closed my eyes and opened them again. Everything around me slowly reeled: the standard lamp beside me with its big yellow shade, Jonathan's blurred face, the drinks table with its bottles and glasses.

"Sorry – I need the loo," I whispered.

On my way to the bathroom I heard music coming from the piano room. I looked inside. Clara was playing and there were people standing around her, singing. I listened for a moment, steadying myself against the door frame before moving on.

The bathroom was occupied – but the door to the bedroom with our coats was wide open. There was no one inside. It was dark with only the light from the street filtering through the curtains. I pushed the coats aside and sat down on the bed, hoping I wouldn't have to be sick. I sat there for quite a long time, head in my hands, waiting for the nausea to pass – maybe I even dozed off for a while. When I heard someone at the door I raised my head. It was Clara.

"What are you doing here all alone in the dark?" she said.

"I had a bit too much to drink."

"Oh dear." She looked at me expectantly. "It's officially allowed tonight. Who cares? We're having a bit of a sing-song. Why don't you come and join us? You can play for us if you like."

"Not really." I inhaled deeply through my nose. "I wouldn't be able to play. Not now."

"Who cares if you make mistakes?"

The room was whirling again. She remained in the doorway, as if waiting for an answer.

"I'm not at ease playing in public."

"Yes, you said. You told me that you stopped playing after your sister died." Her voice was quiet and even. She didn't move. "What was she like, your sister?"

"She was older than me, only by a couple of years," I said,

surprised she remembered. "She was really clever and much prettier than me. She had a lot of friends."

"Was she musical too?"

"Yes, but she didn't play. She didn't have time with everything else she did."

"How did she die?"

"Meningitis." I paused, staring at her. I hadn't talked about it for years. I could see that she was watching me. Her pupils were dilated and her eyes looked large and dark in her white face. I bit my tongue, trying to hold back the tears. I bit so hard that it hurt, but it didn't work. I could feel them brimming over and rolling down my cheeks.

"It was my fault," I said, trying to keep a steady voice. "We shared a room. She was burning with fever when I got up in the morning. I should have told my parents, but I was rushing to get to my rehearsal. I had a competition coming up. I always wanted to be more successful than her. And when I came home, she had died." I didn't wipe my eyes, hoping she wouldn't notice.

"That's awful. It must have been so sad for you all." She paused. "Are you coming? We're in the music room."

I waited a while after she had gone, then returned to the hall to find the bathroom was empty. It was a large room with an old-fashioned dressing table and a wicker chair. Catching my reflection in the mirror over the sink, I stared at my red eyes. I took quite some time, holding my hands under the running cold water and splashing it onto my face. Eventually I flushed the loo and left. In the hall I ran into Dr Turner.

"Are you all right?" he asked, with a look of concern.

"Of course." I managed a smile. "I'm fine." But it wasn't true. I was still a bit shaky. What if I started crying again? There was no way I could stay on. I had to tell Amy that I was leaving.

She was still in the living room, talking to Philip who was listening attentively. She smiled at me as I walked over.

"Where have you been?" she asked. She turned to Philip. "This is my friend, Kate. We live together. You probably know her from college. She's a pianist."

"I don't think we've met." He looked at me, vaguely interested. "You study the piano? Who is your teacher?"

"I don't have a teacher yet," I said, flustered. "I'm not really studying the piano, not at a professional level."

"No?" He looked at me with amazement, like one might look at an animal in the zoo. "What are you doing at college?"

"I'm more interested in the academic side of it." Before I had finished the sentence, I realised it was a mistake. Dr Turner had joined the group; they were all looking at me now.

"That's what we like to hear," Dr Turner said with that ironic smile of his. "What are you interested in?"

"Nothing in particular. The eighteenth century." I stopped, my face burning.

"Which composer?"

"There are so many," I said weakly. "I like Handel and Bach."

"Who doesn't?" He let out a congenial laugh.

"I've got to go," I said to no one in particular. I was acutely aware that my clammy hands were still clutching the tissue I'd used in the bathroom earlier on.

"Why? What's wrong?" Amy rested her hand on my shoulder. "Are you not feeling well?"

"Nothing to worry about. I'm just a bit tired."

"That's a shame." Philip regarded me in the same puzzled way he had done before. "The party has only just started."

"I thought you looked a bit under the weather," Dr Turner chipped in.

"You don't have to come with me," I said to Amy. "Why

don't you stay a bit longer?" She shook her head. No one said a word. I turned away, staring at the bookshelf next to me.

"You have a lot of German books," I interrupted the awkward silence. "You must be good at it."

"I am." Philip furrowed his brows. "My mother is German. I suppose I am what people call bilingual." He looked around the room. "Where has everyone gone? Has anyone seen Clara? I'd better see where she is. I think it's about time to have some champagne."

"She's in the music room," I said, but he was already strolling off. Dr Turner gave me a pitying look and followed suit. Only now did I realise that the piano music had stopped. There were voices and laughter in the kitchen and the pop of a champagne bottle being opened. Through the open door I could see them all gathered around the table, holding glasses.

"I'm getting my stuff," I said to Amy. I walked off and she followed me down the corridor.

"Let's at least say goodbye," she said when we had put on our coats and were ready to leave.

"You do that," I said. "They know I'm going. I'm waiting outside."

IT TOOK ABOUT ten minutes until she came out of the house.

"Dr Turner was worried about you," she said. "He asked me if something was wrong."

"What did you say?"

"Nothing, only that you had too much to drink. What else could I say? They all knew anyway."

I crossed my arms against the cold. It was a clear night with a myriad of stars all over the sky. My heart was heavy. How embarrassing to make a fool of myself! In my mind, I went over what I had said to Clara, the way I had burst into tears.

"Don't worry." Amy interrupted my gloomy thoughts. "It wasn't so bad, but you shouldn't have had that second gin."

"I was just a bit nervous."

"Maybe you shouldn't put yourself through it again if you think you'll have to drink so much."

"There won't be another time." I knew I had squandered my only chance. After the show I'd made of myself, they would not invite me to one of their parties again.

"Did you know that your Dr Turner is carrying on with the pianist?" Amy asked as we were walking down the road.

"The girl who played this evening?"

"Yes. They were in the garden, smoking, and I saw them from the kitchen window. He had his arm around her – they looked very cosy. He must be fifteen years older than her."

"Well, that's not unusual," I said, accelerating my gait. "Most men at his age would go for a younger woman if they could choose. And he's of course no exception." I swallowed, disconcerted by the bitterness in my voice.

6

The following week I made an appointment with the chief librarian for an interview about the job.

"Let's have an informal chat in my office," she said encouragingly on the phone. "Lillian will be there until two, so what about half past one?"

Lillian was her part-time colleague who worked in the mornings from Monday to Friday. She was a stout woman in her early forties with long blonde hair that was turning grey and frizzy – which made her look a bit hippy and probably wilder than she really was. When I came for my interview, she was standing behind the checkout desk, looking for something on the computer.

"Margaret is in the office," she said in a hushed voice, directing me to a little windowless room behind the counter. The door was open.

She was on the phone, speaking in a low urgent voice, in what sounded like a private conversation. There were two desks facing each other, computers and piles of papers stacked up, a corkboard on the wall with picture postcards and family photos of children somewhere at the seaside.

When she saw me hesitating at the door, Margaret beck-oned me in and finished the call.

"Sorry for making you wait," she said with a sigh. "My son has had an accident. Nothing serious, thank God, but the car is ruined, and they want to keep him for more tests. At least no one else was hurt." She looked pale and tired as she explained what had happened. Her son had crashed the car into a road sign. It was not the first time he'd driven under the influence of alcohol or drugs. She began fidgeting with a rubber band, nervously winding and unwinding it around her finger.

With her short white hair, the woolly skirt and matching blazer, she looked somewhat familiar, not unlike Ros, my former colleague in Carlisle. Their personalities, however, couldn't have been more different. Whereas Ros, who'd lived on her own without a partner or children, had hardly ever talked about her private life, Margaret shared freely. Within the next half hour, she had told me all about her son, how they had adopted him when he was a baby, trying to give him the best start in life. He'd been the most adorable child with the sweetest smile and curly blond hair. And then the first disappointments as he got older, the constant backtalk and revolt against everything that she thought mattered.

"'No one else goes to church anymore – and why do I have to play that boring piano?'" She laughed, but I could see how much she cared for him and how upset she was.

It turned out that she had to leave at two – and that, with all her talking, there was hardly any time left for the inter-view. It didn't seem to matter though.

"I'm so glad you want to drag yourself here on Saturdays. We'll be lucky to have you with your experience and knowl-edge of music. I was wondering if you could hold the fort for us this afternoon. Lillian has got other obligations, and I really feel I should go to the hospital. He sounded a bit spaced out on the phone; he might have concussion and need a lift home."

Pleased to have secured the job, I agreed. After Margaret had hurried off, Lillian showed me the computer-based system – how they kept records of their books and of the people who borrowed them. It was not much different from the system I had worked with in Carlisle. She assured me that I didn't have to finish the book search she had started and that I just had to be at the counter and check people out.

It was a beautiful day outside, and the library felt empty with only a few students scattered here and there, reading and making notes. Some were sitting at the computer termi-nals – there was the familiar tapping at a keyboard, the scratch of pencils and clicking of pens. I wondered what I could do to pass the time. There was a trolley with returned books near the checkout desk, so I started to put them back onto the shelves, a task we always recommended to new assistants in Carlisle to get their bearings. The books were already sorted according to their codes.

As I pushed the trolley in the direction of the vocal scores, which were right at the back, I was taken aback to see Philip working at a desk, hidden between the opera scores and reference books. His crumpled linen jacket was hung over the back of his chair and he had taken off his silver framed glasses. He sat with his elbows on the table, his face cupped in his hands, staring at the open book in front of him. It was an encyclopaedia, one of those heavy volumes the students weren't allowed to take out. He looked different without his glasses, his face incomplete, pale and drained in the harsh electric light. I noticed again the darkness around his eyes. Maybe he wasn't sleeping enough.

My heart was beating so hard I could feel the pulse against my chest. I remembered keenly how I had made a fool of myself at the party and the way he had looked at me.

The normality of college life had helped me to forget, but seeing him there brought it all back. Luckily he was too absorbed to notice me.

I left the trolley where it was, turned around and went back to the checkout desk. For a brief moment I wondered if I should hide in the office but it was not an option. I had to be there for the students. The only thing I could do was to carry on as if nothing had happened. Maybe it would be distracting to do some work. I hadn't even started the essay I had to deliver in less than two weeks for Composition, a course led by Dr Peterson, a composer of film music himself. The assignment was a two-page essay about composers reworking existing pieces.

I googled Gustav Mahler and started reading up on how he had borrowed traditional tunes and worked them into his symphonies. As I glanced up, I saw Philip emerging from behind the shelves. Long and thin, his loose-fitting shirt flapping over his trousers, he crossed the room without even glancing at me. It was impossible to tell from his face whether he had chosen to ignore me or just hadn't seen me yet.

It struck me that I had never seen him with anyone but Clara. Was he too arrogant to socialise? I felt reminded of Gemma's gossip – maybe there was something to it after all. He hadn't even talked with his PhD student at the party. But why invite people at all when he couldn't be bothered with them?

As the door fell shut behind him, I tried to concentrate on my article again. Ten minutes later he was back, smelling of cigarette smoke. I saw his beige trousers and felt him hesitating at the desk, but I didn't look up.

"There's an interesting Mahler biography out," he said. He was standing right in front of me, peering at the screen.

"I don't really need a biography." I reared up from my

seat. "I'm only reading it for my composition essay. I just remembered that Mahler used a lot of traditional tunes."

"The composition essay?" He frowned. "I haven't seen you in my course."

"I'm an undergraduate."

"Of course, I remember you said..." Again, he looked at me as if I were an unusual and exotic creature. "Anyway, you can borrow the book if you like. I've got it at home." He glanced at his watch. "I've got to catch my bus."

I watched as he walked across the library to get his things. He hadn't seemed the slightest bit surprised to see me behind the checkout desk.

"There's something else," he said on his way out. "Clara and I have agreed to do one of those lunch-time concerts of Schubert songs in a couple of weeks. Unfortunately, I don't know yet if I can make it. I might have to be in New York. We were wondering if you could step in and accompany her on the piano. Clara wanted to ask you herself, but as I'm seeing you now..." He paused expectantly.

"Are you sure they would have me?" Panic rose within me. The lunch-time concerts were organised by the college but open to the general public in addition to university students and staff. You had to be very good to take part.

"Clara seems to think you're good enough." His tone sounded detached and emotionless.

"Well, I could try."

"OK, that's settled then. She can give you the music at choir rehearsal." He glanced again at his watch. "Or rather, why don't you come to our place? Have a meal with us on Sunday, and we can talk things through."

When he was gone I tried to go on with my reading. I gazed at the computer screen without absorbing anything. I could still pull out – I hadn't said anything definite yet. They would see that I wasn't quite up to it and Philip would find someone else if he couldn't do it himself. But it was an opportunity. It had been Clara's idea. Wasn't it a sign that she still wanted to be in touch and that I hadn't messed up after all? Or was she just feeling sorry for me? The students left one after another until I was on my own. No sound, only the humming of the electric light, cold and sober in the airless room. I was relieved when the porter came to lock up.

"Shame to be cooped up in here," he said, his loud voice cutting through the stillness. "It'll be hot tomorrow again. Indian summer."

At eight o'clock it was already getting dark. The bin outside was overflowing with Styrofoam cups and there were dog-ends and sweet wrappers on the grass where people had been sitting. A cool breeze had replaced the warmth of the day and I shivered in my thin blouse. In the gathering darkness I could see the first stars in the sky. It smelled of burning wood again. I quickened my steps, taking in deep breaths of the evening air. Maybe this day would mark a turning point, if I would only let it happen.

AMY CAME to the door when she heard my key turn in the lock. "How was the interview? Where on earth have you been? Did you get the job?"

I explained what had happened.

"And you had to work straight away? My goodness, they don't half take advantage of you. To be honest, I'm not surprised. I thought you'd have a good chance with your experience. I expected it. That's why I bought the chocolate cake to celebrate. When you didn't come home, I thought I would have to eat it by myself." She grinned, gently patting her belly. "And that would have been a very bad idea." Her purple roll-neck jumper indeed looked quite tight around the waist. I hadn't noticed before how flabby she was because she'd always worn that loose, chequered shirt.

I followed her into the kitchen. The cake was on the table, looking moist, with layers of mousse and frosted with shiny chocolate ganache.

"How lovely," I said. "You shouldn't have." I watched her cut the cake and hand me a plate with a more than generous slice.

"My pleasure. What are friends for?" She chuckled, leading the way to the living room.

"How much will you earn?" she asked, once we were seated on the sofa. "I hope you're not going to move somewhere more fancy now."

"Of course not. Anyway, it's just on Saturdays and maybe covering if someone is off sick during the week."

Amy put a forkful of cake into her mouth. "Give them a finger, and they'll take the whole hand." She laughed. "No, honestly. Don't let them push you around."

It took me a moment to respond. The cake was a bit greasy and sweet for my liking, but it was the thought that counted. "Don't worry about it, the librarian is very nice."

"What's she like?"

"Just a lovely middle-aged woman." I changed the subject: "Philip was in the library. He wants me to accompany Clara at a concert, but I'm not sure. It's open to the public."

Amy, her mouth full, shook her head. She swallowed. "I would think about it if I were you. You know how performing stresses you out."

"I know. It's a pain, but it's also an opportunity. I can't always avoid these challenges. Philip would do it, but he might be in New York. I'll probably go to their flat to practise. I think it's really nice of them to ask me after the show I made of myself..." I trailed off.

"Well, it's up to you, but why put yourself under so much

pressure? I thought accompanying the choir was bad enough." She licked her fingers and picked up the crumbs from her plate.

"I know it's nerve-racking, but the tablets really helped last time. And I could have lessons with the piano teacher at college. Jack Turner said he's really good."

"*Jack* Turner." She chuckled. "How long have you been calling him Jack?" She grinned at me, her lips parted, chocolate on her front teeth. "Is there anything you haven't told me?"

"Don't be silly. I haven't even seen him since the party. There was no lecture on Friday."

"What happened?"

"He didn't come in."

"Why not?"

"I don't know. Maybe he wasn't well. Maybe he had a doctor's appointment."

"Or an appointment with his solicitor."

"Why would he?"

"Maybe he's sleeping around with his students again."

"Don't be silly," I said sharply.

"But you told me that he had been suspended before." She giggled. "No reason to get upset. I was only joking."

I stared at her, taken aback. "When did I tell you that?"

"After the party." She looked at me with narrowed eyes. "Don't tell me you can't remember. My mum never did when she was drunk..."

"But I'm not your mother," I said, trying to keep my calm. "Anyway, it's none of our business."

"What does it matter, no reason to get worked up about it." She got up. "Let's put the kettle on and have a cup of tea. It's really nice of your friends to invite you around. I wouldn't mind seeing them again. There's something I want to ask Philip. He was quite interested to hear about my book. Are you going to the Mackintosh tomorrow after the rehearsal? I could come over."

"I'm probably not going to the pub again. It was too noisy, and we're going to rehearse soon anyway." I got up as well. "Thanks, but no tea for me. I need to go to bed."

"All right then, sleep tight."

"Thanks again for the cake."

"Glad you liked it." She switched on the TV and started channel hopping with the sound off, staring at the screen. Leaving the room, I could hear her finally settling for one of her hospital soaps.

My room still smelled of paint despite having left the window open. The naked 40-watt bulb spread a miserable light. Looking out into the dark, overgrown garden, I saw the mildewed apple tree swaying in the breeze. I felt a chill inside as Amy's words came back to me: "She never did when she was drunk." I had been fooling myself: getting rid of that hideous old-fashioned paper had not been enough. The memory of her mother would always linger in the house, especially in this room! There'd always be an echo of her sad life.

I drew the curtains and went to sleep. After a couple of hours I woke up. I'd had a terrible dream: the house was empty when I came back from college. The electricity was gone and it was pitch dark inside because I couldn't switch on the light. My footsteps echoed as I climbed the stairs to get to my room. I knew that I had a candle and matches somewhere in my dresser and rummaged through the drawers to find them. There were clothes inside, soft fabrics, silk and velvet garments. I knew they weren't mine, but I kept digging my way through them, sure that the candle had to be there. Suddenly I heard someone breathing and turned around. Staring into the dark, I knew in a moment of terror that there was someone else in the room – that someone else was lying in my bed.

The glowing hands of my alarm clock said that it was one o'clock. It was windy outside. Still dazed, I lay on my side, thinking about the dream. The red velvet curtains billowed in, creating swaying shadows on the wall. After a while I got up and closed the window. It took me a long time to go to sleep again.

After many hours of fitful sleep with more disturbing dreams I eventually woke up at half past ten – too late to make it to Composition.

AMY WAS in the kitchen when I went downstairs; she was drinking a cup of tea with her broad back to me, looking out into the back garden.

"Morning," she said without turning around. "How are you?"

"Fine. A bit tired. I overslept."

"I'm not surprised."

"Why?" I turned on the tap and began filling the kettle.

"I heard you in the night."

"What did you hear?"

"You were walking around and talking."

"When was that?"

"Half past two. I had to get up to go to the loo. It sounded as if you were upset or arguing with someone."

"Half past two? I was asleep. You probably heard someone outside. Maybe drunken students?"

"No, it was definitely you." She looked at me, her face set into an expression of irritable concern. "There was no other voice. I listened at your door. You were walking up and down, muttering to yourself. I knocked, but you didn't take any notice. I remembered what you had said about your sleepwalking. I thought I'd better not disturb you. In the end I just went back to bed again."

"But I haven't had an episode for years." With an unsteady hand I put the kettle down. "I only did it after my sister died, because I was so upset." I looked out of the window; there were two blackbirds fighting in the garden, making a hell of a noise.

"But how would you know when you lived on your own?" Amy put her dirty mug in the sink. "Sorry, I wasn't sure if I should mention it. Can you really not remember?"

I shook my head, confused.

"It must have been sleepwalking then. Perhaps it was the stress, all that pressure with your playing."

"Thanks for telling me." I didn't look at her. One bird had left and the other one was hopping around the decomposing apples underneath the tree, tugging worms.

"No worries," she said. "I'm not angry with you. Just thought I'd let you know. Anyway, I've got to go. I'm meeting a friend. I'm not sure when I'll be back – could be late. Don't wait up for me." I could hear her in the hall, putting on her coat and then the front door clicked shut.

I drank my tea and made my way upstairs. I stood a long time under the shower, letting the hot water beat down on me. I remembered the first time my mother had told me about my sleepwalking at home. I could still recall the exact words she had used.

"You scared the life out of me: floating in your white nightie, eyes wide open, roaming the house like a ghost." Had I ever talked while I was asleep? I couldn't remember her mentioning it. Had she been protecting me by holding something back?

When I came out of the bathroom, it was already twenty past eleven. I blow-dried my hair, got dressed and had a quick sandwich in the kitchen, eating on my feet and looking out of the window again. The apple tree stood still, its branches powdery and white. The birds had flown away.

At twenty to twelve I put on my coat and went upstairs to fetch my bag for the choir accompaniment, a flat leather briefcase big enough to hold my notes. It wasn't hanging on the hook behind the door as usual, nor was it on the floor near the desk or in my cupboard. I went back downstairs to have a look in the hall but couldn't find it there either.

In my mind, I ran through the places where it could possibly be. When had I last practised the Mozart at college? Had I left it in the practice room the other day? Time was running out, and I had to leave without it in the end, hoping that someone had handed it in at the porter's lodge. It did not only contain the score I needed – the tranquillisers were in there as well.

THE PORTER SHRUGGED when I asked about my bag. "No, nothing has been handed in. No idea where it could be." He bent his head, returning to his *Daily Mirror*. I peered through the window, hoping that he was wrong, but couldn't see the briefcase anywhere.

I looked in all the empty practice rooms and even knocked on closed doors, but it wasn't there. No one had seen it. There was nothing else I could do but get a new score from the library.

Margaret greeted me at the checkout desk like an old friend and told me all about the court process. Her son had been disqualified from driving for a year. They had to pay a hefty fine, but she seemed pleased that he wasn't going to drive for a while.

"He's going to ride a bike instead." She shook her head, a half-amused smile on her face. "Something else to worry about, I suppose."

I nodded, my thoughts elsewhere.

I sat down in one of the empty rooms and stared at the upright piano. Would I be able to play without the tranquillisers? A panic came over me. For a moment I just sat there, imagining the worst. My hands felt stiff and cold.

I looked out of the window. It was a sunny day again; a lot of students were sitting outside on the grass. The street was busy with passing cars. For a couple of minutes I imagined running into the traffic and being hit by one of them. The thought brought a strange relief. I would be off the hook! It seemed the lesser evil: people would make a fuss – they would look after me – I wouldn't have to go through with it.

Pull yourself together. You can do it, I tried to brace myself. *Just play through it again. What does it matter if you make mistakes?* But my heart was racing so hard I thought I might be having an attack. There were voices in the corridor outside my door. I played a few bars to keep them out.

Maybe I could still get out of it. I really felt awful after the night I'd had. I'd been to the toilet earlier on, my face had looked sweaty and pale in the mirror. Maybe I could still cry off sick.

By rehearsal time, I was in such a state that even Dr Turner cottoned on that something was not right.

"Oh dear," he said, when I mumbled something about coming down with a cold. "I appreciate that you want to play anyway." He rummaged in his briefcase, getting out a box of aspirins. "Have a couple of those," he said.

Clara was already waiting at the piano to turn the pages for me.

"You look a bit peaky," she said.

"I'm not feeling too good." I glanced at Dr Turner. It was too late now – I should have told him I had to go home. When he raised his hand there was nothing else I could do but leap into it. My fingers were so damp that I feared they would slide off the keyboard, but I managed somehow and it seemed not too bad for the first two pages. But as soon as I thought it was going all right I messed up the allegro and halted, my knees shaking uncontrollably.

"Let's take that again," he said, without looking at me. "From the beginning please."

This time I managed to carry on, despite my shaking, and made it to the end. We ploughed through it another three times. By the end my face was burning up.

"I should have sent you home," Dr Turner said, as I was gathering up my things. "You really do look unwell." He shook his head. "I hope it's nothing too serious."

Clara was waiting for me in the foyer. "You're coming to the pub?" she asked.

"No, I'm going home." I suddenly had to hold back my tears. "Look," I said. "I'm really sorry – I was rubbish today. I'd understand if you want someone else to accompany you at the concert."

"Don't worry." She touched my arm. "You just need a good night's sleep." She smiled. "Are you still coming on Sunday? Philip is cooking a meal. I just wanted to warn you: he doesn't follow recipes. Is there anything you don't like?"

I felt a bit lighter on my way home – my headache almost gone. I wondered what Amy would say – but when I arrived at the house all the windows were dark. The place had an empty feel and her coat was not in the hall. She was probably still with her friend. It was the first time she hadn't been there waiting for me.

7

Amy's dirty breakfast bowl was in the sink, but I saw no other mugs or dishes – a sign that she hadn't been back. I was beginning to wonder where she was. Who was that friend she was with?

A gust of wind came through the window and made me shudder with cold. It had started raining. Maybe the weather was changing. It had been unusually warm over the last few days. I looked out. The wind was getting stronger: the apple tree was swaying to and fro. I could hear the creaking of the wood. A second fierce gust bent its branches over so badly I thought they were going to snap. Was Amy out there somewhere, taking shelter, waiting for the rain to stop?

I went to bed early but couldn't relax. The wind kept on lashing against the house, keeping me awake. "You were walking up and down, talking to yourself." I had been too busy all day to think about it. Amy's face surged up in my mind, her slightly suspicious glance.

My mother had looked at me in a similar way. The way she made light of my sleepwalking couldn't conceal what she really thought. "You were roaming the house, walking in and out of rooms in your white nightie like an angel," she had joked, but she was obviously worried and afraid that there was something wrong with me. No wonder. I had become a different person after my sister died. I frequently hid in my room and was withdrawn and quiet at family meals.

For my mother, the worst thing was that I had stopped going to church. I hadn't been to confession for months. She probably thought that the devil had snatched my soul. Father O'Leary came over to find out what was going on in my mind, but I clammed up. What was there to say? Shirley was dead, and I didn't understand how God had allowed it to happen.

One night our neighbour saw me standing in my open bedroom window. She came running over and hammered on the door, anxious to alert my mum.

"She looks as if she's going to jump," she said, "the way she is standing on the sill, her arms wide open, like someone in a horror film."

I was still at the window when they burst into my room to save my life.

"God has saved you this time," my mother said the next day, "but you must never do it again." Maybe she thought that God was punishing me for abandoning Him. For a month she made me sleep downstairs on the hard, green pull-out sofa in the living room. She was fed up with me – we hardly talked. It was not fair that I was making trouble as well – as if the loss of her other daughter wasn't enough. Keeping busy was her way of coping. Her mind was always preoccupied, always busy with her duties in the church, the flower arrangements and Bible classes. She was permanently on the phone with other parishioners or Father O'Leary, as if she couldn't bear to be quiet or allow herself a moment's silence. That way she gave herself no opportunity, no room to think.

The wind was still roaring outside. It was driving the rain harder against the window and I could hear a low rumble in the distance. Sitting up, I saw a white zigzag through the curtains followed by a sudden explosion of thunder. The crash was so loud that I wondered if the lightning had stuck somewhere nearby, but I didn't dare get up to have a look.

My father spent more and more time in his shop after closing time, going over his books or just killing time; anything was better than the miserable quiet evenings with us. Father O'Leary had taken his place, sitting near the fire, sipping my mother's tea. He seemed a smaller, somewhat diminished figure, different from his presence in church, where he loomed over us from the pulpit in his long-sleeved black robe. His sermons were usually uplifting and inspirational. He told us that in testing our faith God only wanted our best. It was allowed to doubt now and then. Some people were weaker than others and got lost like sheep. But He would forgive them as long as they repented and came back.

He was different – more passionate and agitated – when he preached about Hell. His voice grew louder and fiercer. Hell was having to live through our sins again and again – so that the pain we had inflicted would become our own. God saw through our lies and punished us. He could open the gates of Hell and engulf the sinner in its darkness any time. It sometimes felt as if he was looking at me. Did he know that Shirley was dead because of what I had done? Priests were like God. They knew when people lied about things. I was too afraid to go to confession and in the end I stopped going to church altogether. The retribution was too terrible to think about.

I had seen pictures of Hell in my father's study depicting the demons as they captured the sinners and threw them into the fire. They showed the fierce world of my nightmares, all darkness and pain: the demon with two faces, the devil with horns and barbed tails, the casting out of the damned.

"It's her overactive imagination," I once heard my mother

saying to a friend. "She's always been afraid of monsters. She sees them in the shadows at night – in the corners of her room. And now that sleepwalking as well... as if there wasn't enough to worry about." She often told me off for "making things up".

I woke up in the middle of the night. The gale was still howling, tearing at the branches of the tree. The wrath of an angry God! Rain was pattering against the window. There was a banging downstairs. I thought that Amy had lost her keys and was knocking at the door. But when I went downstairs to have a look, it was only the kitchen window rattling in its frame.

I somehow managed to go to sleep again and by the time I woke up the wind had died down. It was just after nine. The garden was a devastated mess. There was rubbish everywhere: plastic bags, soaked paper, debris and broken off twigs. Surprisingly, the apple tree had survived the storm and even kept some of its curled-up leaves.

The heating was off, and it was cold downstairs in the kitchen. There was a mug with grey cold tea on the table. It hadn't been there when I'd been up in the night. What time had Amy come home?

I saw her on the landing later on. She'd only just got up and I was on my way out. I was in a hurry to get to Dr Peterson's class and didn't ask her where she had been. She didn't volunteer any information and so I left it at that. Had she met someone through an ad, I wondered. Had it been a disappointing encounter? Was that the reason she didn't want to talk about it?

I DIDN'T SEE much of her over the next few days. When I did, she said that she'd wasted too much time and had to get on with her novel to make some money. I could hear her typing upstairs. She hardly came out of her room, and I was quite pleased that she gave me more space.

I too had things to get on with. The Composition essay had to be in by the end of the week. It was good to have something to take my mind off things. With time I was getting more relaxed. The library had a calming effect, the familiar musty smell and hushed voices. It rained a lot. I worked in a corner at the back, hidden behind the shelves of the reference section with its thick dictionaries and rows of encyclopaedias. My desk was heaped with books and pages of ideas I had jotted down and my essay was gradually taking shape.

The rehearsal had gone badly – but so what? I'd have to do better next time. I had found my bag with the tranquillisers on the coat rack in the hall. It had been hidden behind one of the coats. I had been too stressed to search for it properly. I just had to take it easy from now on.

There were other students from Composition working in the library; sometimes I had a coffee with Gemma or the other girls. Clara had given me the Schubert score for her concert. Whenever I had a break between tutorials, lectures and my essay writing I withdrew into one of the practice rooms to play through it for Friday night. I needed to be prepared. After what had happened at the rehearsal, I didn't want to mess up again. I only hoped that Clara wouldn't feel obliged to take me on just because she had suggested it.

I managed to more or less finish the essay on Friday. My eyes hurt from staring at the computer screen and that bright artificial overhead lighting. I went home about half past five, which left me enough time to wash my hair and get changed. On the way back I popped into Oddbins and picked up a nice bottle of Bordeaux the shop assistant recommended. She carefully wrapped it in paper for me.

· · ·

AMY WAS in the kitchen when I arrived home.

"Hi," she said, glancing at my bottle. "Something to celebrate?"

"Not really," I said self-consciously. "I'm going to Clara's to practise for the concert."

"Will you be able to play after that?" She chuckled, nodding at the wrapped-up wine.

"I'm not drinking it on my own," I said, feeling a bit annoyed that I had to explain and justify myself. "Anyway, what's the big deal? You have a drink now and then."

"Everything in moderation. I just remember last time." She shrugged. "I know it's not my business. But I would be careful."

"Nothing to worry about." I turned my face away. "It's just polite to bring a bottle. That's all."

As I did my hair and make-up, I could hear the television blaring in the living room downstairs – the volume turned up. On my way out I just shouted "goodbye". I didn't want her to see that I was wearing the purple velvet jacket – that I had gone back to Cardiff market and bought it after all.

I GOT THERE JUST BEFORE eight. Clara opened the door, and I gave her the wine.

"Thanks," she said, giving me a light kiss on the cheek. Her breath smelled faintly of wine. She didn't smile, and I could feel a touch of apprehension as she quietly led the way into the living room. A fire was crackling in the hearth and the table was laid with Chinese porcelain and silverware.

"Just a moment," she said, "I'll open the bottle." She disappeared into the kitchen, and I could hear her saying something in a low voice. I glanced around. The books and papers they'd cleared from the table were now stacked on the floor. The room seemed more worn and run-down than before. I noticed stains on the Persian carpet and there were a lot of dirty cups and glasses everywhere. A half-empty bottle of whisky sat on the mantelpiece. After what seemed like ages she came back with the bottle of Bordeaux and glasses.

"Philip is making a stew," she said, pouring the wine. "His own creation with lamb and lots of spices." She was wearing a crisp white blouse again, and her hair was neat. There was an absent look in her eyes, as if her thoughts were somewhere else. We were both quiet for a moment, sipping wine.

"People are putting their names down for the Christmas concert now," she said eventually. "Have you thought about what you want to perform?"

"Not really." Christmas seemed a long time away. Was she just making conversation? "Have you?"

"Perhaps we'll sing some Brahms... if Philip is back from New York," she trailed off. There was another silence and I was beginning to wonder if there was something wrong. Had they had an argument? Was it awkward for them having me over for dinner?

I was relieved when Philip came in.

"Hi," he greeted me brightly, putting a salad bowl on the table. "The stew is simmering away. It needs a bit more time, so let's have the salad first." He took off his steamed-up glasses and elaborately cleaned them with a paper handkerchief. "How are you getting on with your essay? Wasn't it about Mahler reworking existing pieces?"

"I finished it the other day." I was surprised he remembered.

He nodded, helping himself to some salad, tomatoes and mixed leaves.

"There's a lot of that in Mahler's symphonies," he said, looking even more dishevelled than usual. I sensed that his mind was somewhere else. "And in his songs of course." He sat down at the table, downed his wine and straight away refilled his glass. His white shirt was dirty around the collar, and he had the sleeves rolled up. His forearms were pale but sinewy and strong, leading to long angular hands.

"We were talking about the Christmas concert," Clara said. "We should think ahead and plan it now. There're only so many slots."

Philip was just about to start eating when his mobile rang. He glanced at Clara, his head slightly swaying. Then he got up and walked out of the room. I could hear him talking as he went up the stairs.

"His mum," Clara said in a flat voice. "The third time today."

"Is she not well?"

"I suppose you could say that." She looked at the hearth where the flames flickered and crackled. "She's taking those tablets again."

"What sort of tablets?"

"I don't know. Tranquillisers probably." She shrugged. "She always knocks herself out when she's in trouble. Last time she ended up in hospital. Philip thinks he might have to go over there and look after her."

"What's wrong?"

"Boyfriend trouble." She gave a dry laugh. "It happens now and then." She took a long sip of her wine. "He really loves her, but she drives him crazy."

"Boyfriend trouble?" I said, surprised. "How old is she?"

"Fifty-eight. She had him when she was still a kid herself." Clara raised her eyes to the ceiling, and we listened to the sound of his footsteps above crossing the room and then back again.

"He's too tense to sit down," she said. "He's been in a terrible state all day." She looked as if she wanted to say something else, but then picked up her fork and started eating. She'd hardly touched her salad before.

There was a long moment of silence broken only by the crackling of the fire and Philip's footsteps above. I listened to the low sound of his voice, rising and falling. I wondered if Philip's mum had chosen the furniture: the wooden book-shelves lining every wall, the faded brocade of the sofa, the red velvet curtains and standard lamps with their hand-embroidered shades. What a difference to Amy's house where everything was drab and sad.

"We're having a party next month," Clara interrupted my thoughts. "Philip's fortieth. I hope he's going to be back by then. We thought of having some people over. Nothing spec-tacular, just drinks and music." She topped up our glasses. "Jack is coming," she said, "with his new partner."

"The pianist?"

"Yes, how did you know? They've only been together since the concert."

"He told me that she used to be his student."

"Yes, I suppose she was, a few years ago. I hope it works out. He's had a lot of bad luck over the years."

"Gemma said he was married before. She said that he got into trouble." I took a sip of my wine.

"He got divorced a few years ago," she said sharply. "Don't believe everything you hear. There's a lot of silly gossip going around. He went through a bad time after his divorce – that's all." Her expression had changed. She drew her cardigan across her chest. "I think the fire is dying," she said and got up.

"I don't know much about it. It's just something I heard," I said quickly, wishing I hadn't mentioned it. "She is very talented – and beautiful."

"Jack is a good friend to Philip and me," she said. "Philip nearly gave up music altogether, but Jack coaxed him back. We both owe him a lot. Without him I wouldn't be at college either."

"How long have you been teaching?"

"A couple of years. Just a few hours a week." She shrugged. "Not exactly what you would call a successful career. I suppose I'm not very ambitious. That's certainly what Philip's mother thinks."

"Do you mind?"

She shook her head, but I could see that she was upset. She drew in a long breath.

"It wouldn't be so bad if we could pay our way, but I don't know how we would get by without the house. Philip is teaching part-time. He needs a lot of time for his composing, and his mother doesn't understand that. She thinks he should have a proper career. She probably thinks that I'm a bad influence."

"What is she doing in New York?"

"She runs a music agency. Very successfully, in fact. She makes a lot of money."

"What sort of music? Isn't that useful for Philip. Couldn't she help him to make a name for himself?"

"Maybe." She shrugged. "But she seems to think that he's wasting his time, and he doesn't want her to get involved. He needs to do his own thing."

"What about you? You have a beautiful voice. I heard that you used to be in the Welsh Opera chorus."

"A long time ago." She stared at me. "Who told you that?" She suddenly looked tired and defeated. "It was stressful," she said. "I found it difficult. There was a lot of backbiting, and I didn't have much confidence..."

"Really? You seem so at ease."

"Well, thank you." She got up, her back straight. "Maybe we should have a go at the Schubert."

"Good idea." I followed her into the music room. Maybe it was just shyness that made her seem aloof and absent-minded now and then.

Clara's confession had put my own problems into perspective. I was a bit drowsy after the wine, but when I sat down at the piano and ran my fingers across the keys, I knew that I would be all right. It felt as if something inside me had loosened up.

The Schubert suited her voice. I watched her over the piano. The light from the ceiling lamp fell onto her hair and on the dress she was wearing – a satiny fabric of greenish-blue. Halfway through *Meine Rhuh ist hin, Mein Herz ist schwer*, I realised that Philip was standing in the doorway, watching us.

"Very nice. Thanks for helping out." He steadied himself against the frame, holding an empty glass. His voice was raised and oddly theatrical. "But it won't be necessary now. I'm not going to New York after all. My mother has decided to come over and honour us with her presence instead."

"When is she coming?" Clara asked as we went into the living room, her face pale with the shock.

"As soon as she gets a flight." He reached in his pocket and pulled out a pack of cigarettes. Lighting up, he inhaled deeply and then blew the blue-grey smoke against the ceiling. "She could be here at the end of the week for all I know."

He glanced at me, his expression as unreadable as ever. "Have you ever thought about moving? We have a spare bedroom upstairs. My mum sleeps there when she's in Cardiff, but she could easily go to a hotel. It would be better for everyone."

"He's just being silly." Clara got a new bottle of wine from the kitchen and refilled our glasses. "He always comes up with these ridiculous ideas. Did she say how long she is going to stay?"

"Who says that we can't rent it out?" He let the smoke ease off his mouth. "It might be worth thinking about." His face was flushed. He seemed more drunk than I had thought at first. "Let's at least finish our meal," he said. "I saw you haven't touched the food. Who is going to serve?"

Clara and I went into the kitchen and warmed up the stew. For the next half hour we were busy eating. It was delicious. Philip who gulped down more wine made light of the drama. The last time he'd been to New York, he'd met his mother's boyfriend who was about ten years younger than himself. We all cracked up laughing when he told us how dismayed they had been because Philip had woken them up in the night, coming back from the pub. "You should have seen him sitting next to her at the kitchen table, telling me off – he hardly looked twenty-five. They get younger every time."

We had a couple of straight whiskies after the meal and moved back to the piano room. Clara dug out some sheet music from the stool and Philip started playing jazz songs: *What a Wonderful World* and *My Favourite Things*. And then we went on to Kurt Weill. We sang along from behind the piano: "Oh the shark has pretty teeth dear, and he shows them pearly white."

When Philip played *Blame it on the Boogie*, Clara smiled at me. She put her hands around my waist, and we moved to the music. "I just can't, I just can't, I just can't control my feet." We were singing and completely out of breath – it was hysterical and slightly mad, a release from the tension before. She spun me around until I tripped and dragged her down to the floor. She was laughing, her eyes sparkling next to mine.

At about half past one Clara ordered a taxi for me. We were all quite drunk by the time we said goodbye. Philip insisted that I stay, but I had to do a shift for Margaret in the library the next day. Clara's cheek brushed mine. I remember staring out of the window at the dazzling car lights, at the blurred brightness of their merging colours. I remember feeling giddy and very excited. I remember wondering what the future had in store for me.

8

The following morning, I woke up late. My mouth was dry, and the bright daylight streaming through the window hurt my eyes. My alarm told me it was gone ten, well past my usual wake-up time. I curled under my blanket and closed my eyes again, wondering how many glasses of wine I'd had. I listened to the faint rumble of a passing freight train, and then I heard Amy downstairs in the kitchen, running water and slamming a door.

Soon after there were footsteps on the stairs followed by an energetic knock.

"Kate?" Amy called.

"What's the matter?"

"That's what I was going to ask you." She stood in the doorway, fixing me with an unblinking stare.

"Why?"

"Did you have a good time yesterday?"

"Yes." I sat up. "It was a good rehearsal."

"No food or drink?"

"Why? Philip made a stew."

"And then you thought you'd have some more."

"Why?" I stared back at her, searching for an indication that she was joking, but she looked deadly serious.

"You could have killed us both. You left the cooker on all night with no flame burning. The smell of gas woke me up. Thank God I didn't switch on the light. There would have been a massive explosion: the house gone – a pile of rubble!" She turned around and thundered downstairs.

I put on my dressing gown and followed her. It was cold. All the windows were wide open. She was in the kitchen, her heavy body kneeling on the sticky floor, digging for something in the cupboard underneath the sink. She turned around, her thick neck strained.

"So, what do you have to say for yourself?" She handed over a bottle of bleach. "Do you think I should clear up your mess? Is that what you think?"

There was a charred crust stuck to the frying pan. Someone had smashed an egg, and the yolk had run down the kitchen unit and onto the floor.

"It wasn't me." I stared at the chaos. "I went straight upstairs. And there's no way I would have left the cooker on!"

"So, who was it then? Because it wasn't me either." She crossed her strong arms in front of her chest. "Do you think someone broke in? Someone who wanted to blow us up? Only I haven't seen any evidence of a break-in. Would you like me to have a look if anything is missing?"

Stunned by her sarcasm, I was momentarily lost for words.

"Well?" she said, looking at me. "I would love to hear your idea of what really happened."

"This is ridiculous," I said, my voice raised. "If there wasn't anyone else in the house it could just as well have been you. We had a lovely meal... I was tired... we had wine..."

"Yes, I could hear that." She shook her head. "The way

you stumbled up the stairs. But the wine at dinner was obviously not enough."

"What are you talking about?"

"I'm talking about my bottle of wine – the Pinot Grigio. It was in the fridge last night when I went to bed. It wasn't cheap. You could at least have asked. I bought it for a special occasion."

I swallowed. My mouth was so dry it hurt to speak. All I wanted was a glass of water and a couple more hours of sleep. "Look," I said, trying to stay calm, "I really didn't drink your wine. I don't know what's going on. But if you've got so little trust in me, perhaps I should move out. I'm sure you can find someone better than me." I paused, watching her expression. "Actually, Philip suggested that I could move in with them, and maybe that's not such a bad idea." It felt good, lashing out. I knew moving out wasn't really an option, but my threat certainly had an effect on her. Her face had turned pale.

"Go ahead then. I'm better off without you anyway!" She abruptly turned around and disappeared into the living room.

I got myself a glass of water from the tap and drank it in front of the window. Children were playing hopscotch on the street, laughing and screaming. I couldn't remember ever being so angry. What on earth had all that been about? I breathed in deeply and drank in controlled little sips to calm myself down. Then I went back to my room.

Lying down on my bed again, I mulled over what had been said. Maybe I'd have to look around for somewhere else to live. I raked the fringe of the rug with my fingers when I suddenly felt something damp. There was a wet patch – some liquid had been spilled. I bent over, almost touching it with my nose. The smell, fruity and sharp, made me feel nauseous. Leaning over a bit further, I peered under the bed. There was something at the back but I couldn't see much in the dark. I got up and lay down on the floor to have a better look. It was the shape of a bottle. I reached for it. My throat felt tight. Glancing at it more closely, I held my breath. My mind was numb. There was no doubt: it was Amy's wine. The Pinot Grigio she had been talking about. It had been in the fridge for quite some time.

I felt a rush of blood to my head and had to sit down again. Why was it in my room? Had I been the one to shove it underneath the bed?

I went to the bathroom and splashed cold water on my face. Looking into the mirror, my red-rimmed eyes stared back at me. There was no glass in my room. Had I drunk the wine straight from the bottle, drooling and spluttering half of it onto the carpet? There was nothing I could hold on to, not even fragments of a dream. I lay my forehead against the cold mirror, begging my mind to remember. But there was nothing. For moment I just stood there, imagining it: how I had crept downstairs and taken the bottle out of the fridge... What if there had been a gas explosion? The scene began to take shape in my mind: windows shattering, the noise, pieces of brick and glass raining down, the spreading flames and billowing black smoke! It made me feel weak at the knees.

There was no time for a shower. I put on some clothes and with a heavy heart made my way downstairs. The kitchen was still in a mess. I put the dirty pan in the sink and filled it with hot soapy water. Then I threw away the rubbish, the bits of eggshell and bacon, the half-eaten toast on the sideboard. The smell of the raw eggs made me gag, but it didn't trigger the memory I was waiting for.

I scrubbed the cooker until the smell of bleach became unbearable. I tried to steady myself, holding my hands under cold running water. My head was sore. How could I have left the gas on all night? I wiped the work surfaces again and left the pan in the sink to soak. When there was nothing left to do, I knew I couldn't put it off any longer.

There was no sound coming from the living room, and I wondered if Amy had gone out. But when I put my head around the door I saw her on the sofa, legs stretched out, having a cup of tea and reading one of her library books. Sensing my presence, she lifted her eyes, looking at me through her oversized glasses.

"Sorry," I said, my voice dry with the embarrassment I felt. "I found the empty bottle in my room." I cast my eyes to the floor. "I suppose I must have drunk it after all."

"I'm glad you've come to your senses," she said. "It's not about the bottle at all. We can always buy another one. But, my God, we could have died! I was angry because you were denying it." Her eyes were misty with the hurt I'd caused her, and I felt another pang of guilt.

"I'm sorry," I said again. "But I wasn't denying it. I know now that it was me, but I really can't remember what happened."

"Oh, dearie me." She looked at me. "That's really worrying. I didn't know it was so bad. But at least you've made the first step. It's always the most difficult one: to admit that you have a problem."

"What problem?"

"Well, I'm sorry. I didn't want to..." She looked a bit sheepish, her head cocked to one side. "What do your friends make of it?"

"Make of what?"

"Well, you had a lot to drink yesterday, and you were wasted at the party last time, but I suppose they don't know the half of it. How could you drink another bottle at home?" She sighed.

"Sorry." I bit my tongue to hold back the tears.

"There's no need to be upset now." Amy put her hand on

my shoulder. Her breath smelt of chocolate and tea. "Please don't worry. We'll deal with it. It'll all come out in the wash. I heard you clearing up the mess. That was all you needed to do."

She directed me to the sofa and made me sit down. "I can see that you're not well. You look feverish, if you don't mind me saying so. All glassy-eyed. My word! As though you had flu." She shook her head. "What you need is a nice cup of tea and something to eat to line your poor stomach. What about a nice fried egg sandwich?" She chuckled. "I saw that there are some eggs left. Thank God. I think even I could rustle that up for you." She got up. "Let's see what I can do."

I nodded though I felt nauseous again. The smell of raw eggs! The sun was shining outside. I looked at the light filtering through the dirty window, the particles of dust floating around in the air and wished that it was dark and time to go to bed. The oblivion of sleep was all I needed now. If I could just sleep a few more hours and wake up to see that it had all been a dream.

I heard Amy in the kitchen, making the sandwich, banging the fridge door and humming along to something on the radio. I glanced at the book she had left behind on the sofa. There was a doe-eyed little girl on the cover. It was one of those memoirs she had taken out from the library to inspire her own writing. It didn't take very long until she was back. She handed over a plate with a fried egg on toast.

"I like my fried eggs well done," she said. "I hope you don't mind. I wait until the whites are done and then I flip. My mother always praised my fried egg sandwiches. They were yummy, she said, the best ones she'd ever had." She watched me expectantly as I took a bite.

"Thanks – exactly what I needed," I said. "I can't believe I left the cooker on. That's so dangerous! Maybe I was sleep-walking again."

"Well, I guess it had something to do with your drinking. But don't worry." She took a sip of her cold tea. "Let's not talk about it anymore. To new beginnings." She gave me a smile. "You've done a good job in the kitchen. The frying pan looks cleaner than before."

"I don't know what got into me," I said, eating. I was beginning to feel a bit better now. The sandwich was actually quite nice: the white brown and crispy around the edge and the toast underneath not soggy at all.

"Well, there are things you can do," she said. "People who can help. Have you ever been to one of those groups?"

"What groups?"

"AA meetings." She shrugged. "Nothing to be embarrassed about. Lots of people go there—famous people like Daniel Radcliffe, people you wouldn't think had a problem. I used to go with my mum in the beginning," she added, "when we still thought she could turn it around."

"And could she?"

"Well, yes, for a short while. But she soon enough got fed up with the meetings. She thought that she could still control her drinking then, that she could do it on her own."

"What were the meetings like?"

"I only went a couple of times," she said. "They met up in a community hall in town. Mostly middle-aged people and lots of empty chairs. Everyone had to introduce themselves. I remember a woman. She looked like a schoolteacher, prim and proper. I couldn't believe it when she told us how she had lost her husband and everything else because of her drinking. She stole a handbag off an old woman and took a lot of money from her bank account. She found out where her husband had moved to and went to his house. He wasn't there, but she smashed a window and broke in. When she woke up the next day she couldn't remember anything. But the police caught up with her."

"That's terrible." I swallowed. "But I really don't think I have a drink problem like that."

"That's what you keep saying." She sighed, shaking her head. "Whatever. I'm here for you if you need help. Admitting you have a problem is the first step. They told my mum that the only way forward was absolute honesty and the sincere wish to change, but she didn't want to know…"

"Well, thanks for the sandwich. Please don't worry. It's not that bad. I really don't think that alcohol is a problem." I stood and glanced at my watch. "I'd better get going. I have to cover for Margaret in the library."

"Are you sure you're well enough?" She looked disappointed. "They don't half take advantage. Can't you just phone in and tell them that you're not well?"

"Yes, but there wouldn't be anyone else to do the job. They'd have to close the library." It wasn't true. Lillian would probably stand in for me, if necessary, but I would have said anything at that moment to get away. Amy's well-meant words were really getting me down. I felt so low and weakened anyway – too weak to stand up for myself. It would be such a relief to see other people and forget about what had happened, at least for a while.

THE LIBRARY WAS BUSY. There were more students than usual: all desks were taken and all computers in use. A haven of sanity! Or did it only seem that way? Were there other students struggling? I thought about the woman Amy had talked about earlier on. No one would have guessed what she'd been doing. No one knew as long as you kept up appearances. Were there other music students who like me did crazy things, without people knowing? I quickly brushed away the thought. Normality was what I needed. The familiar sounds had a soothing effect. Some of the students were working together in clusters and there was the typical low-level background chat, voices and computer tapping and laughter. I couldn't make out anyone I knew.

Lillian was checking out books, dealing with a long-haired student.

"Hi," she said, briefly looking up. "I'm glad you're here. I need to go to the dentist. Margaret is in the office." She smiled at the student, handing his card and book across the counter.

Margaret was already in her sensible rainproof jacket, ready to leave.

"Thanks for coming in," she said when she saw me in the door. "You must be busy with your studies. It's so good of you to help me out. I'm really sorry to rely on you so much."

Though she was obviously in a hurry, she took her time to tell me about her latest concerns. It was her son again.

"He scared me out of my wits last night," she said, shaking her head. "I'm really worried about him."

He had apparently come home, his face covered in bloody cuts and bruises. The fact that he was banned from driving had unfortunately not deterred him from drinking or taking drugs. Rather the opposite: going everywhere on his old mountain bike had felt to him like a licence to get legless every night. And now some lowlife was after him, threatening to kill him if he didn't give him the money he owed.

"More than a thousand pounds," she whispered. "He wouldn't have told me if he'd been sober. He usually keeps these things hidden from me. I'm so glad he confessed it now. But the weirdest thing is that he couldn't remember in the morning – not a word of what we talked about yesterday." She sighed. "I hope I can get the money from the bank."

I assured her that I was perfectly able to hold the fort, that I didn't mind covering for her and that there was absolutely no need to feel guilty. She gave me a grateful hug and rushed

off. I was suddenly sad to see her go. Her friendship meant a
lot to me. Her openness was always reassuring.

When Lillian left a few moments later, I was on my own. I
sat down behind the checkout desk. The tension I had felt all
day had developed into a radiating pain around my head. I
breathed in deeply, trying to loosen up, lolling my head in a
circle and unclenching my hands. A student looked over and
gave me a smile. You couldn't help but see the funny side of it.
What would Margaret have thought if I had told her how
drunk I had been – that I had been just as wasted as her
wayward son and couldn't remember anything either?

A girl with long red hair returned some overdue books
and had to pay a hefty fine. When she was gone, I googled
"alcohol and memory lapse" and stared at the screen.

*The alcoholic will experience memory gaps and blackouts
as a result of his binge drinking. He may have a conversation with someone and be aware of it at the time, but later
be unable to recall what was said. Sometimes the alcoholic
will forget small details, and at other times he might not
retain any memory at all. He might not recall where he
has been or with whom he has been drinking. Reminders or
prompting are often inadequate to fill in these memory
gaps. During a complete blackout, a binge drinker fails to
transfer his present memory to long-term storage.*

But how did that apply to me? I had drunk too much with
Clara and Philip, but I could remember everything, even the
taxi ride home. I had gone straight upstairs, quietly, trying
not to wake Amy up. And what about the time when she had
heard me in my room, walking up and down and talking to
myself? That night I didn't have a drink at all. Sleepwalking
seemed far more likely. But maybe the alcohol had made it
worse.

I started another search and found an article confirming my suspicion. Sleepwalking could apparently be triggered by a whole range of factors, amongst them alcohol. There was another, longer article about sleepwalking in general. It said that sleepwalkers could perform activities as simple as sitting up in bed or walking around. Other people had even been cooking or driving. My hair stood on end as I read on. There had been violent gestures reported, grabbing at hallucinated objects and even murder. Going down that route I found a rather gruesome report of homicidal sleepwalking. I devoured the story of Gerard Greener who had killed his father after a heavy night of boozing with his friends. His family had a long history of sleepwalking and his episodes had also been brought on by drinking.

Engrossed in my reading, I wasn't aware that someone was watching me. Only when I heard a slight cough did I look up to see Dr Turner standing in front of the counter. Embarrassed, I clicked the article off.

"Hello there," he said with a broad smile. "I didn't want to interrupt. Don't tell me you're reading the showbiz gossip! Don't worry. We've all been guilty of it." He leaned closer to read the headline on my screen. "Very intriguing. Who is this murderous somnambulist? Anyone important?"

"Not at all." I felt the heat rising to my cheeks. "I was just looking something up," I said quickly, wishing he would leave me alone. Why could I not be more at ease? He couldn't miss how embarrassed I was.

"Never mind," he said. I could feel what he was thinking, how he marked me out again as socially incompetent. "Sorry for interrupting your research." There was an ironic glint in his eyes. "Is everything all right with you? I was wondering how you were. Will you be able to play for the choir tomorrow?"

"Of course."

"Are you sure? You still look a bit off colour. There's a lot of it about. I should have sent you home last week."

"No, it's absolutely fine." I tried to keep an even voice. "I'm much better now."

"I'm very glad to hear it." His lips curled into a teasing smile. "It's good of you to help out in the library. Margaret said what a treasure you are. There was something else..." He raised his eyes to the ceiling. "What was it again I wanted to say? Oh yes, of course. The tutorial tomorrow. Will you be coming? It's essential for first year students. Maybe there's something you want to talk about? Questions about your coursework? We'll take it in groups of twos and threes."

I watched how he went over to a student sitting in a corner at the back. Her desk was heaped with books and photocopies marked with highlighter pen. I knew her from his history course. She was tall and very pretty with long blonde hair and black designer glasses. She shook her head and her long hair swung as she laughed at something he said. As if sensing that I was staring at him, he suddenly turned around. I could feel myself blushing again and quickly averted my eyes, disconcerted by his perspicacious look.

9

The house was dark when I got back. I had been shopping in Lidl's on the way home to replace the food I had taken from the fridge: eggs, bacon, bread, butter and a bottle of the most expensive Pinot Grigio I could find. It was the least I could do to make amends.

There was still the scent of burnt food in the kitchen and I opened a window to let in fresh air. The warm weather was definitely over now; the recent storms had caused widespread damage (a man had been injured and another one killed when a tree fell on their car) and now the weather had turned unseasonably cold. There was hoar frost in the morning and at night the temperatures always sank beneath zero. To save money we had so far avoided putting on the heating. But it was getting increasingly uncomfortable now. There was the gas fire in the living room, which gave off a little warmth, but the sofa was Amy's domain and I would never have thought of sitting there on my own.

Putting the shopping away, I wondered where Amy was. Was she out again with her friend? I glanced out of the

window into the overgrown wilderness outside. The storm
had left behind fallen branches and scattered rubbish. The
broken garden cherub had disappeared under a pile of debris
and leaves, and there was an old plastic bag that had been
blown over the fence.

I was exhausted and needed an early night. It was dark in
the hall – the light bulb had gone dead. I went up the stairs
slowly, feeling my way along the banister when I heard a
noise, a faint crash, as if a door or window had fallen shut.

I stopped and listened, but there was nothing but the
distant rumble of a freight train going past. Or was Amy in
her room after all, I wondered. No light shone from underneath her door but I knocked anyway. When I turned the
knob it was locked. She always locked the door when she
went out. Only once or twice had I caught a glimpse of the
mess inside.

I had left the window open in my room because of the
lingering smell of paint and it was so freezing cold I could see
my breath. I tucked myself in, but my feet were icy, and it took
me quite some time to go to sleep.

THROUGH THE FOG of my sleep someone was hammering on
my door – it was Amy. "Get up," she shouted. "They're all
downstairs. I want you to meet my mother. It's just the right
light for it now."

I jumped out of bed. With no time to get dressed, I put on
my old dressing gown over the pyjamas I was wearing. Amy
was waiting on the landing. The bulb had been replaced and
I noticed that there were portraits on the wall – faces that
seemed to belong to another world, pale with small dark eyes
– and amongst them was the picture of her mother, the one I
had found outside. But there was something different about

her face. I went over to have a closer look. Startled, I saw that her eyes had clouded over and turned milky white.

"Hurry up," Amy said. "Quick! They're waiting for us." I followed her down the stairs and then into the living room. The curtains were drawn to block out the light. There was a large round table in the middle of the room – the other furniture was pushed aside. Half a dozen people were seated around it, women and men. They all looked very pale but I couldn't really see their faces. Only one woman stood out. She was sitting near the electric fire. She was very fat, and her big red face was glistening with sweat.

"Don't stare at her," Amy hissed. We sat down at the table and she took my hand. As if on command the others started holding hands as well.

"About time," said the man on my other side. He was sweating under the arms of his white shirt, and his hand was moist and limp in mine. I recognised his deep sonorous voice; it was Jeremy's. "Don't talk to me," he whispered in my ear. "Be careful. I'll tell them all that you're stalking me."

The woman by the fire got up.

"I've just been in touch with Amy's mother. She has agreed to speak through Kate," she said in a high, commanding voice. She stretched her chubby arm as if reaching out for something above. "Say something," she screeched. "We want to know what has happened to you."

"Yes, why don't you tell us?" Amy said, pressing my hand. "Tell us why you drink so much."

"Be quiet," I hissed back, trying to wriggle out of her grip. I didn't look up because I knew that everyone was staring at me.

"What on earth are you waiting for?" The fat woman shot me an angry look, then turned to Amy. "Close your eyes and summon the image of your mother, child!"

"But she's here," Amy whimpered. "She's sitting right next to me." She squeezed my hand again. "I know it's her. She sleeps upstairs in her room. I can hear her walk around at night."

"Leave me alone!" I screamed and jumped up from my chair. Jeremy hadn't let go of my hand, and in a terrible moment of horror I realised that I had torn off his arm. He sank down in his chair, his face lifeless and pale. His eyes were puckered and clouded. There was no doubt that he was dead. The others were also limp and lifeless in their chairs and it suddenly struck me that they'd been dead all along.

I woke up with a start. My heart was thumping in my chest, and my pyjamas were wet with cold sweat. It was half past five and still dark. I stared at the ceiling for a moment to gather my thoughts. What on earth had all that been about?

I went downstairs and drank a glass of water at the kitchen sink, wondering if Amy was in her room.

It was a moonless night, pitch dark. Back in my room, I tried to get to sleep again but couldn't relax. I closed my eyes, conscious of breathing more slowly, unable to suppress the thoughts racing through my mind. The awful dream haunted me.

Tossing and turning, I thought about Jeremy again – the time when he had summoned me to that café to have it out with me. He'd had wet patches under the arms of his white shirt, just like the Jeremy in my dream. "How can you not remember what you said to me?" he'd said under his breath, glancing around to see if anyone was listening. I'd always thought that Jeremy had been exaggerating those "drunken rages" as he referred to my nightly calls. But what if Amy was right? Maybe there had been memory gaps and blackouts before. I always seemed to remember what I had done, but how could I be so certain when there was no one else to tell me otherwise? Maybe Jeremy had been right to shine a light on it. And what had I done? I had dismissed it as self-serving lies and then – click! – the light had gone off again, and I was back in the dark, unable to see.

Father O'Leary had often talked about the dark. I used to be scared of his tall figure on the pulpit preaching how Satan operated in this world to bring about his own black ends. When he came to have tea and biscuits in our living room, he looked a different person, shrunken to a normal size, sitting in my father's wing chair by the fire with tired eyes.

For months he had turned up every week to help me with my sleepwalking. He had said that he wanted me to see the light and be happy again. Matthew 6:22 was his favourite quote: "If your eyes are healthy, your whole body will be full of light. But if your eyes are unhealthy, your whole body will be full of darkness. If then the light within you is darkness, how great is that darkness!"

The hands of my alarm clock glowed in the dark. How would I be able to make it through the day without a proper rest? I'd have to accompany the choir in the evening and there was the tutorial and Dr Turner's course. It was nearly dawn when I finally drifted off to sleep.

Daylight was streaming in through the gap between the curtains when I woke up. I opened my eyes. There was something odd about the quality of the light, its brightness. I sat bolt upright in bed. It was quarter past ten. I had missed the tutorial! And it was too late for Dr Turner's course. He had especially told me to come. Now he would probably think that I was lazy and couldn't be bothered. I'd have to make up an excuse, phone him and tell him that I wasn't well.

On the landing, I heard Amy typing in her room. So she had come back last night after all. I stopped for a moment and listened. Brushing my teeth in the bathroom, I caught my reflection in the mirror on the wall. I hardly recognised myself: the red face, my sweaty tousled hair, the staring feverish eyes.

I quietly walked downstairs. Putting the kettle on in the kitchen, I started thinking about the call I was going to make. His course had only just started – his mobile would be switched off. It was the perfect excuse to leave a message on his voicemail. A message would be so much easier than talking directly with him. A short and precise message, with no room for interpretation.

I sat down at the table and got out my phone. My fingers were stiff as I tapped in his name. What was I going to say? *Sorry that I couldn't make it to your course.* Or: *I just can't get over this cold.* But wouldn't my voice give me away? It was difficult to fake a stuffy nose. Perhaps a stomach upset would be more convincing.

"I've been up all night with a stomach upset," I said aloud, but it didn't sound right either. Maybe I should cut out the explanations and just say I wasn't well, or even better, just send a text.

In the end I typed into the phone:

Sorry I missed your course and the tutorial. I'm not very well. I won't be able to play for the choir either.

I sent the text, but then straight away wished I hadn't. Maybe it had been too short and sounded brusque.

The kettle was boiling. As I got up to make the tea I saw Amy in the doorway, watching me.

"Hi," she said, "I heard voices. Were you talking to yourself?"

"Of course not. I left a message for Dr Turner." I took a deep breath. "I'm not going to his tutorial because I overslept."

"Did you tell him that?"

"No. I said I wasn't very well."

"And are you?"

"I'm fine." I took a sip of my scalding hot tea, nearly burning my tongue. "I just had a bad night."

She gave me a look of concern. "You still don't look right, if you don't mind me saying so: you're as white as a sheet. You need to look after yourself, recharge your batteries, especially after all that drinking. You should take it easy. Your Dr Turner will understand." She chuckled, touching my arm. "I reckon the stress is getting on top of you. Sometimes you have to carve time out in your schedule that is just for you."

As I rinsed my cup at the sink my mobile rang. Startled, I turned around. It was still sitting on the table, shifting slightly with the vibration. I crossed the room and picked it up, wondering for an anxious moment if it was Dr Turner, returning my call – but it was Clara.

"Hi," she said in a quiet breathless voice. "I'm in town with Philip's mum. She's dragging me round Jacob's Market and driving me crazy. Any chance you could join us later for an early lunch? You'd save my day. I thought we could go to Crumbs in the arcade – they do a nice salad."

"Yes. Why not?" I said, aware that Amy was watching.

"Would twelve be OK?" She lowered her voice to a whisper. "See you there. I can't talk: she's coming back." She hung up.

"Who was that?"

"Clara. She's in town with Philip's mother. She asked me to meet up with them. She said it would do her a favour."

"I thought you needed a rest. Are you sure that would be wise?"

"I'm not ill," I said, a bit impatiently. "I just overslept."

"Because you were exhausted." She shook her head. "It's none of my business, but you have to be careful that people don't take advantage of you. She whistles and you come running. Whatever." She glanced at her watch. "My word! Is it really that late? I'm meeting someone too."

I noticed that she looked different. Her mousy hair was dyed two or three shades lighter and blended with highlights. It had also been straightened and looked glossier than before. She was wearing a new shiny purple blouse with sparkling silver threads running through it – a bit too dressy for my liking. I wasn't sure if I liked her new glamorous look.

"New haircut? Where did you go?"

"Somewhere in town. It wasn't cheap."

"It looks expensive," I said lamely.

"See you later. Watch what you're drinking." I could hear her in the hall, putting on her coat and then walking out and banging the front door. Was she meeting her friend again? Was he the reason for her new expensive hairdo? Had she been with him the night before? Perhaps a relationship would make her life a bit more interesting so that she'd be less bothered with what I was doing.

It was a relief to have the house to myself. I took more care than usual getting ready, had a shower and washed my hair. Then I went through my wardrobe, wondering what to wear. I tried on a few things, regarding myself in the mirror. I thought of the dress Clara had worn, the beautiful vintage fabric of greenish blue. The comfortable slacks and pastel-coloured blouses I had brought with me from Carlisle seemed a bit drab and frumpy now.

I had scheduled a generous half an hour to walk into town. But when I was about to leave I just couldn't find my keys. I checked the pockets of the trench coat I had worn the night before and looked in my leather bag. I went through every room and even searched down the back of the sofa – to no avail. It was getting late and I couldn't afford to waste more time. In the end I pulled the front door shut behind me, hoping that Amy would be there when I came back.

It was busy in town. I hurried along Queen Street, making my way through the crowd. Crumbs was in one of the arcades. I had forgotten which one it was and had to stop in the Hayes and ask for directions..

In the end I even got there a bit early. There were people queuing up in front of the door. I was just beginning to wonder if I should go inside when I saw them. They were coming down the arcade from the direction I had come myself. Philip's mother was striding ahead. Her energetic, manly gait was slightly at odds with her trendy clothes. She was a tall athletic woman with short, blonde hair and a big, arched nose. She wore a green leather coat, ankle boots and thick black tights. Clara looked strained and pale in her wake.

"Hi," she said when she saw me at the door. "I'm glad you could make it. Sorry, we're late. We couldn't find what we were looking for." She smiled but her voice had a slightly irritated tone.

"I was trying to find a new mirror for the bathroom," Claudia explained. She spoke with a New York accent, no trace of German at all. "I don't know how they put up with the old one. It's so tarnished that you can hardly see yourself. But there was nothing nice, nothing but kitsch and cheap junk…"

She seized my hand. "Clara said you were coming. She's very fond of you. Let's go in," she said. "Clara says the food is decent here."

The queue had disappeared and we went inside to order at the counter. We all chose the potato pie.

"You go ahead – I'll pay," she said, motioning for us to go upstairs.

"Oh my God," Clara said, leading the way to an empty table near the window. "I'm so glad you could make it. I would have killed her if I had to spend another hour in that shop."

"Why? What happened?"

"She's like a dog with a bone, always hounding me about Philip and trying to find out about things."

"About what?"

"His love life, his plans... she can't accept that he makes his own decisions now. He's nearly forty, for God's sake! You should have seen him yesterday. He was in a dreadful state. How old does he have to get before she backs off?"

"Have they fallen out?"

"You could say that. We had a few drinks last night, and she just couldn't let it go. She thinks there's something wrong with him because he doesn't want an academic career. He totally clammed up and went to bed at half past nine."

She lowered her voice. "It's just not working with us together in one house. The best thing would be if Philip and I could find somewhere else. We've thought about renting a house with other musicians. Would you be interested?"

"When?"

"We'll have to look into it when Claudia is gone. There are a lot of student houses in Cathays. Let's see how many we are and what we can afford. We'll have to present it to her as a fait accompli. Otherwise she'd try to interfere. It'll be better like that for everyone."

"She's coming." I looked across the room as Claudia approached with a tray. I reached for my wallet to give her the money.

"Please don't. It's on me this time," she said. "It wasn't much and you're only students after all." She sat down next to me and handed out the cutlery. Her hand was large with long fingers – very similar to Philip's hands. Up close I could see how alike they were: they both had arched noses and small grey eyes. But whereas Philip was quite handsome, the same features seemed hawkish and sharp in her face.

"How do you like it at college?" she asked, watching me. "You won't believe it, but I went there too, in the early eighties, a lifetime ago!"

"It must have been very different then."

"Of course." She laughed. "There can't be anyone left that I know – they're all long retired now." Her gray eyes were sizing me up, as if wondering how to swoop down on me. "What do you want to do with your degree?"

"I'm not sure. Maybe teach?"

"Very sensible." She lifted a forkful of pie to her mouth. "Maybe not quite as thrilling as the artistic professions, but let me tell you: it's a lot safer."

Clara gave me a quick glance, rolling her eyes, as if to say: "Now you'll see for yourself." The light from the window fell on her face, and I thought that she looked tired and a bit washed out.

"Which artistic professions are you talking about?" I asked.

She told me about her agency and all of the ambitious hopefuls she represented, mostly performers, instrumentalists, and singers. "Only a few will make a proper living with their music. The majority will have to earn their money in other ways. You have to be tough to make it. Playing, composing – it's a real struggle." She sighed. "I don't understand why Philip is making his life so difficult when he could have a secure career where he's working now."

Clara, who had finished her salad, looked out of the window, a bored expression on her face, as if she had heard it all several times before. Claudia didn't take any notice of her.

"He would make a decent academic," she said. "I wish he

was more ambitious. I really don't understand why he's faffing around. He's not getting any younger."

"He *is* ambitious." Clara didn't look at her. "You know how hard he works."

"But how will he make a living with his compositions?" Claudia gave me a sideways glance, probably trying to get me on her side. "It's all my fault," she continued in a grave voice. "I spoilt him. He never had to worry about money in his life. He takes it all for granted: the house, the council tax and everything else. But I won't always be there for him. I'm worried about his future."

When she looked over at Clara she caught her raising her eyebrows at me.

"Sorry; what am I like?" Claudia frowned. "Here I am going on about my worries and I don't know anything about you yet. Clara told me that you're from the north somewhere. What made you choose Cardiff University? And what did you do before? You've hardly said a word."

"Kate is from Carlisle," Clara said. "She's given up everything to make a new start."

"What was that? Family, kids?"

"No, nothing like that," I said quickly. "Just work."

"What did you do?"

"I was a librarian."

"Really?"

I could see that her interest was waning again. "I wasn't happy," I said, looking down at my hands. "I used to go out with a colleague. He was the real reason I needed a new start."

"What did he do to you?" Claudia touched my arm. I took a deep breath, suddenly feeling the prick of tears. The tiredness I had felt all day was getting on top of me now. I stared at the window as if the bright light could help me regain my composure. The waitress came over to our table to pick up the empty plates.

"You poor thing. That must have been so difficult," Claudia said, her hand still on my arm. "I know. It's unbelievable what men can do to you. You'll have to tell me more about it. Why don't we go somewhere else? Let's talk a bit more and have a proper drink."

10

T he City Arms was busy despite it being so early, but we found an empty table in a cosy corner at the back.

"Let's have a bottle of wine." Claudia took off her coat and went to the bar.

There had been a rugby match earlier on. Wales had lost, but the TV was still on, and the bar was crowded with people. The table was sticky with spilled beer.

"I should really buy this round," I said, pushing a couple of empty dirty glasses aside. I sat down next to Clara on the wooden bench. "She's already paid for the food."

"It's what she wants." Clara shrugged. "She likes to be in charge. Don't worry about it – she's really quite well off. Buy the next round if it makes you feel better." She gave me a sweet smile, all charm, without guile, and I wondered if it was kindness that made her not refer to what I had said before. Maybe she thought I'd get upset again.

I glanced at the pictures on the wall: photos of Cardiff in the forties and fifties when Queen Street had still been busy with cars and a tram going through. There'd been shops with awnings, fishmongers and real butchers.

"If only the houses weren't so expensive now," Clara said. "We can't afford to buy, but maybe we could rent a halfway decent place in Cathays. What about your friend? Would she be interested?"

"Who?" I glanced at the bar where Claudia had inserted herself into the crowd and was ordering the wine.

"Amy. Isn't that her name?"

"She's not renting. She owns the house."

"How many bedrooms have you got? Would there be room for Philip and me to move in?"

"No. It's far too small," I said abruptly. "And it's dark and quite ugly. You wouldn't like it at all."

"But can you just move out and leave her in the lurch? I think she really likes you." She looked at me, slightly puzzled. "She came to look for you in the Mackintosh last Wednesday after choir and asked where you were. She said you had been nervous and that she'd been wondering how it went."

"Really? I told her I would probably not go."

"She said she'd only popped in on her way home. She hadn't really expected you to be there. I think she had a drink with Jack and Philip at the bar."

"What time was that?" I asked, recalling that Wednesday had been the night of the storm.

Before Clara could answer Claudia was back with a bottle of merlot. She filled our glasses.

"To us. Who needs men anyway? What happened in Carlisle?" she asked. "What did this awful colleague do to you?"

"He had someone else." I swallowed. "He didn't tell me; I saw them together. He wasn't honest with me."

"Why do we let them hurt us so much?" She took a sip of

her wine. "Men are cowards when it comes down to it. It happens all the time, but that doesn't make it less painful."

"It doesn't really matter. I've got over it." I glanced at Clara, who had turned away to look at her phone. She had probably decided not to get involved.

"You think you are over it," Claudia said, "but it always leaves a mark. It gets more difficult to trust every time."

Her eyes were swimming as she talked about her own heartbreak. There had been a jazz singer in New York, one of her successful clients.

"He was nearly twenty years younger than me, but we had the most wonderful time together. Until he decided that he wasn't quite ready to be with someone after all – that he needed to be free and independent. And then I heard that he had got married, to a beautiful, much younger woman of course. I always go for the wrong ones." She shrugged. "I just have to get used to being on my own." She downed the rest of her wine.

Clara glanced over at a group of Chinese tourists seated next to us and then returned to her phone, acting as if we weren't there.

Claudia shot her an angry look. "Women should support each other. It was different when I was young. We were all feminists then." She got up and walked over to the jukebox where she looked through the list of songs.

"Top-up?" I asked Clara.

"No, I think I've had enough," she said with a faint smile. She was still glued to her phone, hardly raising her eyes.

I was beginning to wonder if there was something wrong. Did she resent that I was getting on with Claudia? Wasn't that what she had wanted when she asked me to come to her aid?

Claudia came back to *I Will Survive*.

"We danced to that one in the seventies," she said. "The gay anthem. Coming out was a big thing."

"Were you still in Germany then?"

"Yes, until '81. I wanted to do music, but they wouldn't have me in Cologne. You had to be pretty good, and I hadn't been practising enough. It was a blow. In the end I did a business degree instead. I nearly died of boredom, but it came in handy when I started working for the agency." She sighed. "At least I had a lot of friends. We tried to make a difference. There were a lot of women's groups then, and we were there for each other. Shall we have another bottle?"

"Let me go this time." I grabbed my wallet and headed to the bar, pleased to get away. It took a while to get the attention of the busy barmaid. When I returned with the wine they were still not speaking.

Claudia topped up my nearly empty glass.

"There were women with real problems," she said, picking up the conversation from before.

"What sort of problems?"

"I remember a woman who tried to kill herself. She'd cut both her wrists. Her bedding was soaked with blood when the cleaner found her in the morning. A little bit longer and she would have been dead. She'd been in a deep hole for years, not knowing who she was or what she wanted. Her husband had always told her how hopeless and stupid she was – and she had believed every word. She'd lost all sense of who she was. She was still in a bad way when she came to our group. It took quite some time to build her up again, but we got there in the end." She glanced over to Clara who had finished her texting and seemed to be listening at last.

"Don't you think we would help each other?" she said, her eyebrows raised. "Women only joined those groups back then because it was the fashion. I don't think that we're any more selfish now."

"Well, you might be wrong."

Clara didn't answer.

The Sex Pistols erupted from the jukebox, *God Save The Queen* filling the silence. I had been drinking too quickly. A sensation of warmth was spreading through my body, making me feel drowsy and slightly unfocused.

"I do know what you mean," I said over the music. "Women are more career-minded and competitive these days." It sounded like an awful cliché. I had tried to back up Clara, but she didn't even seem to notice.

Claudia stared at me, her hawkish eyes narrowed. "That may be one aspect of it. I'm glad you understand. Young people are different these days. Everything is so different."

I nodded, though I wasn't quite sure what she was trying to say. She was eighteen years older than me.

"What's the plan?" she asked. "Shall we go somewhere else? Or head home for something to eat and another drink?" She wrapped her arm around me.

I glanced at Clara.

"Why not?" she said, getting up. "The more the merrier." It was difficult to tell whether she really meant it. I remembered that I didn't have the key and that Amy would have to unlock the door for me. I was a bit tipsy now, and it was still quite early.

"OK, thanks. I'd love to," I said.

IT WAS DARK OUTSIDE – a fine misty rain was falling. We decided to walk, but by the time we reached the end of Westgate Street it had started pouring down. None of us had brought an umbrella. My hair was drenched within minutes. The rain was getting into my eyes and went down the back of my coat. A girl in front of us let out a scream as a sudden gust of wind blew her umbrella inside out.

Claudia stood at the curb, waving her arms, and managed to stop a taxi. Clara and I climbed into the back. She glanced out of the window – as if not in the mood for talking. Streaks of her wet hair were plastered to her forehead, and her breath smelled of the mint she was sucking. Lights from the passing traffic illuminated her pale face, and I wondered what she was thinking and whether I had said something to make her cross.

THE LIGHTS WERE ON – but Philip wasn't there. Had Clara warned him that we were on our way? Was that the reason he had left? He couldn't have been gone long. There were still some embers glowing in the hearth and it smelled of his cigarettes.

Clara went straight into the kitchen.

"I'll make us tuna sandwiches," she said through the open door. "Nothing else left. And I'm not going out again in this weather."

Claudia poured me a glass of wine and went upstairs to change into dry clothes. The room looked even more dishevelled than last time. The dining table was cluttered with mugs, music scores and empty plates. A newspaper was spread out on the sofa and there were clothes, coats and jackets hanging over the backs of the chairs. The lingering odour of cooking verged on the unpleasant. It struck me that the place was sickening, that its beautiful composure had been disturbed somehow – unsettled by the recent disharmony and tension.

"Have you ever read Simone de Beauvoir?" Claudia re-entered the room and took down a paperback from the shelf. She shoved the paper off the sofa and sat down next to me. "*The Second Sex*. I've just started reading it again. I used to read her books when I was young. She was my leading light. It's all about being free and authentic and not relying on external validation or meaning." She smiled at me. "That's why I fought so hard to have the career I wanted. I couldn't stand being told what to do." She filled her glass and topped up mine. "But there's of course much more to it..."

Clara came from the kitchen with a plate of sandwiches for us and another one for herself. "I hope you don't mind," she said, "but I want to finish that thriller I started last night – I recorded the ending. Couldn't keep my eyes open, but it was hugely exciting." She gave me a complicit smile.

I watched her as she crossed the room and snuggled down into one of the chunky old armchairs in front of the TV. When she switched it on, the sound was so quiet that you couldn't understand a word. It looked like the news to me. I was surprised and slightly annoyed by her choice of words: "Hugely exciting." Why, then, was she now watching something else? She was sitting with her back to us, her eyes fixed upon the screen. She was obviously avoiding us.

"I often think of that woman I told you about," Claudia said. "She became a writer in the end. There must be millions of women like her, women who live their whole life pleasing others, trying to avoid criticism and resentment. They become so used to self-editing everything they think and do that they lose all sense of who they are." She sighed. "An authentic life means more than just making your own decisions at work."

I nodded, biting into my tuna sandwich. I was beginning to feel a bit nauseous from all the wine.

"You value the man's opinions and see the world through his eyes, but then he starts judging you. You feel like an object under his gaze. The trouble is, you can't ignore it, and you end up believing you are the person he sees. One should never give a man so much power."

My thoughts wandered back to what Clara had told me before. Why had Amy been in the pub, looking for me? What had she talked about with Philip and Dr Turner? And why had she not mentioned it to me? My horrible dream came back to my mind – the creepy way she had squeezed my hand and said, "Tell us why you're drinking so much."

"And then you look in the mirror and notice all those signs of ageing," Claudia said, "the loose skin and dark spots on your face and hands – all those telltale signs you had been able to ignore before."

"Do you think a house can have an influence on you?" I interrupted her out of the blue.

"What house?"

"Any house." I sat up straight. "I was just wondering if strong emotions can linger on in a house after a person has died – if thoughts can filter into someone else living there later on."

"Are you talking about yourself?" She gave me a startled look.

"Amy's mother was in a bad way. I live in her room."

"Was she ill?"

"She drank herself to death."

"That's terrible." She was going to say something else when the door opened and Philip walked in.

"Where have you been in this weather?" she asked, staring at him.

"Just walking, clearing my head." He only briefly glanced at me. The rain was still beating against the window but he looked surprisingly unscathed. His dark coat looked damp at the sleeves, but his glasses and hair were dry.

"Where did you go?"

"Nowhere in particular." He spoke in a stilted, deliberate way, as if not quite sober, and I wondered if he had been drinking in the pub next door.

"On your own?"

"It's hellish out there." He ignored her question, looking right through her. He crossed the room and sat down in the armchair next to Clara. I watched him light up one of his Marlboro Lights. He inhaled deeply and blew out the smoke. Ash sprinkled upon the carpet as he leant forward and spoke to Clara in a low voice.

"Why don't you both come over and sit with us?" Claudia said. "Have something to eat. We can open another bottle."

"No thanks. I'm tired. I'm going to bed." He got up, his face a mask of controlled emotions, and walked out of the door.

"I sometimes don't know what's the matter with him," Claudia said to me. "He's so secretive about everything these days. He's always observing, but never taking part. I worry about him."

Clara switched off the TV and came over. "I'm turning in as well," she said with a yawn. "God, I'm nearly falling asleep. But don't let me spoil it for you." She bent over and gave me a little peck on the cheek. "It was nice you could come over. We'll have to do it again. Goodnight, everyone." I heard her in the kitchen – the clatter of dishes in the sink, the running water – and then her footsteps on the stairs.

Claudia leant over to top up my glass, but I shook my head. Her face was blurred. I stared at her in a daze.

"I'm getting fed up with New York," she said. "Nothing matters but who knows who and if you're invited to launches and parties. No one is really interested in anyone else."

I got up to go to the loo. The floor was swaying slightly underneath me but I somehow managed to get upstairs and find the bathroom. My face was burning. I splashed it with water to sober up.

"I've been thinking about moving back to Cardiff," she said when I returned. "I could open a café with food and performances, jazz and classical music, book launches, that kind of thing. I'd have a curry night once a week. What do you think? You could play the piano or help with the organisation." Her voice seemed to come from far away. I closed my eyes for a moment. She leant over, looking at me more closely now. "Are you all right?"

"I've got to go home and sleep it off – if I can get in." I told her about the key.

"You can sleep on the sofa. What if she's out?" Claudia got up too. "No problem at all. I've got to be up at eight to go to the dentist, but I'll let you sleep."

I'd had too much to drink to politely disagree. I watched her pick up the coffee table and put it aside. Then she pulled out the sofa bed, retrieved the bedding and stretched a white sheet over the mattress.

"I think someone might have slept in that before. I hope you don't mind." She gave me a brisk hug. "Sleep well. Sweet dreams."

I woke up from a fitful sleep, my blankets tangled and halfway on the floor. My throat was dry. The thick, velvet curtains were drawn, and the room looked drab and cheerless in the murky light. I heard Claudia in the kitchen having breakfast, then running water and making tea. I reached for my watch. It was half past eight. I closed my eyes again and lay there for some time, listening to the sounds coming from the kitchen. Words and images came floating back to me. I had hardly talked to Clara or Philip. They didn't even know that I had stayed the night. After a while, I heard Claudia in the hall. She lingered a moment, perhaps putting on her coat. Eventually the front door clicked shut, and she was gone.

I sat up and glanced around the room. My clothes and shoes were scattered on the floor. I took a deep breath. My handbag had fallen open, and the contents had spilled all over the place: crumpled receipts, lip gloss, mints, my mobile and loose change. When had that happened? I stared at it, suddenly frozen with apprehension. Had I tripped over it? Had I been sleepwalking again? The bottle of merlot sat on the table, looking empty.

How much wine did we have? I tried to figure it out but couldn't remember. Had we really finished the bottle? I hauled myself up, got to my feet, but the sudden movement made me feel dizzy. My heart was thumping as I made my way across the room.

I had to force myself to open the kitchen door. There were a lot of empty bottles and foil takeaway containers on the worktops, crumpled tea towels and dirty cups and glasses – but no chaos or real mess at all. Thank God! The cooker was splattered with grease, but there was no sign that I had ravaged the place, no egg yolk or charred frying pan. My heart still racing, I found a glass amongst the dirty dishes in the sink, rinsed it and drank some water from the tap. The black and white tiled floor was cold under my bare feet. I refilled my glass and drained it again, listening to the noisy hum of the fridge. I found a pack of aspirins in the cupboard and swallowed two with more water.

Then I went back to the front room and started tidying up. I put the sofa bed together, stored the sheets and blankets inside, and washed our wine glasses. It had been quiet so far, but now I heard voices upstairs, and after a short while a toilet flushed.

I hesitated for a moment, wondering if I should say good-bye. Claudia would tell them that I had slept on the sofa. It would seem odd if I just disappeared without a word. I waited in the hall until whoever was in the bathroom came out and then gingerly made my way upstairs. I had no idea which one was Clara's bedroom – there were three rooms – only one of them was open, I looked inside. There were books and Philip's glasses on the bedside cabinet. The bed covers were in disarray as if he had just got up. A pair of black jeans and one of his crisp white shirts hung neatly over a straight-backed chair.

I stepped back onto the landing. From the adjacent room came low voices – then a sudden scream. "Your hands are icy," Clara shrieked. I froze, listening. Someone was moaning, and it sounded like Clara again. I stood, paralysed, staring at the door, wondering what was wrong. Then I heard a gasp or a sob. This time it seemed to be Philip. He was panting. I held my breath. There was no doubt what they were doing.

I quickly made my way back. In my haste I tripped over the carpet halfway down the stairs where it had come loose. I gasped with pain. Had they heard me up there? I dared not move. There was an eerie silence – foreboding and tense. Were they both listening as well?

I quietly limped downstairs. My ankle was throbbing as I went into the living room to fetch my bag and coat. Thoughts raced through my mind. With Claudia at the dentist's, they had obviously thought that they were on their own. And now they'd caught me eavesdropping on them. How wrenchingly embarrassing for everyone! Or hadn't they heard me after all? I softly shut the front door as I left. Clara's bedroom over-looked the street. When I raised my gaze I could see a tall figure behind the net curtains. I couldn't see clearly because the rain was getting into my eyes, but I was pretty sure that Philip was standing there, watching me.

———

11

The sky was a uniform shade of grey. It was pouring again, and I was wet within minutes. The cold rain was stinging my face as I walked into town. I caught a bus on Westgate Street. It smelled of damp coats and shoes. I wiped away the condensation and glanced out of the window. The wet pavement had an oily sheen. Had there been signs, I wondered, something I should have noticed? Why had they kept it a secret from me? I thought about the night we'd all got on so well. Was the friendship I had hoped for merely wishful thinking? The doors closed with a gasp of air, and the bus lurched on. The sudden movement made my stomach turn and I sank deeper into my seat. My mind was going round in circles, unable to make any sense of it all.

I got out on Albany Road, the rain in my face again – and only when I turned into my street did I start wondering if Amy would be home. With everything else going on, I had completely forgotten about the key.

It was just after nine, and the curtains in her room upstairs were drawn. I rang a couple of times, hearing the bell chime inside. I was just beginning to wonder if I should try her mobile when I heard footsteps and saw her shadow through the frosted glass.

"Thank God it's you," she said, staring at me. "I was worried when I saw your keys. And then you didn't come home." She was still in her faded old pyjamas, her hair back from the salon-straightened slickness to its usual frizzy mess. "Where on earth have you been?"

"Sorry for waking you up. I stayed over at Clara's last night. Where did you find the keys? I looked everywhere – but then I had to rush off."

"In the kitchen. I haven't moved it, so it must be still there." She shook her head. "You could have given me a ring."

"I'm sorry..."

"It doesn't matter now," she interrupted. "I was just wondering how you'd get in. I stayed up a bit longer than usual, waiting for you, but when I hadn't heard from you by half past twelve, I went to bed anyway."

"So late? I'm really sorry. I should have phoned." She looked tired, bleary-eyed, as if she too hadn't had a lot of sleep.

"Don't worry about it. I watched a good film. I really didn't mind."

I followed her inside, feeling a pang of remorse. It was nice of her to wait up. She seemed to really care for me. What a difference to Clara who couldn't even be bothered to sit with us last night. And here I was, making plans to move in with them, leaving Amy in the lurch. She really didn't deserve to be treated like that.

I looked through the kitchen door. The keys were indeed on the sideboard near the cooker. I picked them up. For a moment I stood staring at the key ring with its light blue laminated tag. How could I have missed it there?

"Have you had breakfast?" Amy asked from the door.

"Let's have a cup of tea and some toast, and you can tell me all about your evening."

I glanced at the kitchen clock. "Thanks – that would be great, but I've got Counterpoint in two hours and I need to do some work." It wasn't strictly true. There was no lecture; I just had to stand in for Margaret later in the afternoon. But I was very tired and far too nauseous to face breakfast with Amy.

"You look done in. Why don't you have a little rest?" she said. "You'll be right as rain after a couple of hours sleep. I think I'll go back to bed as well." She chuckled. "What are we like? Sleeping in the day! Anyway, I'm glad you had a good night out." She gave me a friendly smile and at that moment I had no doubt that she meant it. There seemed to be no reproach in her voice, no insinuating undertones at all.

I went straight upstairs. Catching my reflection in the full-length mirror on the wardrobe door, I stared at myself. My face was pale and tired, and my wet hair clung to my scalp. I pulled the curtains and lay on my bed without taking off my clothes or shoes.

When I closed my eyes, the image of Philip surged up – his shadowy figure behind the curtains. Would things change between us now I had found out? Why hadn't they trusted me, I wondered. Did they think I would tell Claudia? Amy's words came back to me: *Clara calls and you come running.* Had she just taken advantage of me to keep Claudia off their backs? Had they only asked me to move in with them because it would be more affordable – because they needed someone to share the rent? Going over and over what had happened, I dozed off in the end. My shallow sleep was restless and full of disconcerting dreams: a concert in which I was supposed to perform. The concert hall was gigantic and the audience was getting impatient because I was late and had forgotten to bring my music.

The beeping of my mobile woke me up. It was still in my

bag on the hook behind the door. I jumped out of bed, feeling dizzy again. My poor stomach lurched; it was in need of food. It was half past two. I had slept for nearly five hours. It was still raining outside; the clouds were so heavy that it seemed to be already getting dark. I checked my messages. There were two from Dr Turner, one from the previous day, a reply to my text:

Sorry to hear you're sick.

The second one, which had been sent just now, sounded urgent:

There's something I'd like to talk about. Can you see me before Reading Week? I'm in my office all day.

I had forgotten that next week was Reading Week. There would be no tutorials or lectures while students studied, and only the library would be open. What was so urgent that he wanted to see me today? I hauled myself up and put on fresh clothes. While brushing my teeth, I wondered whether I should knock on Amy's door and say goodbye. She was in her bedroom, typing again. I decided not to disturb her. Quietly I made my way downstairs, grabbed an apple from the kitchen and left through the front door.

THE CAMPUS WAS QUIET, the foyer and corridors deserted, as if the weekend had already begun. Gareth, the porter on duty, was in his lodge reading *The Sun*. As I went past, he raised his head and beckoned me nearer.

"Margaret was looking for you," he said. "Dr Turner told her you were sick. She was worried that you wouldn't come in."

"Is she in the library?" Standing in the doorway of his lodge, I got a whiff of his lunch, chicken from the takeaway across the road, nothing but the greasy skin and bones left on the plastic tray. Bits of it were in his greying beard. I've never been fond of meat, and the sight of it was more than I could bear. I turned away, but he caught the look of revulsion on my face and grinned.

"And Dr Turner wants to talk to you," he said. "Said I should send you upstairs You've just missed him. He was in the foyer chatting. The girls are all over him. I don't know how he does it. He could have his pick." He rustled his paper.

"Not every man has a one-track mind," I said, annoyed, glancing at the Page Three girl, a big-busted blonde.

"You may think that!" He laughed, his fat belly shaking. "There are a lot of pretty ones this year."

I turned around and walked away.

Margaret was in the office, working at her computer. "Dr Turner wants to talk to you," she said. "Why don't you go to his office now and see what he wants? It's quiet anyway, and it'll take me at least another half hour to order these books for next term. You'd better get it out of the way before you're on your own later on."

I didn't even look at Gareth as I passed his lodge again and made my way to the second floor. A spindly woman in a blue uniform was polishing the shiny floor. The hum of her buffer mingled with the sound of a violin coming from one of the practice rooms. It smelled of the cleaning fluid she was using.

Dr Turner's door was shut. I took a deep breath, knocked and waited until he called me inside.

"Good to see you," he said, getting up from his desk. He was wearing a crisp pink shirt I hadn't seen on him before. He motioned me to the sofa at the back and sat down in an armchair, facing me. "Are you feeling a bit better now?"

I caught a scent of his aftershave as he leant towards me. His eyes were fixed on mine.

"Yes, I'm sorry, I had a stomach bug, but I'm much better now." Aware that it didn't sound very convincing, I trailed off.

"Thanks for letting me know. I wouldn't have bothered you, but Margaret said she was expecting you downstairs." He cleared his throat. "Well, there's a lot of it about. I'm glad you're over it now. It's a pity you couldn't come to my tutorial."

"I'm sorry."

"I was wondering... how is it going? How have you settled in? I know it can be stressful. There's a lot of pressure on students. Are you all right?"

I nodded. There was something probing behind his friendly banter and I was beginning to wonder where this was leading.

"How are you getting on with the essay for my course? Is it coming along?"

"Yes, no problem." I looked down at my perspiring hands. I had been so busy with the Mahler and everything else that I hadn't even decided on a subject yet.

"Good," he nodded. "What are you going to write?"

"Probably early eighteenth century. I haven't started it yet."

"Well, there's still a bit of time." He sank back into his seat, but I could feel that he was watching me. "How is it going in the library?"

I raised my eyes. "Very well. I'm glad I can help out." His expression had changed. There was a hardened, serious look in his eyes.

"Maybe we should start taking the pressure off. Have you met Alicia Green?"

"I don't think so."

"She played for the choir to cover for you. She told me

that she enjoyed the challenge and would like to continue. I was wondering what you would think about that."

"Of course – I don't mind." I couldn't take my eyes off his pink shirt. Who on earth was Alicia Green? "I'm sure she plays much better than me."

"No, I wouldn't say that." He gravely shook his head. "But she's available, and as you have been under so much pressure recently..." He stood up. "I'm glad that's settled then. We don't want to make you ill with our unreasonable demands. Now you've got the time to concentrate fully on your academic work. I'm looking forward to reading your essay when it's finished, and I'm always happy to help if you encounter any problems on the way. We know that academic writing can be challenging." He gave a reassuring laugh. "Don't worry. It'll be fine."

I nodded and stood up. "Thanks. I'd better go. Margaret is waiting downstairs."

"She's lucky to have you," he said, "an experienced librarian from Carlisle. Don't let her take advantage of you." He lightly touched my shoulder. "Very interesting city, Carlisle. I remember the cathedral. I went to a conference there a few years ago."

Margaret was standing behind the checkout desk when I came in.

"Oh dear," she said. "Is everything all right with you?"

I nodded, avoiding her eyes.

"You'd better sit down." She led me into the office and directed me to sit in her swivel chair.

"Are you still under the weather? You're as white as a sheet!" She shook her head. "Did you see Dr Turner?"

"I'm just a bit tired."

"What did he say?" She didn't give up easily.

"Nothing much, just that he's found someone else to play for the choir."

"Do you mind?"

"No, of course not. I'm sure she's much better than me."

"I wouldn't be so sure." She looked at me, her face soft with sympathy. "Did he tell you that?"

"No." I swallowed. "He didn't have to. He clearly doesn't think I'm good enough."

"Well," she shook her head, "as long as you don't take it personally." She frowned. "I don't know if I should tell you." She glanced at the door and lowered her voice. "Something similar happened a couple of years ago."

"Really?"

"I can't remember her name, but she was a lovely girl. She was supposed to sing the soprano solo in one of his concerts. I think it was Haydn. She even had extra lessons for it. And then halfway through rehearsals he gave the solo to someone else. She was in tears when she told me. She said that the other student didn't have the voice, but that he liked her better." She sighed. "I don't think that's very likely, but he really can be a bit insensitive. I don't think that he handles these things very well."

"Don't worry, it really doesn't matter," I said, trying to keep my voice light. To divert her attention, I enquired about her son.

"Oh, he's absolutely fine," she said with deliberate cheerfulness. "I don't worry anymore. He's probably still in bed, sleeping it off. It must have been three when he came in last night. But what can I do? Throwing him out would only make things worse. What would he eat, and where would he end up sleeping? It would kill me to see him on the street." She let out an unhappy laugh. "He doesn't listen to anything I say, so I might as well give up and stop fretting about it." She looked at her watch. "Good grief, is that the time?"

I watched as she put on her coat. She bent down and gave me a little hug.

"I hope you feel better soon. Don't worry about the choir," she said, smiling. "There will be other opportunities. Don't take it to heart." And then she was gone.

The library felt desolate with hardly anyone about. Only a couple of students were sitting at tables, working. There was no sound – except for the eerie hum of the overhead lighting. A woman in a thick Norwegian jumper was leafing through the *Music Quarterly*, silently turning the pages.

To keep myself busy I spent some time pushing around the trolley, shelving returned books. Turning into the reference section I caught a faint scent of cigarettes. Startled, I stood there for a moment, trying to find out where it was coming from. It seemed to be lingering around the encyclopaedias where Philip had sat the other day. Or had he been in today? There was an open dictionary on the table. Maybe he had only gone out for a smoke.

My heart started pounding. It would be awful to make conversation – what was there to say? How could I pretend that nothing had happened?

I resumed my place behind the checkout desk, switched on the computer and started reading an article on Handel's early operas. The door creaked and someone came in. I held my breath. There was that whiff of cigarettes again. I kept my eyes fixed on the screen. When I dared a surreptitious look, I saw, to my relief, that it was someone else. A man with longish greasy hair was sitting at Philip's desk. I had never seen him in the library before. He was hunched over the dictionary, his lips moving as he was reading. A strand of his lank hair kept falling into his face, and he kept pushing it back behind his ear. As he sensed my stare, he glanced up and gave me a steely look.

He didn't look like a student to me. Perhaps he was afraid

that I would throw him out. I turned away. No one needed me for returning or checking out books and I managed to concentrate on my article and even made some notes.

At about half past six the telephone rang in the office. I darted inside to answer it. It was Claudia.

"Sorry to bother you," she said in an urgent voice. "I tried your mobile – and then I rang your landline. Your friend, Amy, said you might be in the library. I was wondering." She paused to catch her breath. "Do you know where Philip and Clara are? I was supposed to cook lunch, but when I came home from the dentist they were gone. No message at all. What did they say in the morning?"

"Nothing – I think they were still asleep."

"Did you go that early?"

"Just after you left."

"Sorry, if I woke you up." She sighed. "Never mind, they'll be back."

"Where are you?" I could hear traffic noises in the background.

"Cathedral Road. I'm walking into town. Look, why don't we have a chat later on? I can pick you up. Or even better I could meet you in the Mackintosh."

"I don't know." I hesitated, feeling my heart beating faster again. "I think I need an early night."

"Just for a couple of hours." She raised her voice. "I promise you'll be in bed by ten."

"OK, but just a couple of hours." I hung up and just sat there for a while, staring at the gray, old-fashioned phone.

I returned to my computer screen, but the call had thrown me off balance, and I found it difficult to focus. The students had gone. At half past seven I started tidying up. I put books back on shelves and threw sweet wrappers and empty cups in the bin.

Claudia had sounded quite alarmed. Would she catch on

that I was hiding something? There was no way I could tell her I had heard Clara and Philip together. What they were up to was none of her business – and it was certainly not my place to let her in on the secret – especially as they obviously didn't want her to know.

When it was finally eight o'clock I locked up. Returning the key to the porter's lodge, I found Gareth asleep in his chair, a little drool coming from the corner of his mouth. I stood there for a moment, staring at his belly rising and falling under his uniform shirt, wondering if I should wake him up. But then I just left the key on his desk and stepped outside.

IT HAD STOPPED RAINING at last, but it was freezing cold, and a thick fog had formed. The yellow light of the moon was watery and vague. A wall of warm air hit my face as I entered the pub. It was busy with young people, their voices competing with thumping loud music. Claudia, who was sitting near the fire, waved me over.

"You do look tired," she said. "Promise, I won't keep you long. Drink?" There was an opened bottle of red wine on the table. She poured me a generous glass. "Have you still not heard from them?"

"No. Have you?"

"Not a word. I've sent umpteen messages but they haven't replied. I hope nothing has happened." She bent forward, her voice high and shrill with tension. "Do you think they are avoiding me?"

"I don't know." I took a sip of my wine. It wasn't such a good idea; it made me feel hot and nauseous again. "Maybe you should back off a bit. You know what Philip is like."

"Am I really that bad?" She stared at me, flushed and

glassy-eyed, and I briefly wondered how much she'd been drinking before I arrived.

"I know they want their own space," she said. "Philip is so sensitive these days. They've done it before, but then they'd always been in touch and told me where they were. It's so worrying. Why don't they answer my texts?" She stared at her mobile as if she could will it into ringing. "Do you think they're angry with me? Did Clara say something yesterday?"

I shrugged. "Maybe you should stop texting them. You know Philip doesn't like to be pushed."

"You could say that." She took a sip of her wine. A muscle in her eyelid twitched. "I know I'm terrible to live with. But it's just so difficult... I can't help myself giving advice. Philip with his composing – how will he make a living with that?"

"Maybe he won't, but he's old enough to know what he wants. I think you should leave him alone. Perhaps he'll find out one day that he's not quite Stockhausen after all."

"But he is really good – he's excellent," she said grimly. "That's the trouble. He won a competition last year – a couple of grand. Heard of the Rappaport Prize? They had to fly over to Boston to collect it."

"Really? That's a prestigious award." I was impressed.

"I know. He never makes a fuss about his achievements. Of course he should carry on, but he could have a career as well. He just can't be bothered with his academic job. Preparing his courses, marking – it's all too much for him. I really don't understand why he doesn't want to do it. There are a lot of academics who compose in their spare time."

"You should let him work it out for himself."

"I know. I'm terrible and overbearing, and you're right." Her face crumpled and for a moment she looked as if she was going to cry. She topped up our glasses. "At least he's not on his own. I'm sorry for going on about it. How was your day?"

"Fine." Why was she so shaken? I was beginning to wonder if there was something I didn't know.

To take her mind off things I told her about my meeting with Dr Turner.

"And you just put up with it?" She raised her brows. "That's unbelievable. He didn't even ask you what you wanted. I thought he was all right. Clara likes him – they're friends. But this is really out of order, to replace you with someone else... Shall I ask Clara to have a word with him?"

"No. Please don't." I stared at her in horror. "He's made up his mind. Of course it's not nice to be sacked. But I'm in a way relieved. It was very stressful for me." I glanced at my watch. "I'm sorry, but I have to go. I'm exhausted."

"I understand." She got up. "What about if I come with you? I need an early night as well."

It was still foggy outside. Claudia took my arm as we quietly walked down the road, heading towards the railway bridge.

"Thanks for coming," she said as we said goodbye on Crwys Road. "You're a real friend. I'll let you know what happens."

12

Amy was in the living room watching TV when I came home, and didn't hear me come in. When I put my head around the door she was nestled in her usual corner of the sofa, her legs covered with a blanket, eyes glued to the screen. Dramatic orchestral music created a tense, dark mood as Lauren Bacall in a dress with a plunging neckline paced up and down a room. In the half-light Amy could have been part of the film herself: her face pale and vacant, her lips stained dark from the red wine she had been drinking.

"Any good?"

"Oh, dearie me! It's you," she said, startled. She turned the volume off. "It's an old potboiler. I wasn't really watching anyway. There's some wine left." She grinned at me. "I shouldn't really tempt you, but you're welcome to a glass if you fancy it."

"No, thanks. I think I've had enough."

"Have you been out again?"

"Just a quick glass with Claudia in the Mackintosh."

"Of course. I talked to her earlier on." Amy stood up. "I

told her that you were at college and gave her the extension for the library. I hope that was OK. I wasn't sure if you had choir tonight."

"It's on Thursday, but I'm not doing it anymore."

"Really? Since when? Did you tell him that you've had enough?"

"No. He's found someone else. He was probably annoyed that I phoned in sick last time."

"Well, maybe it's for the best." She looked at me. "Are you sure you don't mind? You do look upset. Why don't you sit down for a moment? I'll make us a nice cup of tea."

The damp fog outside had turned into heavy rain. While she was putting the kettle on, I sat and listened to the downpour lashing against the windows. It suddenly felt safer to be inside. In the warm glow of the standard lamp, the room almost felt cosy. It seemed a haven from all the chaos outside. Amy's motherly concern was comforting. She would be so disappointed if she knew that I had halfway agreed to move out.

A moment later she returned with two mugs of sweet, milky tea.

"So who is accompanying the choir now?"

"Alicia Green. I'm sure she's a much better pianist."

"Or maybe she fluttered her eyelashes at him." Amy chuckled. "It wouldn't be a surprise, knowing his track record."

"I don't think so."

"Well," she shook her head. "How can you be so sure? A leopard doesn't change its spots. I bet she's young and pretty. That's what men are like." She sighed. "I can understand why you're upset."

"But I'm not. Not really." I paused. "Look, it really doesn't bother me. In fact, he's done me a favour."

"And why don't I believe you?" She looked straight into

my eyes. "I can see it in your face. You don't have to pretend with me. I saw how you were looking at him at the concert. Don't worry. Your secret is safe with me."

"You're making it all up again." I said with a light-hearted laugh, but it sounded false even to my own ears.

"You'll get over it," she said, turning back to the film. "I suppose it's one less thing to worry about."

"Yeah, you're absolutely right." I finished my tea. "I better have an early night. I'm falling asleep." A wave of fatigue had come over me, and my eyes felt heavy. I hauled myself up.

"All you need is a good night's rest," she said. "You'll be right as rain in the morning."

I dragged myself upstairs and went to bed without even washing or brushing my teeth and almost instantly fell asleep.

I WOKE up the next morning in a sleepy haze. I shut my eyes again against the light. I had no idea what it was that had woken me up. It was only half past seven. For a moment I just lay there, thinking about the dream I'd had. Clara and I had been lost in a tall office building, walking down a long and gloomy corridor, anxious to find a way out. My mouth was dry and tasted of metal. I had slept nearly nine hours, but I felt spaced out and tired, as if I'd been up drinking all night.

Slowly and reluctantly, I got up to brush my teeth. When I was on the landing Amy came out of her room.

"Couldn't you sleep?" she asked.

"Why?"

"I heard you downstairs."

"What time? What do you mean?" For some strange reason it made me laugh.

"Just after five. At first, I thought it was the radio," she said, unsmiling. "But then I recognised your voice. It sounded like an argument. You were shouting like that time when I heard you before."

I stared at her.

"I'm so sorry," she said. "I thought I should tell you." She shook her head. "Maybe you can do something about it." With another look of unease she withdrew back into her room.

My heart was pounding. Was this something now haunting me on a regular basis: the fear every morning of what crazy things I had done in the night? I made my way downstairs. The door to the kitchen was open. It was quite dark inside. Beneath my naked feet the linoleum was cold and sticky. Everything seemed to be in its usual place: the odd assortment of chipped mugs on the windowsill, the dirt-encrusted cooker, the old tea towels, the wobbly wooden table. I switched on the light and froze, staring at the kitchen wall. What I saw made me gasp.

Painted in huge black letters was Dr Turner's name:

JACK TURNER

It was crossed out – a big angry X brushed through it. The paint had dried; the dirty paintbrush was still on the floor with the tin of black paint. I had seen it in the cupboard before. I picked it up and weighed it in my hand, trying to remember. And then I saw the splash of black on my sleeve. There was no doubt: it was the same paint, the same nauseating smell.

I brought my hand to my mouth, suppressing a scream. *Focus*, I said to myself. *Don't panic! You have to get rid of it somehow.* Kneeling down, I opened the cupboard under the sink. Amy kept a box with cleaning stuff in there. The paint was probably water-soluble. Maybe I could wash it off.

I found scouring pads and a roll of kitchen paper and

made a start. Dark diluted paint ran down my arms and all over my pyjamas, but I kept on scrubbing at the wall. After half an hour, the letters were smeared but still clearly visible. I carried on, regardless, my fingers getting sore, until I heard Amy on the stairs.

"Morning," she said, coming into the kitchen. "What are you doing?"

"Nothing." I turned my back to the wall, trying to conceal the mess.

She came nearer and gently pushed me out of the way. "Let's see," she said. "Oh my word!" For a moment she just stood there, staring at the wall.

"I'm really sorry." My chin trembled. I tried to hold back the tears, but something in me collapsed. Hiding my face in my hands I could feel the hot tears running down my cheeks. I turned away but couldn't stop crying. I heard my own sobbing, raw and distressed.

"Don't cry," Amy said in a soothing voice. I felt her chubby hand on my back, patting and rubbing me. She put her arm around my shoulder and firmly guided me into the living room.

I didn't mind. It was comforting to be looked after and I was so relieved that she wasn't angry with me. She made me sit on the sofa and sat down next to me.

"You didn't seem that bothered yesterday," she said. "I don't understand. And then you're up all night painting his name onto the wall. You must be really mad with him to do such a thing."

"I don't know," I sobbed. "I really don't know." It was terrifying me: how could I not remember? Was there a dark side in me I didn't know anything about? Was there a destructive force, a buried anger that wanted out and bubbled over the moment my guard was down?

"I worry about you," she said softly, patting my arm. "The

mess doesn't matter. I'm just wondering what makes you do these weird things. Maybe it's the drink..."

"But I didn't have that much." I took the tissue she handed me and wiped my eyes. "Just the one glass in the pub."

"Maybe that was too much. Perhaps you should stop drinking altogether and see how it goes. Or maybe it's the stress you're under. Did you do anything like this before?"

I shook my head.

"Perhaps you just don't remember." She sighed. "Who knows what you did when you lived on your own? You could have wandered around the streets at night. How would you know? That's so dangerous!" She hesitated. "Maybe you should talk to your GP."

"I don't think that's necessary." I blew my nose. "But I promise I'm going to cut down the drinking. At least that's something I can control."

THE LIBRARY WAS open during Reading Week, but there were no lectures, and most students had gone home. It was very quiet with hardly anyone about. Even Margaret had taken the week off. I missed the chats with her, the distraction they usually brought. I had to cover for her most afternoons. There was nothing else to do but sit at the checkout desk and work at the computer.

I had to get on with the essay for Dr Turner but couldn't really concentrate on my research. Instead of reading about Handel's oratorios I surfed the net. The notion of myself, shouting and writing on the kitchen wall, was still haunting me.

I read an article about suppressed aggression, how it could result in destructive relationships, alcoholism and depression. The image of Jeremy surged up – the crushing shame I used to feel the morning after our arguments. There had been some memory gaps, but I always remembered that I had phoned. Never had the experience been utterly wiped out.

Then I looked up sleepwalking and alcohol again. There seemed to be a connection. Drinking could apparently be a trigger. Amy was right. There was no other way: I had to stop altogether.

AMY WAS VERY KIND and tried to help. She painted over the writing when I was working at college, using the same black paint. There wasn't much left, just about enough to cover one side of the wall. Having one black side in the kitchen was a sinister reminder of what had happened, but I really appreciated her effort. It was certainly better than the dreadful sight of Dr Turner's crossed out name. I was grateful that she didn't go on about it. We got on better than before, and I quite enjoyed spending more time with her.

The weather had improved a lot; it was very mild. The following Saturday we took the bus to Southerndown. The sun was out as we made our way down to the grassy cliffs. We bought ice cream from the pink van and sat on a bench looking out to sea. Amy told me about her dream of going to Blackpool one day and seeing the illuminations, the promenade lit up with thousands of lights.

"I've always wanted to go," she said, a longing look in her eyes. The cries of seagulls seemed to mock her from above. A plane left a thin vapour trail in its wake, white against a sky of the palest blue.

On our way back we had coffee and cake in Bridgend. Amy loved cream cakes and all things sweet. When I told her that I preferred home-baked biscuits she was silent for a while.

"I could bake you some biscuits," she eventually said, licking cream off her finger. "It can't be so difficult."

She'd never shown any interest or talent for cooking before and I was very surprised when I came home from college on Monday and the house smelled of baking. She proudly showed me the rows of chocolate biscuits lined up on the tray.

"Try one. I found the recipe in that old cookbook on the shelf."

"Wow. It smells wonderful. I'm impressed."

We carried them into the living room with cups of tea and watched a comedy programme together. They were delicious: crunchy, full of chocolate pieces and not too sweet.

"They must be the nicest biscuits I've ever had," I said before I went to bed. "But after what I've done to your kitchen, I really don't deserve them. Thanks for being such a good mate."

THE FEELING of impending doom began to lift a bit as time went by and I dropped the habit of walking around the house first thing in the morning to check that everything was OK. I had my essay to worry about.

I started working in the library again, but the muffled stillness, the humming of the fluorescent light, was distracting and my thoughts kept wandering off. Claudia had given me a ring. Clara and Philip had been in touch. They were in Cornwall over Reading Week. When would they return, I wondered? Clara would have to be back for her teaching. Towards the end of the week, I half-expected to see her at college.

It struck me how little I knew about them. Gemma had told me in the beginning how aloof they were. I had dismissed her talk as idle gossip, but now I thought about it again. I pictured Clara, her intimidating silences – the way she had been in the pub. She hadn't even listened, let alone taken part in the conversation. Just as later on when she had blatantly ignored us both, watching television in that armchair with her back to us.

Had she just been nice and polite to keep me around for Claudia's sake? I had thought that she was shy. Perhaps I had been wrong and she was just cold and distant after all. She had bothered with me as long as I served her own ends. Was she afraid I would tell Claudia? Or was she just embarrassed for not telling me the truth? Was that the reason she hadn't been in touch?

One day I thought I smelt Philip's cigarettes again. I didn't come across him in the library, but that afternoon I glimpsed his thin, tall figure at the porter's lodge. I waited behind the swing door, looking through the glass, unsure whether I should go over and say hello. But then he turned around... and I saw it was clearly someone else.

I thought about the evening I had spent with them, the meal, the singing and laughing. He had loosened up and shown a different side when he was usually so self-controlled. I remembered what Claudia had said about his composing, how brilliant he was.

Back in the library, I googled him. I don't know what I was looking for. Perhaps something in his biography that would cast a light on what was going on between them. Why did they keep their relationship secret? Why didn't he just stand up to his mother and tell her the truth?

An article on Wikipedia showed a picture of him from the waist up, wearing a formal white shirt with a narrow tie. He looked young and serious. I read that he had been born in London. He had studied at the Royal College and later earned his PhD in composition in Cardiff. He was appointed to the staff in 2015. The list of his compositions included mostly orchestral work and chamber music. There was a considerable gap between the time he had started at the Royal College and his PhD in Cardiff. What had he done in between? I remembered that Clara had said how stressful the Royal College had been for him and that he had nearly given up music altogether.

I was still reading when Dr Turner came in.

"Good to see you," he said, slightly out of breath. "How are you doing? Was there anything you wanted to talk about?"

"Not really," I said, surprised and a bit confused.

"I only thought..." He hesitated. "I was under the impression that you tried to send me a text the other day. I received two empty messages from you."

"I didn't text you." I felt a flush of adrenaline, a sudden flutter of my heart.

He shook his head, a puzzled look on his face. "The pitfalls of technology! Tell me about it. Yesterday I sent an email to my own address. 'From the spirits that I called deliver me!'" He laughed, but it sounded a bit forced.

"It must have been a mistake..." I trailed off.

"Never mind. I'd better press on. Time is ticking. There's a pile of essays waiting for me on my desk and no excuse to put it off any longer. I see you're busy too." He looked at the computer. "Are you working on the essay? How is it going? Let me know if there's a problem."

My eyes followed him as he opened the door and left. How strange. I was quite sure that I hadn't written to him since the day I had cried off sick. With trembling hands, I switched on my phone and opened the sent folder. There was, indeed, a text message to Dr Turner, sent on November tenth at ten to twelve – the day I had met Claudia after work. The night I had roamed the house and written his name on the wall! My mind raced. Thank God the message had been empty! I recalled his expression: the jovial smile, his laugh. Had he just been putting it on? What did he really think of me?

AMY WAS in the kitchen when I came home. A scent of cinnamon and nutmeg filled the air.

"I'm trying a new recipe," she said. "Christmas biscuits… It's a bit early." She chuckled. "But what does it matter?".

"I've just seen Dr Turner," I said, still shaken. I stood in the doorway, stunned by the mess she'd made. There was a broken egg on the floor, and the work surface was smeared with dough.

"And?" She wiped her sticky hands on a kitchen towel.

"He said I sent him an empty message."

"And did you?"

"Yes. The night I was sleepwalking." I swallowed. "I can't believe I did that."

She shrugged. "I'm not surprised. You did a lot of crazy things that night. But at least you've stopped drinking, so let's hope it won't happen again. Try not to worry about it now."

"But it's so embarrassing," I groaned. "God knows what he thinks of me. I can't afford to fall out with him. And what if I send another text, something more compromising? He is my personal tutor. I have to pass the exams somehow. I don't know what's the matter with me. Everything I do is so ridiculous. I haven't even properly started on the essay yet."

"Who cares? You're putting yourself under too much pressure. No wonder you're at sixes and sevens; your head is all over the place! You'll have to slow down, or maybe leave college and do something else."

"But it's what I really want to do." I stared at her in disbelief. "I've given everything up for this. I've spent all my savings! I left my old job. I can't go back there now. What else would I do?"

"You could work in another library or give piano lessons. There's a lot you could do."

"But I want to become a teacher. It's important to me."

"No reason to get so worked up." She looked at me with narrowed eyes. "It's that Dr Turner, isn't it? He's the reason why your nerves are frayed. I don't know why you put up with him."

"He's just a tutor," I said, trying to keep my calm. "There's nothing wrong with him. He only wants the best for me. He's not putting me under too much pressure. He really hasn't done anything wrong."

"I know it's not easy." She gave me a serious look. There was a new authority to her voice. "I know how much you like him, and I understand why you're defending him, but he has let you down. You have to face it. He replaced you with a younger, more attractive girl. Wasn't that what your sleep-walking was all about? If you want to get better you'll have to admit to yourself how upset you really are."

She directed me into the living room again. We had a cup of tea together and I had to eat a couple of her cinnamon biscuits before I could finally go upstairs.

I sank down on the bed and got out my mobile phone. What if Amy was right and I was really harbouring a grudge? There'd always be that danger of sending another message now... unless I put it somewhere safe. I climbed on the chair and reached for the box on the wardrobe. It was still stuffed with towels and summer clothes I hadn't unpacked. I wrapped the phone in a kitchen towel and hid it underneath a pile of blouses. There was no way I would allow this to happen again. It would be difficult to get it out of there while asleep – not impossible, but at least I'd see in the morning if I had moved the chair.

13

Amy's suggestion to give it all up was a wake-up call. I had to increase my effort if I wanted to finish the essay in time! I had only a couple of weeks. Perhaps I would just about make it if I got up early and put in more hours.

When I told Amy she seemed impressed. She even gave me her alarm clock to make sure I wouldn't oversleep. I would set it for seven and was out of the house before she got up. Being the first one in the library as soon as it opened at eight o'clock gave me a sense of being in control.

I sat in a corner, hidden behind the reference books, not far from where Philip had sat before. I still hadn't seen either of them though Reading Week was over and lectures had started again. Sometimes I wondered if I should give Claudia a ring to find out if they'd come back, but then I always put it off again.

I was writing about Handel's oratorios. I had done my research and the essay was progressing well. I was beginning to feel more focused and relaxed again. There were other students from Dr Turner's course working in the library;

sometimes I had a coffee with Rachel on the steps outside. She was pretty and quite tall with short dark hair and we chatted a lot about Handel, as she had also chosen to write about him, focusing on *Semele*.

I would work until the library closed at nine. Back home, I usually had a quick sandwich in the kitchen and a cup of tea with Amy who was always happy to have a chat.

"Are you sure you're eating enough?" she kept asking. "You have to keep up your strength when you're working all the hours God sends. You still look a bit peaky, if you don't mind me saying so."

I made a big thing about how much progress I'd made with the essay and that I felt more optimistic now, but in fact I was quite exhausted. Was it the new routine, was I working too hard? Or was I coming down with something, I wondered.

I was feeling tired all the time. At the library I found it hard to concentrate. My mind seemed fogged up, often unable to take in what I was reading. Was it some sort of flu – a nasty virus? It wasn't the kind of tiredness that just needed a good night's sleep. Sleeping wasn't the problem. As soon as I went to bed at night I went out like a light and I stayed asleep for at least eight hours without getting up or going to the loo. In fact, I slept too deeply, it seemed. I found it increasingly difficult to wake up. It took the persistent ringing of both alarm clocks to rouse me from my comatose sleep. Everything was blurry, my head hurt as I dully fumbled for the button to turn off the buzzer. I got into the habit of having long showers, letting the stream of piping hot water pour down on my face, but neither that nor the strong coffee I had with my breakfast could properly wake me up.

I carried on regardless all through the week and the essay was coming along in spite of my sluggish mind. But the fatigue was getting worse from one day to the next. By Friday

I found it increasingly hard to keep my eyes open. I was reading at my usual desk, when suddenly my jaw went slack. I could feel the saliva dribble out of my mouth and my head sink onto my chest. I woke up with a start after what felt like seconds but could have been half an hour or more. Although it was only early afternoon I decided to go home and have a rest.

To carry on with my essay over the weekend I needed the book I'd been working with. It was a big encyclopaedia, one of those heavy volumes the students weren't supposed to take out. I decided to break the rules and put it in my leather rucksack anyway. The plan was to return it on Monday morning before anyone noticed.

"Oh, dear me!" Amy said when I got back. "You do look under the weather. Have you got a temperature? Let me make you a Lemsip. Why don't you go to bed and I'll bring it upstairs?"

Entering my room, I caught my reflection in the full-length mirror on my wardrobe and stopped for a moment to have a closer look. I really didn't look well; I had lost weight and my face looked gaunt and pale. There was a lot of darkness around my eyes. Something was definitely wrong with me. I felt a bit nauseous again and desperate to go to bed. Amy brought me sandwiches and tea – I was grateful that she was looking after me.

The weekend went by in a blur. I drifted in and out of sleep, hardly aware of the passing of time, nauseous and dizzy whenever I had to get up to go to the loo.

"You can't go to college in that state," Amy said on Monday morning when she came to see how I felt. "I was wondering if we should call a doctor. Maybe you need medication."

"No, I'm much better already." I hauled myself up. "I have to go and return the book I've taken out." I hadn't even looked at the relevant chapter, or taken the book out of my bag, but when I opened my rucksack it was empty. I searched everywhere in my room, even under the bed, then in the kitchen and living room. It was thick and leather-bound and so could hardly slip behind somewhere and disappear. I broke out in a sweat. How could I explain to Margaret that it was lost?

On my way to college, I thought about what I could possibly say to apologise. Margaret was behind the checkout desk. She was busy looking at something on the computer.

"What book are you talking about?" she said distractedly. "An encyclopaedia? There was one on the desk when I came back from lunch on Saturday." She pointed at the trolley with returned books, and there it was: a large encyclopaedia, bound in black leather, cracked and dry with age. There was no doubt that it was the one. I ran my fingers over the gold lettering:

Encyclopaedia of 18th Century Music

"How silly of me," I said, startled. I had been so sure, so absolutely convinced, that I had carried it home. Even now I could feel the weight on my shoulders. What was happening to me? It wasn't just the sleepwalking. Was I beginning to lose my mind?

That afternoon Dr Turner came in and stopped at my desk.

"Everything going all right?" he asked. I told him about my essay plan and showed him what I had done so far.

"Sounds like a really good structure. Good idea to focus on the Oratorios. Don't forget to give a summary of the historical background and note other composers who helped develop the style." He smiled, and for the first time I had the impression that he was genuinely pleased and not mocking me.

"You look a bit peaky," said Margaret when I saw her later on. "Maybe you've caught the bug that's going around. Go home. You look as if you could do with an early night."

I followed her advice and went home at half past three. Amy was in her room but came downstairs when she heard me at the door.

"Hi," she said in a cheerful voice. "There was a phone call for you. Your friend, Clara."

"You talked with her?"

"Yes, we had a nice chat. She phoned the landline after she tried your mobile."

"What time was that?" I took off my wet coat.

"About half an hour ago. Don't you ever answer your phone? I tried to ring you as well."

"I don't know where it is," I lied. For a moment I thought she might have heard it ringing on top of my wardrobe, but I knew it was switched off and securely buried beneath my summer blouses. I could feel heat rising to my head. I didn't like lying to her, and I wasn't sure why I felt I needed to do so.

"She said she'd try again."

"Anything else?"

"They're back from their holiday. She wanted to remind you of the concert – the one with Philip and her. She asked me to come as well."

"Really?"

"Yes. They're going for a pizza afterwards. But she said she needed to talk to you before then. Are you feeling a bit better now?" She gave me a sceptical look.

"Yes, thanks. Much better."

"You don't look it." She shook her head. "Anyway, she said you should ring her back."

"I will later." I went straight upstairs, closed the door and sat down on my bed. My heart pounded against my ribcage. What did Clara need to speak to me about so urgently? Was she trying to find out if I had told anyone else about her and Philip?

I dialled her number, and she answered straight away, sounding out of breath. "Did you get my message? We're home again."

"Yes, Amy told me." I heard voices in the background. "When did you get back?"

"Last night. It's beautiful down there, but I'll never go again in November. The weather was dreadful. It rained every day." She told me about the little village and that their hotel had been right near the sea – and the whole time, I could hear Claudia and Philip chatting. Maybe they were sitting in the living room. When their voices faded a few moments later, she lowered her voice. "I need to talk to you. Later today. I can meet you in the Albany at five."

"Yes, fine," I said.

I sat for several minutes, staring into space. What was going on? Were Philip and Claudia not supposed to know about her meeting me? Why the secrecy? I could hear Amy outside, first in the bathroom flushing the loo and then going into her room. An icy gust of wind came through the open window, twirling the curtains. I shuddered again with cold. For a terrible moment it felt as if a freezing hand was touching me.

THE ALBANY WAS a Victorian pub with wooden interior, red velvet curtains and brocade-upholstered seats. Clara was sitting at a table in the lounge waiting for me.

"I haven't ordered yet," she said. "I wasn't sure what to get. Is it too early for wine?" She hesitated. "Amy is concerned about your health…"

"What did she say?" I stared at her.

"Nothing really – only that you hadn't been sleeping very

well and that you're staying off the booze for a while. She was a bit worried, I think."

"Drinking is not a problem," I said. "I haven't had a glass of wine for nearly two weeks now."

"So, what do think? Shall we have a bottle?"

"Go on then, why not?"

"Great." She looked well, her face slightly tanned in spite of the rain. I watched her as she ordered at the bar. She carried herself very straight and for a moment I wondered if she was as tense as me.

"I'm glad you could make it," she said when she came back with the wine. "We're really very grateful."

"What for?"

"That you didn't tell Claudia our little secret." She smiled wryly. "I think we owe you an apology."

"Don't be silly."

"Yes, I think we do. For not being straight with you, for letting you believe... It wasn't because we were ashamed..." She trailed off.

"You just thought I wouldn't keep it to myself..."

"Yes maybe there was that – but we know now that we were wrong. Philip was worried because you were getting on so well with Claudia."

"It wasn't my choice. But why is she not supposed to know? I don't understand. She thought that Philip was gay and now he's not? What's the problem? Why don't you tell her the truth? Is it because you don't get on?"

Clara leant forward to fill our glasses. "It's not my decision. Philip doesn't want her to know. He is afraid that she would interfere, so he doesn't tell her anything about his emotional life."

"Why?"

"They were very close when he was young – too close."

She shrugged. "It's a long story. Are you sure you want to know?"

She told me about his childhood, how well he had played from early on and how Claudia had been proud of him.

"And he loved pleasing her. He played at every school concert. Everyone said how brilliant he was, and he bathed in the attention. He didn't even have to practise very much. But then he got accepted at the Royal College in London, and things changed."

"Why?"

"It was a shock for him to see that there were so many students better than him, students who had started earlier and practised harder. Some of them were already making a name for themselves. He realised that he had to put in more work if he wanted to rise to the top. He was quite ambitious in those days, and Claudia fired him on. His father had left by then. It was only natural for Philip to keep on living with her. She was already in the music business, running her own agency; she had connections and talked to his teachers. Under her supervision he practised ridiculous hours. There was no time for anything else. Of course he didn't make friends. His fellow students had their own places or lived together in the halls of residence."

She sighed. "It didn't take long before he cracked up. At the beginning he had problems sleeping. His piano teacher had arranged for him to play in a competition. It was open to the general public and he knew that his mother and his teacher would be watching. Claudia was excited for him. She provided him with recordings of the piece and books to read. It didn't take long until he began to suffer from headaches, and then he developed a terrible tremor in his right hand. Claudia made him see her GP who put him on antidepressants. He could sleep again, but his mind was numb and sluggish. When he stopped the tablets, the tremor came back. He knew that he wouldn't be able to perform in that state, but he didn't tell Claudia. You don't imagine how close they were then. He'd always lived for her approval back then. He was under terrible pressure – and then something in him snapped and he just packed his bag and left."

"Where did he go?"

"Berlin. You know that he speaks German, right? He found a job in a pub and earned enough to get by, but he didn't tell anyone where he was for a while. Claudia was beside herself; she thought he had killed himself. He phoned her after a couple of weeks, and she pleaded with him to come back, but he wouldn't have any of it."

"How long did he stay?"

"Eight years. He never talks about it. I only know that he worked behind the bar for all that time. He gave up the piano completely. It was the only way he could cope. There was nothing Claudia could do about it. He hardly ever phoned and never told her anything that mattered. She had to accept it. Around that time, she had the opportunity to move her business to New York. She told Philip on the phone that she would sell the family house if he didn't want to come back and live there himself. It was another attempt to coax him back, but he told her to go ahead and sell it."

Clara topped up our glasses. "By then he had met Franz. He had never been in a relationship before and threw himself completely into it. I think he was a bit naïve. Franz wasn't really committed and was seeing other men as well. Philip was distraught when he found out. That's when he first thought about going back to London. With his mother gone, it suddenly seemed possible again and he really needed to make a new start."

"Did he think of going back to college?"

"The Royal College? No, they wouldn't have him after all that time. He was completely out of practice. But he didn't want to anyway – that was all in the past for him now. Frankly, I don't think he had any plans for the future. He was depressed and lost. It was a very difficult time. I remember the first time I saw him. He was staying with Jack Turner. I knew Jack and his wife through my singing teacher. They invited me round for a meal one night. Maybe Jack thought it would cheer Philip up. I remember his lank hair and the smelly old grey jumper he used to wear all the time. He drank a lot that evening and told me about some book he had read. All he did in those days was read novels and smoke. It was extremely kind of Jack to let him stay. He had no money and nowhere else to go. But it caused problems with Jack's wife. By the time I went round to see them, the tension was obvious. She was fed up with him lying on her sofa all day.

"And then he moved in with you?"

"My marriage had just come to an end, and I felt lonely on my own. The deal was that he would find a job and help me with the rent. I knew that he played the piano but had no idea how good he had been. When I asked him to accompany my singing, he refused at first, worried that his problems would come back. But then he helped me out anyway and gradually got back into it."

"Did Claudia know he was back in London?"

"No, she didn't. He still hadn't told her. He hadn't seen her for over eight years. I nagged him until he phoned her in New York. He actually made peace with her and she came over to meet up. He was terribly tense. I don't know what they talked about, only that he told her that he was gay and that he wouldn't go back to New York with her."

"How did you end up in Cardiff?"

"When Jack got his job at Cardiff University we moved there too. Philip found a job and with Jack's help he studied music again and finally did his PhD in composition. We couldn't have done it without him. When I got the teaching job at college Claudia bought the house. The prices were low and she said it was a good investment for her. But it was really just a way to get into his life again. We shouldn't have gone along with it." She sighed. "We were short of money. It seemed a good idea at first because she lived so far away, but she visits more often now and stays longer every time..."

I thought about what Claudia had said the other day: that she wanted to move back to Cardiff, wondering if I should let Clara know.

"Is she coming to the concert?" I asked instead.

"She wouldn't miss it, especially as Philip is playing. There's nothing we can do about it." We were quiet for a moment, listening to the crashing of someone stacking crates behind the bar.

"Amy said you invited her too," I said.

"Yes, I asked her earlier on when I talked to her on the phone. She was very chatty. She asked me if we were still planning to move in together."

I froze. "What did you say?"

"That it wouldn't happen before Christmas, but that it's still on the cards. Didn't you say that she'd be OK with it?"

"I hope so, but I haven't mentioned it to her again. You should have talked to me first."

"Why? She said that she was expecting it and that you had told her a while ago. I don't think there's a problem. She said she'd always find someone else."

"I thought she would be more upset," I said uneasily.

"You worry too much. A friend of Philip's might be interested in living with us as well. We should all meet up and get to know each other. The more of us there, the more affordable it'll be. There are some beautiful Victorian houses in Roath with original features, ceiling roses and stucco." She glanced at her watch. "I've got a lesson in half an hour, but thanks for coming. And again, I'm sorry for not telling you.

Try not to worry too much. Make sure you get the rest you need. Everything seems more worrying when you don't sleep."

At the door she hugged me goodbye. My eyes followed her as she walked to her car. Should I have told her about my sleepwalking, I wondered. Or had Amy mentioned that to her as well?

IT WAS JUST after seven when I got home. I could hear Amy in the kitchen. The door was open. She was busy scrubbing a pot under running hot water. It smelled of her baking again. There was music on the radio; she had obviously not heard me come in. I stood for a moment in the doorway, wondering what to say.

"Hi," I said. "I'm back."

Her face was flushed and her glasses fogged. "Back from where?"

"I met Clara in the Albany. We had a chat."

"Did you have a drink?" she asked. There was an indignant tone to her voice.

"Yes, why?"

"I could smell it the moment you came through the door." She carried on with her scrubbing. I stared at her broad back, wondering what she had said to Clara about my health.

"I only had a couple of glasses. Nothing to worry about. I'm really feeling much better. We had a nice chat. Clara told me all about their holiday in Cornwall."

"Well, I'm glad you had a good time." She turned around, gazing at me through her fogged-up glasses. She drew a long breath. "Sorry for snapping. I just had one of those days. I couldn't find my glasses... I looked everywhere, blind as a bat. That's why I forgot to see to the biscuits. They were all burnt to a cinder. I had to throw the whole tray away. What an awful waste! If that's not enough to drive anyone mad." She sighed. "Let's put the kettle on. What we need is a nice cup of tea."

We didn't talk about my moving out, and I was glad she didn't mention it. A wave of tiredness came over me as we were watching TV in the living room. I finished my tea and went straight to bed.

14

I woke up with a start, not knowing where I was. It was pitch black apart from the light of several black-wicked candles, flickering in the draught from a half open window. I got up, my heart thumping, and made a few hesitant steps towards the light. Getting nearer I recognised the wrought-iron candelabra from the piano downstairs. A gust of wind was billowing the curtains towards the flames. I quickly blew them out and switched on the ceiling light.

Only then did I see a picture frame on my desk. The protective glass was smashed and scattered around. The picture itself was cut up into several pieces. Amy's kitchen scissors were next to it, one blade bent, as if they had been used with force – maybe to edge the frame open.

Startled, I didn't notice the bin bag next to the desk and nearly stumbled over it. It was the dirty wet bin bag from the back garden. I held my breath. How had it got into my room? With stiff, cold fingers I brushed the glass aside and picked up the scraps, trying to match them together. Some of the edges looked burnt. It was the photo of Amy's mother – there was no doubt. I recognised fragments of her pale face and that beautiful red hair. There were matches, a whole pile of them – at least twenty next to an empty box. They had all been struck, but some of the heads were broken off. Had I tried to burn that picture? Why?

I glanced around, shivering. Nothing else had changed. My coat was on the back of the chair, the usual pile of books on the desk. Had I been downstairs and gone into the garden, sleepwalking again? The photo was damp – was that the reason it hadn't caught fire. Frozen to the spot, I imagined it all. I must have struck the matches against the sandpaper strip of the box, lighting them one after another, watching the flames flare up in the darkness. What if the photo hadn't been wet? A horrific scene arose in my mind: high flames engulfing me and setting the curtains alight, a gust of wind fanning and spreading the fire.

I was still holding the empty box of matches in my hand. Panic swelled within me. It was only half past seven. I had to get rid of it all quickly before Amy got up. She would be terrified by how I had nearly killed us both. And she would of course blame the drinking again.

I picked up the glass and the fragments of the picture, grabbed the frame and stuffed it all together with the broken scissors into the bag. Quietly I made my way downstairs. The 40-watt bulb was burning and swinging from the kitchen ceiling. The door to the garden was wide open. It was dark and quite windy outside. I left the bag near the apple tree where it had been before and closed the door.

With shaky hands I made myself a cup of tea and sipped it as I looked out the window. My heart was pounding. *We could have died!* my brain kept screaming. *We could have died in the fire!* How could I do a thing like that, and why on earth had I tried to burn the picture? I'd only had a couple of glasses of wine with Clara before, but Amy was right: it had obviously been too much.

I could hear her on the stairs. A moment later, she put her head around the kitchen door.

"You're up early. What are you doing, standing here in the cold? Fancy some breakfast? We can have it in the living room. I'll put the fire on. I bought some eggs for my baking." She smiled. "Fried egg sandwich again?"

"No, thanks. I'll have something later," I said, managing a smile. "I have to press on. Got to get on with my essay."

"Sure, but don't you think you need to line your stomach first?" Her eyes rested on mine. "Are you sure you're all right? You look done in again."

"No, honestly, I'm absolutely fine." I quickly left before she could say anything else.

I WELCOMED THE COLD. The rain had ceased, but the day was dark and overcast. I needed a walk to clear my head. A strong wind was roaring in the bare trees along the recreation ground. I had not planned where I was going, but it soon became clear that I was heading towards the lake. My mind was racing. What could I do to stop this nightmare happening again? Should I talk to someone, a doctor or psychiatrist? What would they do? Put me on drugs or lock me up somewhere to protect me from myself? Maybe I had no other choice.

I sat down on a bench near the lake. The water was choppy and muddy, its colour, mirroring the sky above. The swans were sleeping or hiding from the cold, their bills buried in their feathers. I don't know how long I sat there, staring at the lake. Amy's mother was on my mind. She had been so beautiful. How could she have gone from that to the wreck she had been in her later years, lying in bed all day long, drinking herself to an early death?

And now I lived in that room. Was I slowly going mad as

she had? Was that why I had fetched the bag from outside and tried to burn that photo of her? There had to be something about that room, some awful spell that made me do those things. What was happening to me? Was there something bad inside of me, a dark side that took over when my guard was down? Was I normal just by day and at night the other, evil side took over?

Images of my childhood surged up. After my sister died I soon stopped going to confession. They couldn't make me, but my mother refused to give up on me. For a while I still let her drag me to church with her. There was a painting on the stained-glass window, the oval shaped blue eye of God. I knew that He was watching me. There was no hiding. He knew what I had done.

Father O'Leary, too, looked right into my soul. His face was red and angry when he warned against evil. There was a war for our soul between God and the devil, a battle of good and evil within ourselves. He was always out to get us. We had to resist him like Jesus whom he tempted with the kingdoms of this world if he would fall and worship him. And now he went after us, the poor and broken souls. "The devil wants us to spend eternity in hell and wants our life on this earth to be a living hell!" Father O'Leary droned on from the pulpit. I always felt as if he was talking straight at me, as if he had found me out.

The clouds were getting thicker and darker and after a while I could feel the first thick drops of rain. In seconds it was pouring down. The bare trees offered no shelter and the icy rain hurt my face. I made my way towards the café but was drenched before I even got halfway there.

It was warm and dry inside. There were other people queuing up in their wet coats. Behind the glass-fronted counter was a display of various cakes, but there was also warm food on the menu: chips, sausages, burgers and chicken curry. I realised how hungry I was and ordered a mug of tea and fried eggs with toast.

Eating my late breakfast, I looked out of the blurred window onto the lake. The rain continued hammering down on the roof. I tried to gather my thoughts and come up with some sort of plan. The house was getting me down. Clara had told Amy that I was going to move out after Christmas. It would be for the best. Living with other musicians would be a welcome distraction.

Maybe the sleepwalking would stop then on its own account. Until then I had to just get on with it. It was still three weeks until the Christmas holidays – time enough to find a house. I had a bit of extra money now through my library work and could afford a more expensive place. It was good to know that Amy knew about it and didn't seem to mind. But why hadn't she mentioned it at all? I couldn't shake off a terrible feeling of dread and foreboding as I trudged back under the tall, dripping trees, making my way home.

AMY WAS IN THE KITCHEN, rummaging through the cupboard.

"Hi," she said, turning around when she heard me at the door. "You're back early."

"I forgot the laptop."

"Deary me." She grinned. "And you had to go all the way back in this weather! You'll forget your head one day." She brushed a strand of hair away from her hot face. "You don't happen to know where the scissors are? I've been looking everywhere."

"What scissors?" I asked, feeling the heat rising to my head.

"The old ones from drawer. I need them for the baking. Where on earth can they be...?" She let out a little chuckle. "Maybe I'll have a look through the rubbish." She gave me a searching look. "No time for a cuppa? Never mind. I know, you're busy again."

Later, on my way back from college, I bought a new pair of scissors. They were nothing like the old ones, but I put them in the drawer with the cutlery anyway, hoping that Amy wouldn't notice. To my surprise she never mentioned them again. Nor did she ask me about my plans to move in with Clara and Philip. I wondered if she hadn't taken them seriously. She was amiable and good-tempered, and we didn't talk about my "problem" anymore.

My essay for Dr Turner was almost finished. I was still feeling tired and muzzy most of the time, but I kept at it. By the end of the week the basic work was done. I just had to review it once more and check the annotations.

I was surprised and a bit flustered when I saw Philip in the library a few days later. He was reading a book about William Mathias in Welsh and needed the dictionaries. When he went for his cigarette break, he asked me to come along. We sat on the steps at the back of the college and chatted about Handel. He was friendlier, more gentle. I had never felt so at ease with him before. We talked about the opera productions we had seen, and he told me about a *Semele* performance in New York in which the audience had laughed at the most inappropriate moments. He even suggested that we all go to London to visit the house where Handel had lived and written most of his works. He'd apparently been there with Clara before.

"We could make it a couple of nights and go to the museums. There's so much to do."

He wanted to know about Carlisle, about my last job, and why I had chosen Cardiff to do my degree. I asked about his plans, but he didn't give much away. I wondered if Clara had told him about our chat – or if he had any idea how much I knew about him. We also talked about the upcoming concert.

Clara had been unwell with a cold and was apparently worried that her voice would not be up to it.

"You know what singers are like. I'm sure she'll be all right." He took a deep draw of his cigarette, holding it between his thumb and index finger. "And don't forget my birthday party next Saturday. Clara said you were coming. I've invited Chris, a friend of mine who is quite keen on sharing a house with us. You should get to know each other."

I managed to finish the essay that afternoon, but decided to have one last look at it before emailing it to Dr Turner. As I was getting ready to go home, Margaret announced that Claudia was on the phone for me.

"I've got amazing news." Her voice was high and excited. "I found the ideal place for the café bar in Roath. It's a wool shop now, but we could easily make some changes. The location is ideal for an art café there, and it's affordable as well. I'll have to show you the photos. Can we meet up tonight? There is an excellent Italian restaurant in the Bay? My treat."

"I'm not sure," I said reluctantly. "I'm quite busy actually." I trailed off.

"I won't take much of your time," Claudia said. "I would really like to discuss it with you. It would mean a lot."

"OK, but just a couple of hours." I gave in, aware that Margaret was listening. We agreed to meet at Signor Valentino's at the waterfront.

When I got there at just before eight she was already standing at the door, waiting for me. I saw her tall thin figure from afar. She was wearing her green leather coat and a long black scarf. Coming nearer I could see that she had dyed her short hair red.

She greeted me with a hug. "I'm so glad you dragged

yourself here. I really need to hear your opinion. Come on in. They do lovely food. I was here with a client a while ago."

It was a traditional trattoria with red-and-white chequered tablecloths, flowers on each table and the menu written on a blackboard on the wall. A mirror behind the bar reflected shelves of various bottles. Claudia had booked a table at the window overlooking the bay. The waitress came over with the menu, and Claudia ordered a bottle of Valpolicella. I glanced at the prices. It was not cheap; the main courses started at £15.

"Please choose whatever you like," Claudia said as if reading my thoughts. "My treat. I recommend the salmon. It was excellent last time."

When the waitress returned with the wine, we ordered side salads and marinated vegetables as starters.

"Would you like the side salad with your main course?" the waitress asked. She was in her early twenties and obviously Italian.

"No, as I said before: we'd like it for the starter please – if that's possible at all," Claudia said politely enough. But her voice had a sharp edge to it and the girl looked a bit embarrassed as she walked away.

Claudia got out her mobile.

"I can't wait to show you the pictures," she said. I could feel her excitement like a nervous kind of energy. "Look," she said, her eyes alight. "What do you think?" She handed over the phone. The photo showed a big Victorian corner house. The glass-fronted shop was downstairs. There was a display of wool and jumpers behind the large shop window.

"How big is it inside?" I asked.

"There are two large rooms, but we can knock down the dividing wall and make it one. It would be a fantastic space for concerts. I thought we'd have one jazz night a week, snacks, and maybe classical music. We have to suss it out –

see what goes. A lot of students live around there. The area is up and coming. We could even have poetry readings and book launches. We'll get a core clientele..." Her hawkish eyes were boring into mine.

"But won't it be really expensive to make all those changes?" I took a big sip of my wine.

The waitress came with the starters along with bread and garlic butter.

"Don't worry about money," Claudia said when she was gone. "I don't expect you to invest. There's a lot you could do, help me with the management, cook or play the piano. I thought you were keen."

I didn't answer. We helped ourselves to the salad. There was a long silence. I knew my lack of enthusiasm was disappointing her, but how could I possibly take part? Clara and Philip had no idea that she was planning to come back for good, and I was planning to move in with them. There was no way I could work so closely together with her. I couldn't remember agreeing to anything when she had told me about it in the first place.

I took a deep breath. "I don't think I'll have the time. I'm planning to be a teacher. How could I commit to this as well?"

"Don't worry. You wouldn't have to share the workload or really commit to anything. It would just be nice if you could do an hour here or there." She sighed. "To be frank, I had hoped to get you on board because of Philip and Clara."

"What do you mean?"

"Maybe they'll come round and take part as well when they see that you're involved and realise it's going well. You're friends with them... You could talk them into it. Philip likes playing jazz..." she trailed off.

"But I won't have the time."

"It would be fun," she said, ignoring me. "And it's a real goldmine! We could make serious money."

She topped up my glass. I noticed that the bottle was already empty. How could she be so insensitive? She was of course used to getting her own way. I should have known she wouldn't take no for an answer.

"You don't have to decide now," she said. "You think about it."

When the waitress came with the salmon, Claudia ordered a second bottle, and I didn't protest. Seeing her so set on her plan made me increasingly tense. It wasn't my place to say that Clara and Philip didn't want to live with her. Clara had told me all those things in confidence. And Claudia would be so upset if she knew. I was beginning to feel a bit sorry for her.

I finished my glass. The wine took the edge off a little.

"Really excellent food," I said, trying a forkful of salmon. "It really is worth every penny. Thanks for inviting me."

"Yes, isn't it great?" She smiled. "As I said, you don't have to make a decision now. Let's talk about something else. Are you coming to the concert tomorrow? I'm so glad that Philip is performing again." She looked at me expectantly.

I nodded.

"How are you anyway? Have you had a word with Dr Turner about that accompaniment?"

"No, but I'm not really bothered anymore."

"You should be though," she said. "I would have given him a piece of my mind." She grinned at me. "I remember sorting things out for Philip at music school. He could be a bit of a pushover then."

It struck me again how similar they looked. Philip was like a paler, feebler version of her. It was almost as if she hadn't given him the room to grow.

I took another big sip of my wine, which made me feel a bit giddy. Glancing out of the window, I saw the lights of the Turkish restaurant across reflecting on the water, and the colours blurred in front of my eyes. There was a hen party at the neighbouring table, a lot of women with bright red wigs – and it was suddenly quite noisy with raised voices and shrieks of laughter.

Claudia needed the loo and I watched her wind her way through the tables. When she came back, she looked exhausted and pale.

"Let's finish the wine and go for a walk," she said.

Claudia paid the bill. She took my arm and we walked along the bay. She told me about New York, about the horrendous property prices there. She was wondering how much she would get for her flat in Brooklyn. "It will pay for the art café," she said. It was a moonless, cold night – with no hint left of the Indian summer feel of the day. The air was chill and the breath from our mouths looked like smoke. It was about half past ten. I remember going home in a taxi with her. I sat in the front next to the driver because she had to get out first. We stopped in Pontcanna at her house. It must have been eleven when the driver let me out at Chapel Road.

AMY WAS STILL up when I got in.

"You smell of wine again," she said. "Oh my word. How much have you had?" She took my arm and led me to the sofa. "Sit down for a moment. What you need is a nice cup of tea. It'll help dilute it a bit." She disappeared and I closed my eyes for moment. It didn't take long until she was back. "I put extra sugar in it," she said, leaning against the doorway, watching me.

My hands gripped the mug as I sipped the strong sweet tea. All of a sudden the room started reeling.

"Where did you go?" Her voice sounded far away. "What's the matter, Kate?"

I tried to get up, but my legs were too weak. I got hold of

the armrest and lifted myself up a bit, but almost immediately fell back again. There was blackness at the edges of my vision. Amy had come over from the door; her face above me was blurred.

"I'm going to throw up," I whispered. Amy took my arm and I staggered with her towards the door, but stumbled over something and fell on my knees.

"Get up," she shouted.

The vomit came up suddenly, chunks of half-digested salmon together with wine and the tea I just had. Resting my palms against the floor, I took in a deep breath before my stomach lurched again and more liquid dribbled from my lips.

"For God's sake, pull yourself together."

I couldn't stop heaving. Amy grabbed my arm again and helped me up. I nearly slipped on my own sick, but she somehow managed to drag me with her into the kitchen.

Leaning over the sink, it started all over again; another violent wave of vomit came up. I retched and retched until there was nothing left but acid bile. Next door I could hear Amy with a mop and bucket, clearing up. I opened the tap to let the water run to rinse off the mess. I was so cold my teeth were chattering.

"It smells terrible," said Amy when she came back. "Oh my word, what have you been drinking?"

She refilled her bucket and disappeared into the living room again. Afraid that it wasn't quite over, I desperately clung on to the sink. After what seemed like ages she came back.

"Are you feeling better?" she asked, her tone a bit more friendly now. "We'll have to get you upstairs somehow. You'll have to take off your clothes." She was right: my trousers were soiled with vomit and the sleeves of my blouse were dripping wet. My legs felt like giving way but with her help I made it to the stairs. Everything started reeling again. I had to go on all fours, my hands flat on the step above, dragging myself up step by step.

Back in my room, I took off my clothes and fell onto the bed.

"Try not to make a mess in here as well," she said. "Oh my Lord, how much did you have?" She put the bucket next to my bed. "Sleep tight," she said. "I hope you're better in the morning." My eyes were shut but I could feel that she was still standing there watching me.

15

I sank into unconsciousness. I slept and slept. Night became day and the morning turned into the afternoon until eventually the sleep became more shallow. Dreams and images were triggered by the sounds that seeped in from outside: Amy's muttering and sighing. I dreamt that there was someone in the room with me, trying to tell me something important, but I couldn't raise my head and hear what it was.

The banging of my door finally woke me up. Opening my eyes, I saw Amy standing at the window: her broad shoulders a dark silhouette against the incoming light.

"What time is it?" I asked. My throat was sore and there was a horrible taste in my mouth.

"I made you a drink," she said. "You got me worried. I thought you'd never wake up. You must be thirsty."

I nodded, suddenly remembering. A feeling of dread and shame rose in me.

She handed me a mug of steaming tea. "Drink that," she said in a firm voice. "You are dehydrated; it's important to replenish the fluid you've lost." I had heard nurses speak like that on *Casualty*, Amy's favourite soap. The tea was still hot and swallowing hurt my throat, but I managed to drink it in little sips.

Only now did I see the flesh-coloured bandage wrapped around her wrist and lower arm. But my mouth was still too dry to ask why it was there. There was a chair next to my bed. I wondered if she had brought it in from her room. Had she sat there when I was asleep?

"Well done," she said in her firm nurse's voice. "You will feel better, but it might take a while. Maybe you can eat some chicken later on. We'll have to see if you keep down the tea."

"What time is it?" I asked again.

"Nearly half past four. It'll soon be getting dark again."

"What? So late?" I flung back the duvet and swung my legs out of bed, only the sudden movement made me feel dizzy again. Cold sweat was running down my neck. Defeated, I sank back against the pillow. "I've got to go to Clara's concert!" I mumbled. "I said I would go."

"You can't be serious." Amy gave me a stern look. "No one is expecting that. We were all really worried about you."

"We?"

"Yes. Clara and I thought you were going to die from alcohol poisoning. I nearly called 999, but Clara said I should wait." She glanced down at her bandaged arm. "I thought you might apologise."

"You told Clara?"

"It still really hurts," she said, ignoring my question. "You must have damaged a ligament when you twisted my arm. I should have left you on the floor, but I was worried that you would choke on your vomit."

"I can't remember." I stared at her.

"The state you were in!" She shook her head. "It reminded me of my mother: collapsed on the floor, hardly conscious, mumbling stuff. I couldn't leave you like that, so I hoisted you up. That's when you opened your eyes and screamed at me. You said that I was holding you back, that you wanted to take revenge, or something like that. And then you deliberately wrenched my wrist."

"Oh my God! I'm sorry. Did you tell Clara?"

"No. I'm not a snitch. I just told her that you had too much to drink again and that I was worried. I said that you wouldn't be able to go to the concert."

"Thanks," I said, the relief bringing tears to my eyes.

"God only knows how much you'd had." She let out a heartfelt sigh. "I didn't know that pubs stayed open that late around here."

"But I was home by eleven." A feeling of panic was choking me. "I took a taxi home with Claudia."

"Sorry, but that's not true." She shook her head. "It was after twelve when you came home. Claudia said that you took a taxi at half past ten from the bay and that she was home about ten to eleven. You must have gone somewhere else afterwards. You certainly didn't come home straight away. It sounds like another blackout to me."

"Claudia?"

"Yes. I phoned her up this morning. She said you had two bottles of wine between you. She was very worried too. But please relax. It'll be fine in the end, but you really have to change your ways."

WHEN I WOKE up on Sunday I was drenched in sweat. As soon as I opened my eyes, the guilt was back, weighing heavy on me. A sob tore from my throat. I had twisted Amy's wrist! It was the dark side again – the monster within me that came to the fore when I drank, a destructive force completely out of my control. What terrible thing would I do next?

I tried to piece together what had happened. My bag was

on the floor. I reached for it with clammy hands and emptied it onto the bed. My movements were sluggish. Where had I gone after leaving the taxi? There was some money in my purse – about five pounds in small change. I knew that I had taken forty pounds, two twenty-pound notes. Claudia had insisted on paying for the meal and had even given money to the taxi driver in advance. Where had it all gone? What pub had I been to? Where had I spent those thirty-five pounds?

I felt utterly exhausted. A cup of cold tea sat on my bedside cabinet. I took a sip and sank back onto my pillow. I racked my brain, but there was nothing, not even a feeling or a vague idea. Had the driver stopped at the Woodville pub on the way home? Perhaps someone had stolen the money while I was drunk. I tried to imagine how I had staggered home. Had there been people on the street, witnessing it? Should I be worried about something that I had said or done? If I could only remember where I had been. Had I shouted at people or started a fight?

My stomach lurched and gurgled. I had never felt so bad after drinking. It reminded me of the stomach bugs I'd had at home. It brought it all back: being curled up in bed, clinging to an old plastic bucket, the purposefully darkened room, my mother checking on me. Maybe I had caught a virus and the drinking had just aggravated it.

Amy had left my door open and looked in now and then to see how I was. With her assistance I managed to go to the bathroom. Washing my hands, I caught my reflection in the mirror over the sink: cold sweat glistening on my pale face, my feverish eyes staring back at me. I was glad to be back in my room. She brought me food, soft convalescence food: chicken soup, white bread and eggs. After carefully placing the tray, she sat down next to my bed and watched me eat.

"Maybe I have a stomach bug," I said.

"Don't try to fool yourself." Her face clouded over. "I have never seen you that drunk. You were legless." She shook my pillow, plumping it up. "My mum was like that: always making up excuses. All her illnesses were caused by drink. She nearly died from pancreatitis. Oh my Lord. She was sick just like you; her stomach was on fire. I found her in the bathroom when I came home from school, curled up in pain. Couldn't open the door because her body was in the way. Three long weeks she was in hospital."

I closed my eyes, trying to hide my dismay. My brain was struggling to take it all in.

Later on Amy came in again to say goodnight. She brought me another cup of peppermint tea, fluffed up my pillow again and straightened the sheets. She told me about a fire on Cathedral Road. A big house had burned to the ground and several people had died – the family dog, a German Shepherd, had been trapped in the basement. There had been a long report in the news. She reminded me to be more careful with my sleepwalking. It would be so easy to start a fire, especially if I tried my hand at cooking again.

I woke up late the next day. Amy was in the kitchen – I could hear her banging cupboard doors. Maybe the noise had roused me. I sat up and listened. After a while the front door fell shut, and the house was silent. She had probably gone shopping. It was ten past twelve. Fourteen hours of deep, dreamless sleep had done me a lot of good. I was still a bit queasy but strong enough to get up. Margaret was expecting me to do the afternoon shift.

In the bathroom, I stopped in front of the mirror. The sickness had taken its toll. I looked thinner and older somehow; there was more grey in my unkempt hair. For a while I stood leaning against the tiled wall to steady myself and take in its chill. It took concentration to go through the usual motions: step into the shower, onto the cold, ceramic floor, turn on the water and regulate the temperature until the lukewarm drops began to soak my hair and trickle down my neck.

As I got dressed, I noticed that my jeans that used to hug my waist hung loose on me.

"You shouldn't have come in," Margaret said when I showed my face in the office. "You're still very pale. Dr Turner asked about you. He told me you were poorly. He was wondering if you'd come in." She shook her head. "You shouldn't have dragged yourself here."

"I had a meal out. I think there was something wrong with the food."

"Did you have chicken?" She told me that a friend of hers had been in hospital with Salmonella poisoning. It had started with abdominal pain and terrible cramps.

"Did Dr Turner say why he wants to see me?" I interrupted.

"He said he wanted to discuss something... something to do with your essay, I think. He said it was important. You're very lucky to be back to normal so soon. My friend took more than a week to recover. Two people died on her ward. She was put on strong antibiotics because the infection had gone to her blood."

I nodded absently. How did Dr Turner know that I had been sick? Had Clara told him at the concert, I wondered. Had she said something about my drinking?

"Are you sure you want to stay?" Margaret asked as she put on her coat.

I nodded.

"Give Dr Turner a ring. The list with his number is on the corkboard." Then she was out of the door.

The room was quiet with only a few students studying at the tables, reading and using the computers. A first-year student asked for Mendelssohn's *Elijah*, and I pointed her to the shelves with the choral and opera scores. What was so important that Dr Turner had come down looking for me, I wondered.

After a moment of trepidation, I dialled his number.

"Kate," he said, "I'm glad you've rung. We need to talk."

"Yes, Margaret said. What about?"

"Your essay."

"Is there something wrong with it?"

"I'd rather not discuss it on the phone," he said. "Could you come to my office? I've got a student here at the moment, but I'll be around until half past four. And there was something else as well…" he trailed off.

"No problem," I said. "I'll see you later."

I resumed my place behind the checkout desk, wondering what was wrong. There had been a strange note of urgency in his voice. Why couldn't he talk about it on the phone? I let my gaze wander. Maybe I could leave the library unattended for a few minutes. Hopefully no one would need me for checking out. Better now than later when it would be busier. It was nearly four, and he wouldn't be there for much longer.

I left the library door open. Gareth was in the lodge, and I felt his eyes following me as I crossed the empty foyer and rushed up the stairs to the second floor. As I stopped in front of Dr Turner's office, I heard a woman's voice rising and falling inside. Was it the student he'd mentioned earlier on? It sounded like an informal chat. There was an outburst of laughter. I all but pressed my ear against the door but couldn't make out what she was saying.

To avoid being caught eavesdropping, I began walking up and down the corridor, getting increasingly tense and impatient. It was at least another ten minutes before she came out: Alicia Green, the woman who had taken over the accompaniment. I'd seen her laughing with Dr Turner before. She looked very pretty in a grey, lace dress that brought out the honey blonde of her long hair. A smile on her face, she walked past without even noticing me.

I went up to the door and knocked.

"Come on in," he shouted. "Oh, it's you," he said, taken aback.

"Shall I come back later?"

"Bear with me," he said, gesturing towards his brown leather sofa, "I'll be with you in a moment." He started shuffling papers on his desk, apparently looking for something.

The sofa was still warm where Alicia had been sitting. I furtively glanced around. He really did look busy. The chaos on his desk had spilled onto the floor, and there were stacks of papers everywhere. Music was playing in the background: Bach's Violin Concerto No. 3. I breathed deeply to calm down my nerves.

"I'm glad you've come. We need to talk about your essay." He sat down in the armchair opposite me.

"Is there something wrong with it?"

"Well, you could say that." He glanced at the computer printouts in his hand. "It's incomplete. The second half is missing. Handel's influence on other composers is not even mentioned. What happened? Didn't you manage to finish in time?"

"I don't understand." My face was hot with embarrassment. "I'm sure I sent you the whole essay."

"No, I'm sorry, but you haven't." He crossed his arms in front of his chest as if bracing himself.

"It must have been a mistake," I said. "I've got it on my computer at home. I can send it to you if that's still OK."

"Well..." He looked straight into my eyes. "There's a problem. I don't know if I can accept it. The deadline was last Friday and it wouldn't be right if you'd have had three more days than everyone else." He cleared his throat. "Unless you could give me a doctor's note. I heard that you hadn't been well."

"I had a stomach bug."

"A stomach bug?" He looked at me, slightly amused, his eyebrows raised.

"Yes. All weekend."

There was a long silence.

"There was something else too," he said eventually. "I had a voicemail from you on Friday night. It must have been half past eleven."

"That can't be." I stared at him.

"You don't remember?"

"No, I don't," I said, trying to suppress the tremble in my voice. "What did I say?"

"I'm afraid I couldn't understand you very well," he said coldly. "Your speech was slurred; it was rather incoherent."

"I really can't remember." My stomach felt heavy.

"Maybe you should see a doctor. I thought you'd feel less stressed, now that someone else is doing the accompaniment for the choir. I thought I had taken the pressure off, but it doesn't seem to have done much good. Maybe you should reconsider."

"Reconsider what?"

"Let the doctor decide," he said. "Let them assess you first. Maybe you need a break to sort out your problems before you come back. With a doctor's note you could start again next term."

"But there's nothing wrong with me. I only had a stomach bug."

"Well, as long as you see your GP and produce a note we might be able to accept the rest of your essay." He got up. "And I hope you'll tell me directly if something is bothering you. If you'll excuse me now, I'm very busy."

I left his office, humiliated and dejected. My mind was

racing. Where on earth had I rung him from and left that drunken voicemail? The mobile was still in my bag at home. I had taken it with me on Friday because I thought I'd have to call a taxi later on. Slurred and incoherent, he'd said – in other words, a drunken rant! Had I said something about the accompaniment? I had to fight back the tears burning in my eyes.

Downstairs, I ran into Gareth.

"Where have you been?" he said indignantly. "I thought you'd gone home."

"Why? I was upstairs."

"You can't leave the library without someone in charge." He rattled his big bunch of keys. "One of the lads complained because there was no one to check him out. I had to send them all home."

"Sorry," I said, "I didn't think it would take so long."

"I looked for you. I thought you were on the loo. Where were you anyway?"

"In Dr Turner's office." I stared back at him, unable to hide my dislike.

"So, Dr Turner's office." His eyes looked me up and down. "For all that time?" He let out a fat chuckle. "I wonder what's so interesting up there." His right hand was still holding the keys, the other was in his pocket, scratching at his crotch through the black polyester of his trousers.

"We talked about my essay." I took a deep breath. "Didn't you see my stuff in the office, my bag and my coat?"

"Essay…is that what you call it these days?" He grinned at me.

I followed him to the library where he unlocked the door. Some of the computers were still running. I could have gone back to my place behind the checkout desk, but the man made me feel nauseous.

"I'm going home. I'm not feeling very well," I said. Aware

that he was watching me, I tidied away the books that were lying around and turned off the screens. I put on my coat and switched off the light. And when I was done I walked out of the door, without even looking at him again or saying goodbye.

AT HALF PAST four it was already getting dark. Dark clouds were drifting along the sky, obscuring the light of the moon. It was windy, and I shivered in spite of my coat.

A feeling of shame and panic rose from the pit of my stomach. It hadn't been an illness after all. I'd been raving drunk on Friday night. I neared the Woodville pub with its yellow lighting and stopped to peer through the window. Most of the tables were empty. The barmaid, a middle-aged woman with a yellow perm, was pulling a pint for a local. I wondered if I should go inside. The warm haze of a few drinks was tempting.

Maybe the barmaid would recognise my face and tell me if I had been there on Friday night and what I had done. Even the most embarrassing truth would be better than this limbo of not knowing, but I could hardly go in there and ask. When the barmaid raised her head and glanced in my direction, I quickly turned and walked away.

As I let myself in through the front door, I could hear voices. It wasn't the television. Amy was obviously not alone. She'd never had a visitor before. I stopped in the dark hall, trying to find out what was going on when the door suddenly opened from inside.

"Oh, it's you," Amy peered out, "I thought I heard something. Where have you been?"

"College. I had to be at the library."

"You could have left me a note." She lowered her voice. "Clara is here. She wanted to know how you were."

"Really?" I stared at her, lost for words.

"She's been here for a while. We had a chat. She's really worried about you. We both were. I didn't even know where you were. You could have gone to the pub again for all we knew. To just walk away like that, after all I've done for you..." she said flatly. "Well, I'll leave you to it then."

Clara was sitting on the sofa, flicking through the television magazine. Seeing her there was strange – she looked misplaced in the ugly uninviting room. I suddenly felt ashamed of the shabby furniture, the threadbare carpet and the unfinished walls. The window hadn't been cleaned for years and there were cobwebs hanging from the ceiling. The lingering stale smell of cooking was revolting.

"Hi," she raised her head. "Thought I heard your voice. I was wondering how you were."

"I'm OK – much better anyway."

"I was worried when Amy rang me on Saturday." She gave me a searching look. "How are you, really?"

"Honestly, I'm much better." I sat down next to her. "It must have been a stomach upset – maybe something I ate when I was out with Claudia."

"Amy said you were drunk." She let out an uneasy laugh. "You know I don't mind. I was just worried..." she trailed off.

"I had a bit too much wine with Claudia," I said in a steady voice, "but there must have been something wrong with the food." I was beginning to wonder if she had just come to talk to Amy and find out how bad it really was.

She didn't respond.

"I'm sorry I couldn't make it to the concert," I said. "How did it go?"

"I'd had a bit of a cold, but it went very well. The usual crowd was in the audience, students and parents mostly. Jack Turner was there, and we had a long chat afterwards." She hesitated. "We're all concerned about you. He told me about the voicemail. What was all that about?"

My hand shook as I leaned forward to help myself to one of Amy's biscuits. "I can't remember. I had no reason to phone him. I don't know why I would have left a message."

"You don't remember what you said?"

"No. He told me in his office that it was incoherent. Maybe I had switched the mobile on by mistake when I was talking to someone else."

"I don't think so. That's not what he said." She sighed. "He said you threatened him."

"I threatened him? But he said he couldn't understand."

"Maybe he was just being kind."

"What exactly did I say?"

"Well," she paused, "you said that he was sexually harassing his students and that you'd report him if he carried on."

"That's terrible." I stared at her.

"Don't worry." She put her hand on my arm. "It was probably the drink. Don't you think it's worrying that you can't remember anything at all?"

"Of course." I swallowed. Her hand felt soft and cool. It struck me that she was the only person who would be able to help. "I don't think it's just the drink," I whispered. "I really need to move out. The house is getting me down. I think I'm going mad in here. Amy's mother died in the room where I sleep."

"I understand that, but I'm not so sure if that's a good idea." She sighed again. "You'll have to deal with your drinking first. You can't run away from it. The problem won't go away. I know you tried it before."

"Tried what?"

"Running away from it. Amy said that you did the same thing in Carlisle, that you had to leave because you had fallen out with your colleague – that you had rung him when you were drunk."

"When did she tell you that?" I looked at her, stunned.

"I'm sorry." She sat up straight. "You know I'm not judgmental, but I really think you need to own up to it. You're not mad; it's just a drink problem. Don't get me wrong, I'd like to live with you, but moving in together is probably not an option until you have sorted it out." She looked embarrassed.

"No." I lowered my voice. "Please understand. I'm really going mad in here. Amy's mother drank herself to death, and it's always on my mind. Do you think her presence could have an influence on me?"

"How could she? She's dead." Behind Clara's widened eyes I sensed her panicked thoughts – the worry that I was losing it.

"Strange things happen. I haven't been myself," I whispered. "I never was that bad before."

"Look," she said softly, "you could see your doctor or a therapist, or go to one of those groups. I don't think blaming it on the house or whatever is getting you anywhere. You have to take responsibility. We will all support you. I discussed it with Amy. She said that the stress is getting you down and that you need a break from it all. Maybe she is right. She wants to hire a car and go to the seaside with you. Maybe that's what you need. At least she'd have an eye on you there. But promise me that you'll see your GP as well. Don't worry. It's really nothing to be ashamed of. You know how much Philip and I like a drink. It's just that some people are more likely than others to get hooked. Do you want me to go with you?"

I shook my head.

"Well, give me a ring if you need my support." She got up to leave. "I must be getting on your nerves." She frowned. "Oh, I nearly forgot: the party next weekend! There'll be a lot of booze, and Jack will be there. I understand if you don't want to come. Or you could bring Amy along. She really wants to help. Think about it."

I walked her to the door. She gave me a kiss on the cheek, and I caught a whiff of her shampoo, a fresh lemony scent.

"Everything will be all right," she said with a strained smile. "Trust me. Everything will be just fine."

16

I expected Amy to continue what Clara had started – that she would talk about my problem again and insist that I do something about it. Had Clara told her about the voicemail I had left? Maybe she didn't know. Or maybe she had other, more pressing things to think about. Whatever the reason, she didn't mention my drinking again. It was almost as if it had slipped her mind.

Though Amy hadn't talked about her novel recently, it seemed to be all that mattered to her now. Clara had put her in touch with Claudia, who knew a literary agent in New York.

"I'll have to send her a synopsis and the first chapter," Amy said.

There were two hectic patches of red on her cheeks. She had been typing all day in her room and had only come down to make herself a sandwich. "Claudia said that I'd have a good chance to get it published if that agent takes me on. She'll recommend it to her. I'm really grateful. It could be the making of me."

"That's very kind of her," I said, surprised. Claudia hadn't mentioned it. She had been quite short with me when I'd phoned her to find out about the evening and the taxi drive home.

I tried not to worry. There were other things I had to deal with anyway. I checked the attachment I had sent to Dr Turner, and the second half of the essay was really missing. How on earth could I have deleted half of it without even noticing? I couldn't find it anywhere on my computer, but there had to be a hard copy of it somewhere. I looked through the pile on my table, the various photocopies from my courses, but the essay wasn't amongst them. In the end I managed to dig up some rumpled old papers with an outline of the original draft from my bin. I was determined not to give up. I would do everything necessary to carry on with my degree: make an appointment with my GP to get a note and most importantly write up the second half of that essay again.

At college I soon fell back into my usual routine. No one took any notice of me; no one seemed to know about my voicemail to Dr Turner. He had probably only told Clara. It almost seemed as if he'd forgotten about it already. During his course I hardly looked up behind my curtain of hair, but I needn't have worried. There was nothing unusual in the way he behaved. When I walked up to him afterwards to tell him I would send him the essay again, together with a doctor's note, he just nodded, seemingly unsurprised.

Margaret hadn't mentioned my leaving early the other day. Maybe she didn't know, or maybe she thought it wasn't worth making a fuss about. She was in high spirits when I went to see her after Dr Turner's course. Her son had finally managed to land a job as a chef.

"Who would have thought?" she said with a satisfied smile. "It's only pub food, but it's a start. He always had a real talent for cooking. You should have seen the cakes he baked when he was a boy."

I was relieved for her and grateful for the chat. The library was the only place where I could get away from it all and relax. The weather was dreadful; it poured down every day that week, and with the clouds hanging low it never really seemed to get light. Inside I felt safe. The bright overhead lighting, the familiar sounds: hushed voices, the tapping at keyboards, the quiet flip of pages, Margaret talking in her low voice – all this gave me a sense of normality. I spent a lot of time on the essay, redrafting the second part and then going over and over it again, removing repetition and unnecessary words. Absorbed by what I was doing, I managed for hours to suppress uncomfortable memories and thoughts.

On Thursday I saw Clara. She was returning some books at the checkout desk and chatting with Margaret. She glanced over and our eyes briefly met. I quickly saved what I had done on the computer, but when I looked up again, she was gone.

"She had to be somewhere," Margaret explained. "She said that she was busy. I think she had a singing lesson."

"Oh, never mind," I said lightly. "I know how much she's got on." But I knew that there was more to it. She'd rushed off because she didn't want to talk to me. I'd seen the look in her eyes.

Later that afternoon I rang the surgery and made an appointment for the following day. But what would I say? Would I have to mention the drinking? I hadn't had a drink for nearly a week, and it hadn't bothered me in the least. If I could only make sense of it all!

The reality of the appointment brought it all back to me. I googled memory lapses and sleep disorders again and came across an article about Dissociative Identity Disorder. Someone with DID would have two or more identities ruling their behaviour. Now and then they would do something completely out of character, such as speeding, stealing money or even harming someone else. They wouldn't remember anything about it afterwards. It was a memory loss far worse than simple forgetfulness.

I stared at the screen. Was that what was wrong with me? It said that people with DID often experienced other problems, such as sleepwalking, anxiety, alcohol abuse or depression. My heart raced. I closed my eyes to steady myself. Was I really that mad? Then it would surely be only a matter of time until I started acting like that during the day. The normality of my working routine was nothing but an illusion; the demons were still lurking in the dark, waiting for the moment to take over.

What could I tell the doctor? What on earth could they do to help me with this? Wouldn't they want to lock me away? What if they got me committed – how would I cope on a mental ward? Or could they prescribe me something to make me feel better – something to prevent it happening again?

By the time of my appointment I was in quite a state. I had worried all night and hardly slept at all. I still didn't know exactly what to say. The waiting room was overheated, and I was sweating in my big coat. There were a lot of patients waiting, mostly older people and mothers with their children.

I hadn't asked which doctor I would be seeing and didn't even know if it would be a woman or a man. For a brief moment I felt like turning around and walking away. Instead I sat down on one of the chairs next to a heavy breathing man and stared at the landscape print in front of me: a picture of the sea with rolling waves on idyllic white sand. There were a lot of magazines neatly arranged on a low wooden table, but I knew that I wouldn't be able to read.

I imagined the scene in the consulting room – the doctor asking me why I had come.

"Do you want to know the truth?" I would say. "I'm Dr Jekyll and Mr Hyde. I've got two identities. I do terrible things but can't remember anything about it." What would they say to that? A deep sigh escaped my lips. My gaze was fixed on the picture, but I could feel the old man's eyes on me, his curious look.

It took a while until I was called into one of the consulting rooms. The doctor was an Asian woman in her forties, her hair tied back in a neat bun. She smiled when I came in, an easy professional smile.

"What seems to be the problem?" She glanced at her computer as if the answer was there somehow.

"I have problems sleeping," I said.

"Are there any specific reasons for that?" She looked at me with tired eyes. Maybe she thought I was wasting her time.

"I get up at night," I said. "I do things when I'm asleep, things I can't remember the next day."

"What sort of things?"

"I tried to make fried eggs and left the cooker on. The gas could have caused an explosion and killed us both..." I trailed off.

"Have you been under stress recently?" she asked, apparently unfazed by my confession. She waited, and when I didn't answer glanced at her screen again. A few moments passed. Finally lifting her head, she realised that I was trying to hold back tears.

"Oh dear." She handed me a paper handkerchief. "Do you worry about it?

I nodded, grateful that she seemed to understand. Her movements were unhurried and professional. The thought that I was only one of many patients – someone she would forget about soon – was somehow comforting. She was used to people talking about their problems. Maybe she kept looking at her screen to make me feel more at ease.

I told her about my dread of not being in control, the fear of what might happen. I said how forgetful I was in general and mentioned the problem I'd had with my essay.

"That must be quite worrying," she said, handing me a sheet. "Could you answer these questions for me?"

I read through them. *Do you feel persistently guilty, worthless or helpless? Do you find it difficult to concentrate, remember and make decisions? Do you have problems with sleeping, such as early morning awakening or oversleeping? Have you ever attempted to take your own life?* Apart from the last one, I ticked *yes* every time.

She looked at my answers. "Let's put you on a course of antidepressants," she said, typing the prescription into her computer. "It will ease the stress. They can make you feel a bit drowsy at first, but it's worth persevering."

"What about the sleepwalking?"

"The antidepressants will also suppress your dreams and prevent the somnambulism," she said in a confident voice.

I took the two-month prescription she had printed out for me.

"And it will hopefully help with your forgetfulness," she said as I was getting up. "What kind of things do you forget?"

"Where I have put my keys or if I returned the library books."

"Well," she said, "come back in a month. See how it goes until then. If the forgetfulness remains, we might have to do some tests."

"Tests for what?"

"You're still quite young." She gave me a quick assessing look. "But forgetfulness can be a symptom of something more serious. We'll have to exclude cognitive disorders such as dementia. You can intervene with medication at the early stages. But please don't worry about it. I'm sure it's just the stress you've been under."

IT WAS RAINING HEAVILY OUTSIDE. The wind was so strong I couldn't hold up my umbrella. The gusts carried the rain in diagonal sheets and I was soaked within minutes. The water ran down my face, but I didn't mind or even notice much.

The doctor's last words were on my mind. What if she was right to think of dementia? I had been so convinced that I had taken out that encyclopaedia. How could I have been so wrong? It had nothing to do with my sleepwalking, and I hadn't been under terrible stress – nor had I been drinking. Dementia was too frightening to think about. On my way I popped into Boots and got the tablets she had prescribed.

I COULD HEAR Amy typing in her room when I came home. I changed into dry clothes, a new pair of jeans and warm socks. I briefly considered going back to college, but then decided against it. I would be soaked again by the time I got there. The work I had to do could be done at home. I had to look over the essay once more before submitting it. This time I would personally hand it over. It was Friday afternoon, but I had Dr Turner's home address and could easily walk over to his house in Gelligaer Street.

I sat down on my bed and opened the laptop to check my incoming emails. There was one from Dr Turner, written at eleven that morning:

Just to let you know that I can't extend the deadline for your essay any longer. Sorry about that, but the results have to be in by noon. You're very welcome to repeat the

*module next term. Best wishes and happy Christmas if I
shouldn't see you before.*

I covered my face with my hands. I couldn't think straight;
my brain felt as if it had seized up. All the work I'd put in over
the last week had again been in vain. There was no way he
would accept the essay now. My wet hand trembled as the
tears kept falling and desolate sobs wracked my chest.

When I eventually sat up to blow my nose, I saw Amy in
the doorway. How long had she been standing there,
watching me?

"What's the matter?" she asked. "I heard you crying. Is
there anything I can do?" There was the nurse's tone to her
voice again, but I didn't really mind. I was glad she cared.

"I've just been to the doctor's to get the sick note Dr
Turner wanted," I sobbed. "I needn't have bothered." I
explained to her what had happened.

"Maybe you could have a word with him," she said.

"No, I can't. He said the results had to be in by noon."

"But you could go there and try. Didn't you say he lives in
Gelligaer Street?"

"He wouldn't accept it."

"How can he be so mean?" she said. "You should ask for a
different tutor."

"No, it's complicated." She still didn't know about the
drunken voicemail.

"What's complicated?" A flicker of anger crossed her face.
"The only thing I can see is that he's making your life a
misery. Why don't you come downstairs? I'll make us a cup of
tea. You need cheering up."

I washed my face and put some make-up on my puffy, red
eyes before making my way downstairs.

Amy was sitting on the sofa with her cup of tea. She
had tidied up. There were no dirty mugs and she had

opened the window to air the room; that awful smell of cooking was gone. It was almost cosy in here. She had switched on the standard lamp, which with its yellow shade cast a more intimate glow than the cold ceiling light. I sat down next to her.

"How are you feeling?" She poured me some tea. "What did the doctor say? Did you talk about your drinking?"

"She doesn't think that I'm an alcoholic," I said defiantly. "She prescribed me antidepressants."

"Really?" She looked sceptical. "Does she think you have depression?"

"Yes. I had to fill in a questionnaire. I'm not sure if I will take the tablets though. She said they would make me feel drowsy."

"What are they called?"

"I can't remember. Wait, and I'll get them." I went out to the hall and fetched them from the pocket of my coat. "Seroxat," I said, handing her the packet.

"I know them," she said, to my surprise. "They'll calm you down a bit. My mum used to take them. She even stopped drinking for a while."

"What about the side effects?"

"She got a bit drowsy, but it passed after a few days." She opened the packet. "I'm sure the doctor knows what's best. Why don't you give them a go?" She took a white tablet out of the blister and presented it on her flat palm.

I took it, glad that she had made the decision for me. She watched as I swallowed it with the rest of my sweet milky tea.

"Well done," she said. "You'll be better after a few days. It'll be all right. No wonder the stress is getting you down. What you need is a break from it all. Why don't we go away for a few days? I could rent a car; let's go to the seaside somewhere."

"I can't. There's the theory test on Monday and I have to

sort things out with Dr Turner. Maybe I should show him the doctor's note. Maybe he'll accept the essay after all."

"You and your Dr Turner!" She got up. "After all he's put you through. Tell him that you have depression and that it's his fault for treating you so badly. You owe him nothing."

"But that's not true. He's always been fair to me. I think I'll go to his tutorial next week and explain."

"Whatever." She switched on the TV. *EastEnders* was on. She went to the kitchen to make another cup of tea and then settled down on the sofa again, her eyes fixed on the screen. I couldn't quite read her blank face. Was she angry that I didn't want to go on holiday with her?

I stifled a yawn, suddenly feeling sleepy. Was that because of the tablet, I wondered. I stared at Phil Mitchell, trying to understand what was going on, but my mind was unfocused. My eyelids kept drooping, and I even dozed off for a moment. Amy was right. I was exhausted.

She hardly seemed to notice when I got up and said goodnight. My limbs felt heavy as I dragged myself upstairs. I went to bed without brushing my teeth and fell asleep as soon as my head hit the pillow.

It was late morning when I woke up. For a moment I didn't know where I was. Bright daylight shone into my eyes. Amy was standing at the bed with a freshly brewed cup of tea.

"How are you?" she said. "I thought you'd sleep forever."

"What time is it?" I sat up.

"I heard you walking around again last night. Don't worry," she said quickly, "you didn't make a mess or anything."

"That's good," I mumbled, trying to get my head around what she had said – my mind was still not working properly. My head felt as if it was stuffed with cotton wool.

"It's the party tonight," she said. "Will you be fit enough to go? You can still think about it."

"I'm not sure." My mouth was dry. I took a sip of the hot sweet tea; it tasted odd. I must have had a sleepwalking episode again. I imagined myself: roaming the house, going from room to room. Then I quickly shut my eyes, trying to remove the image from my mind. Exhausted, I sank back against my pillow. The pills had obviously not worked.

"You should take another Seroxat," Amy said, as if reading my thoughts. "It will take a few days until you feel better. You don't have to get up. I'll make you something for breakfast."

I heard her go downstairs to the kitchen. I was still awfully tired, even my heart seemed to be beating more slowly. I was in no fit state to do my Saturday shift in the library, so I phoned Margaret at home.

"Oh dear," she said with her usual warmth and compassion. "You don't sound well at all. You'd better stay in bed and take it easy. No problem. I'll go in. It'll be quiet today."

Amy was kind too. No trace of the irritation she had shown the night before. I noticed again how much she enjoyed looking after me. She brought me easy digestible food: white bread, soft-boiled eggs and yet more tea.

"I've got to do a bit of shopping," she said, carefully wiping my damp forehead with a paper handkerchief. "Will you be OK on your own?"

"Of course," I said.

Nothing seemed to matter anymore. I merely felt hollow inside. For quite a while I just lay there, staring ahead, watching how the sunlight through the branches of the tree outside made moving patterns on the wall. Then I drifted off to sleep again.

The house was quiet when I woke up. I felt very drowsy when I rose to my feet, but, holding onto the banister, made it downstairs. Amy wasn't there. She had been shopping at Lidl's. I was surprised to see how much she had bought. There was a whole bag full of stuff: various cheeses, two litre bottles of German wine and big bags of crisps.

"I bought some stuff for the party – for both of us," she explained when she came back later and popped into my bedroom to check on me. "I might not take everything. I wasn't sure if you'd be fit enough. I will stay, of course, if you need me here. Just say the word." She gave me a look of concern.

"Of course not. Please go. Tell them that I've come down with something – that I've been in bed all day." I was quite pleased to have an excuse. The prospect of making small talk with Dr Turner was so daunting that I probably wouldn't have gone anyway.

Later on, she came in to say goodbye. She looked transformed in her new clothes: a pair of black skinny jeans and a floaty tunic top. She told me that she had found them in a charity shop on Albany Road.

"Are you sure you'll be all right?" she asked. "You can always ring my mobile if you need me."

After bringing me yet another cup of tea and some more fussing with my sheets she tidied away the empty cups and went downstairs. A few minutes later I heard the front door slam and she was gone. My eyes felt heavy. I tried to read but my exhausted mind couldn't focus and I was soon dragged back into the world of my murky dreams.

17

When I woke up, I couldn't tell from the grey half-light if it was very early in the morning or getting dark again. I was shivering with cold – the sheets were drenched in sweat. I sat up – it was five o'clock in the afternoon. I had slept nearly seventeen hours.

My jeans and jumper were on the floor. The jumper looked dirty. I picked it up to have a closer look. I knew straight away that something awful had happened. The stain on my jumper looked like blood. The sleeve was soaked through with it. Had I fallen over and hurt myself? I inspected my hands, but there were no scratches, no bruises.

My heart was thumping. I shut my eyes, trying to piece together what had happened. But there was only darkness, nothing I could remember, nothing, not even a vague sensation, only the gnawing feeling that I had done something terribly wrong. The ticking of my alarm clock cut into the silence. Why had Amy not woken me up? I lay still, listening for her footsteps or the faint sound of her typing, but heard only my own breathing.

I rolled onto my side and reached for my jeans. As I picked them up, I saw that there was something underneath: one of the green litre bottles of German wine that Amy had bought. The bottle was empty, the screw top next to it.

I sat bolt upright. Had I drunk the whole lot? What on earth had I done this time? I staggered to the window to fully open the curtains. I suddenly felt faint again – my legs almost gave way. I gazed into the desolate garden with its chaos of rubbish and leaves. The battered garden cherub stared back at me with dead white eyes.

I put on my dressing gown and slowly made my way downstairs. The house felt empty – there was no sound. The heating was off. There were some dishes stacked in the kitchen sink, but I couldn't remember if they had been there the night before. The cooker was grubby, as always, and smelled of Amy's baking. I shivered in my thin gown. Outside a freight train halted at the signal. The dreadful metallic shriek made me jump.

My wooden clogs echoed through the hallway. The doors to the rooms were open. The piano room with its mouldy wallpaper was damp and cold. I tried not to breathe through my nose; the musty smell made me feel nauseous. The living room was empty too. The television magazine was open on the table next to a half-full mug of grey tea.

As I went back into the hall I heard someone at the gate. I held my breath, wondering if I should creep back upstairs. Instead, I stood, frozen to the spot, expecting the police to ring any moment. But then the key turned in the lock, and Amy walked in.

"What's the matter?" she asked. "You look terrible. Are you still sick?"

"I've only just got up."

"It's very late." She gave me an assessing look. "Sorry I

rushed off in the morning. There was no time to see how you were. I was out with Claudia. We had a long chat about my book. I've just come back from town."

Her face was pink from the cold. She looked relaxed and quite pleased with herself. There was no indication from her expression that she knew what I had done. She hadn't been in my room and had probably no idea that the wine was missing. Maybe I could fill it up with water for now and replace it later on.

It crossed my mind how important it was that she didn't find out. Maybe she'd tell Claudia, now that they were getting on so well. I stared at her big new coat – it was beige with a dark fur collar. Maybe she'd bought that too in the charity shop. It struck me how broad and strong she looked in it.

"How was the party?" I asked.

"Great." She grinned at me. "It's a shame you couldn't come. It was great fun. You would have loved it."

"Did you tell Clara that I wasn't well?"

She nodded. "But it was too noisy for a proper talk. The music was really loud. Some people danced."

"What did you say?"

"Nothing much, just that you were sick. She looked as if she knew that there was more to it. Maybe she thought it was just an excuse. They're all concerned about your drinking. But as I said, it was too noisy to explain. And anyway, she's got other things on her mind."

"What things?"

"Philip and Clara are moving out. Claudia is really angry with them for making plans behind her back. She asked them to leave."

"Really?" I stared at her. "How did she find out?"

She shrugged. "How do I know? They had words. Claudia wants to put the house on the market and rent somewhere smaller for herself if she doesn't stay in New York for good. Clara is so upset. She thinks that you told Claudia about their plans."

"But it wasn't me." I could feel a wave of panic rising in me. Why did she think it was me? Was there something I couldn't remember – had I told Claudia the night we had been out? Maybe on the way home in the taxi...? I shook my head to shoo away the thought. "I'll have to give Clara a ring," I said.

"I wouldn't." Amy flattened her damp, frizzy hair in front of the mirror. "I think they're moving out today."

"But where are they moving? How can they find somewhere so quickly?"

"They're staying with Dr Turner for the time being. He's got a big house. That's what Claudia said anyway."

"Oh well, I'll give Clara a ring tomorrow," I said with all the calm I could muster. "I'm still a bit under the weather. I think I'd better get back to bed."

Back in my room, I stuffed the pullover into a plastic bag. Then I shoved the bag in the bottom drawer of my wardrobe, hiding it behind a pile of socks and underwear. Stepping onto the landing, I could hear the television blaring in the living room. I had to take the opportunity.

Thank God, it had been white wine. I took the bottle to the bathroom and filled it with water. Then I quietly made my way downstairs and put it into the fridge where it had probably been before. I could only hope that Amy wouldn't want a glass later on. There was nothing much else I could do, but go to bed again and rest.

IT WAS STILL DARK when I got up at seven. The hot shower steamed up the bathroom as I turned the metallic dial. I stood for ages under the pouring water, my eyes shut. After a while my mind became foggy and tired again and I felt for a moment that I had only been dreaming and nothing was real. I opened the window to let in some air. My face in the misted mirror was pale. To hide the shadows underneath my eyes, I put on foundation. Then I applied dark eye shadow, eyeliner and mascara, and finished applying rouge to my cheeks. The result was surprising – I looked almost normal again.

Amy was still asleep. I could hear her faint snoring as I walked past her room. It was very cold again downstairs although the kitchen window was shut. The fridge gave off a sour smell, which made me gag. There was nothing in it apart from the bottle of wine and a strawberry yoghurt that was way past its sell-by date. I quickly closed the door and put the kettle on to make myself a cup of tea. I could always have a proper breakfast in Aberdare Hall later on.

When I got to college, the canteen had just opened. There were no other students, only staff: the middle-aged woman behind the counter, chatting with one of the cleaners. It smelled strongly of cleaning fluids. I got myself coffee and a cheese and tomato roll, which I ate at a corner table while reading the *Echo*.

Going through the ads I noticed again how expensive it was to rent a decent house. How much would Clara and Philip be able to contribute, I wondered. If only I could talk to her and tell her that I was feeling much better already, that I had been to the doctor's and that I was taking antidepressants now. She also had to know that it wasn't me who had given away their plans. Why on earth would I tell Claudia about it when I was still hoping to move in with them? It didn't make any sense. I'd have to get in touch with her somehow, even if I had to phone Dr Turner's landline to get hold of her.

I closed my eyes for a moment, feeling tired again despite the strong coffee. If only I could suggest an affordable place! Maybe I'd have more luck in the foyer. There were always cards pinned to the noticeboard offering music lessons and student houses to rent.

When I opened my eyes, I saw Gemma come through the door, accompanied by her red-haired friend and two other girls. I had often seen them in the library, doing their course work together, surrounded by books and piles of papers. I watched how they went to the bar and got coffee, then settled around a table near the front window, talking and laughing. They all listened to something Gemma was saying. It was difficult to say whether she had seen me yet. I wondered if she was ignoring me. We hadn't talked in weeks. At the beginning she had tried to be friends. She'd often sat next to me in lectures, but I hadn't taken much notice of her. No wonder she had given up on me. When she turned her head in my direction, I rose from my seat and slowly walked over.

"How are things?" She glanced at my *Echo*.

"Not too bad. I'm looking for a house to rent. Any ideas?"

"Not really." She frowned. "Have you had a look at the flat-sharing message board online?"

They were all looking at me now.

"Good idea," I said lightly. I knew that they were all sharing a house in Cathays, and it was quite obvious from their expressions that they wouldn't want me there. Not that I was keen to be part of their lives: the pub-crawling at weekends, the pot smoking and permanent clubbing. But I couldn't help feeling a sudden pang of regret. Gemma had always been so affectionate.

"No music history this week," she said, oblivious to my thoughts. "Have you heard?"

"Why?"

"Dr Turner won't be back this term. The porter just told me."

"Not even after Christmas?" I said, startled. "Do you know what's wrong with him?"

"No idea." She shrugged. "It must be something serious. Gareth didn't know." She touched my arm. "What's the matter? You look as if you're going to faint. You'd better sit down."

"No, I can't." I shook my head, the thoughts running riot in my head: *Oh my God,* I thought, *let him be all right; let it not be my fault.*

"Maybe he's had an accident," the red-haired girl suggested.

"Got to go," I mumbled, hardly able to speak. "I've got things to do." I quickly walked off. *The blood on my jumper!* What the hell was going on? Had I something to do with it? There had to be someone who could tell me more.

I saw the police officer when I entered the main building. He was standing at the open door of the porter's lodge, the epitome of order and security with his dark blue uniform and polished shoes. Frozen to the spot, I stared at his thick neck and large shoulders. Then I crossed the foyer to get closer. Pretending to check something in my bag, I strained my ears to hear what he was saying to Gareth, but they were talking in low voices, and I couldn't understand a single word.

THE LIBRARY WAS OPEN. I found Margaret behind the checkout desk, doing something on the computer. She looked surprised to see me.

"Are you feeling better? You're not working today, or are you?" She seemed tired, her gaze distracted and sad.

"Just thought I'd pop in." I cleared my throat. "Someone told me that Dr Turner is off sick. I hope it's nothing serious."

She drew in a long breath and glanced around the room. Assured that there were only a couple of postgrad students around, she ushered me into her office.

"What did they tell you?" She sat down, her big untidy desk between us. Her voice was grave.

"Well, nothing much. Just that he wouldn't come back this term."

"That's all?"

"What's wrong with him?"

She opened her mouth and then shut it again. Her eyes filled with tears. "Awful news," she whispered. "The police were here. The officer said that he's dead. It's just so terrible. They think that someone murdered him."

"Oh my God! It can't be. How?"

"He was stabbed on his own doorstep, probably late at night. His neighbour found him on Sunday morning."

I held my breath. "Do they know who did it?"

"No, they don't. They're asking around, trying to find out if anyone had a grudge against him."

She gazed back at me in a strange unfocused way. "I don't know if I should have told them. She's probably completely innocent. I feel so bad about it now."

"Who are you talking about?"

"There was this student a couple of years ago." A tear rolled down her cheek. "Just a silly girl – thought she could blackmail him. She asked him to accept an essay that was clearly copied from the Internet, hinted that she would make it worth his while... She was used to getting her own way. Jack was not impressed by her plunging necklines and short skirts, but when he rejected her, she turned it around and said that he had molested her. It was very unpleasant. Everyone was talking about it. Jack had just got married too. He nearly lost his job and everything else because of her." She started twisting the leather strap of her necklace. "Of course it was all lies. The truth came out in the end."

"Don't worry," I said, trying to control the panic in my voice. For a moment I felt light-headed again. The windowless room seemed airless – as if the oxygen had been sucked out of it. I looked up at the ceiling – the fluorescent tube gave off a constant hum.

"They asked me if there had been someone with a grievance," she whispered, "and all I could think about was this girl. But I'm sure she's innocent. It was more than two years ago. Now I wish I hadn't mentioned it."

I stared at her seashell pendant necklace, which looked like a present; maybe one of her nieces had made it herself – or even her useless son. It struck me again how decent she was.

"Sorry, but I've got to go," I said, getting up. "I've got to be somewhere." Everything seemed unreal, as if zoomed out of focus: Margaret with her seashell pendant, the stacks of books on her table, the stuffy little room.

Back in the foyer, I took a deep breath, hoping that the fog would clear. Gareth was in his lodge, munching cheese and onion crisps while reading his paper. There were crumbs all over his dark blue jumper. The policeman was gone. Seeing me in the door, he glanced up.

"The library is open," he said. "Margaret's in there."

"I know. I'm not working."

"All right for some," he said, returning to his paper, shoving another handful of crisps into his mouth.

"Margaret told me about Dr Turner." I interrupted his reading. "Is that why the policeman was here?"

He looked at me, chewing. It took him a while until he could speak.

"I bet you'd like to know." He cleared his throat. "But maybe I'm not allowed to tell you."

"But Margaret has told me already."

"Why ask me if you know it all?"

"Margaret said they have a lead."

"Did she now?" He paused. "Maybe they do, but nothing is certain at this point." He glanced over to a group of first-year students milling about near the door, then gave me a sleazy look. "He was a very popular man, but you would know since you were in his office all the time."

"I don't know what you're talking about." I glared back at him. I hadn't talked to him since the day he had closed the library early. I'd never had a chat with him like the other students. I'd never pretended to like him – and the feeling was probably mutual.

"If you say so." He shrugged and carried on reading.

I was just turning away when I heard Clara's voice. I could see her through the open door, talking with the piano teacher. After a couple of minutes, she came inside. She looked around the foyer, her eyes tired and red-rimmed from crying. When she darted a glance in my direction, I raised my hand to say hello, but she turned quickly away. With a heavy feeling in my stomach, I watched how she walked up the stairs until her blue coat disappeared from view. She probably thought it was me. She knew about the voicemail – maybe she had already told the police.

A steady drizzle was falling outside – it had never got light. The overcast sky was one impenetrable grey. At eleven o'clock it was almost as dark as before dawn. The weather matched my mood: hopeless and forlorn. The lawn looked soggy – big puddles had formed. My umbrella was still in Margaret's office – but there was no way I would go back to fetch it. *Someone will tell her that it was me*, I thought, *I'll prob-*

ably never see her again. There was nothing else I could do but go home.

Aмy was in the kitchen. George Michael was singing on the radio. She had turned the volume up. *Wake me up before you go go...* I quietly shut the front door and was just about to sneak upstairs when she came into the hall, a mop in her right hand.

"Thought I'd wash the floor," she said in a vigorous voice. "About time..." She gave me an expectant smile. "I'm having a break from writing. I've finished the first chapter. I can send it to Claudia's friend in New York. But now I really need to do something else. Have you thought about that holiday by the sea? It would do you a world of good – you need a break."

"Maybe," I mumbled. "I'll think about it. I'm still feeling a bit rough – I'll have to lie down." I could feel her eyes following me as I made my way upstairs.

My room was icy cold. I usually left the window open, but the smell of paint had never gone away.

Dr Turner had been stabbed on his doorstep. He was dead. Only now was it beginning to really sink in. Were there no traces apart from my bloodstained jumper? There had been no blood on my hands when I woke up. Had I washed them in the bathroom and even cleaned the sink, wiping away the red spots, cold and cunning, even in my sleep? What a terrible monster I must be to commit such a cold-blooded murder! He had been so kind to me. It wasn't his fault that I failed the course – he had only tried to help. A sickness rose within me, and I sank down onto the bed, still staring at my pale, clean hands.

Had I rung his bell? Had he opened the door and smiled at me before I drove the knife into his chest. Had he screamed or tried to fight me off? How much blood had there been flowing from the wound? *Oh my God! I murdered him*, I thought, *I murdered an innocent man*! It was that darkness in me, that monstrous side. But what had driven me to it? Was it the resemblance to Jeremy, his good looks and patronising ways? Had my muddled unconscious mind taken revenge for what had happened in the past?

I buried my head in my hands. Tears were dripping through my fingers. What on earth should I do? Perhaps it would be safer if they arrested me. I could give myself up and explain about the sleepwalking. My GP would back me up. But wouldn't that be pleading insanity? They would declare me a danger to myself and everyone else and lock me up on a mental ward. They wouldn't let me near knives or scissors, and I'd be forever trapped, drugged up and at the mercy of psychiatric nurses. Wouldn't I rather be dead?

I had to keep a clear head. They'd soon enough find out that the girl was innocent. They only had to check her DNA. I didn't have much time. Listening to Amy rummaging in the kitchen downstairs, I tried to calm my breathing. My head was aching, I couldn't think straight. What options did I have? Maybe somehow I could get a false passport and go abroad. I had read about a fraudster who had changed his appearance and taken on a new identity. Couldn't I also start new somewhere else with a different name? Running away would look bad, but the psychiatric ward would be the end of me... At least I would have a chance. There were always people who disappeared, people who just vanished and were never seen again. Posters came to my mind, the red headings: *Age, Missing since, Last seen location...* There would of course be no way back. I swallowed hard.

Maybe I should tell Amy the truth. She didn't know about the text message I had sent to Dr Turner's phone, nor had I mentioned the bloodstained jumper. I had to tell her that he had been murdered. She was probably the only one who

would stand by me if she knew, the only one who'd understand. She wouldn't be sad that he was gone – that was for
sure. But it would be safer not to tell her straight away – she'd
be less obvious, less likely to draw attention to us.

I don't know how long I sat there, my mind racing, before
I eventually went downstairs.

18

I found Amy in the living room, hoovering the filthy carpet. I hesitated for a moment, waiting in the open door for her to notice me. Her face was flushed and sweaty from the unusual physical work, but she was still in that heightened, exuberant mood. I could hear her humming something over the whining of the old vacuum cleaner. Suddenly she turned around, as if sensing that I was there.

"Hi! Are you going to help me here?" She switched off the hoover, staring at me. "You're white as chalk. What's the matter?"

"Nothing," I said. "I've been thinking about the holiday. Maybe you're right; I could do with a break. College is finished. There's nothing going on until after Christmas."

"Good. I'm glad you've come to your senses." She took my arm and led me to the sofa. "To be honest, I was beginning to get really worried," she said, sitting down next to me. "It's so strange that you don't get better at all although you haven't been drinking that much. Perhaps you should see that doctor again. She could prescribe you something else."

I shook my head. "No, I don't need more pills. I just want a break. College is stressing me out, with that essay and every-thing else."

"Well," she frowned at me, "maybe music college isn't right for you. It's too much pressure, and then you hang out with those ambitious people too. No wonder you're cracking up. I've been wondering for some time if you should leave."

"I think you're right," I said, my voice dwindling. "I'd like to go to a new place, somewhere far away. Maybe abroad?"

"Why abroad?" she looked at me steadily, her eyes slightly narrowed, as if to find out if I was trying to wind her up. "I don't even have a passport." She paused a moment, watching me. "What about Blackpool?"

"Yes, maybe…"

"Would you like to see the illuminations?"

"Why not?"

"Why not?" She stared at me, stunned at my lack of emotion. "It must be absolutely amazing. Six million light bulbs! There's a great view from the open top tram," she said, a faraway look in her eyes. "My mum had a book; I liked the pictures when I was little. There weren't many children's books around," she trailed off, glancing at me with a sudden unease. "I don't think my mum was ever there herself. Anyway, what does it matter? It's too late for the illuminations anyway. They'll be over now – it'll be all dark and miserable again."

"But there are other things you can do – the Tower, the Pleasure Beach and the piers."

"How do you know?" Her expression changed; she looked surprised. "Of course we can go. It's just what you need." She broke into a smile. "Don't worry about money. Let's go tomorrow morning. We'll have to be there in time to find a hotel. I think I'll rent a car. You wait and see: the sea air will do you a world of good." She was talking fast, her face glow-ing. I had never seen her like that.

"Great," I said, getting up. "No time to waste. We'd better pack our things."

Back in my room, I sat down with a heavy feeling in my chest. My glance fell on the green hard-shell suitcase, which had been standing at the foot of my bed for the last three months. I remembered the day I had bought it in Debenhams and how excited I'd been for the future. I pushed it to the floor and opened it. There was still the booklet from the National Careers Service with information on how to become a music teacher. I had read it on the train journey here. I stared at the green writing on the cover:

Career Path and Progression.

It seemed unreal now, almost like looking in from outside, seeing my former self on that train to Cardiff. How full of hope I had been.

And now I could only hope they wouldn't lock me up in prison or some sort of mental institution. *A murderess on the loose!* I stopped for a moment; my hands clenched into fists. A man was dead because of me. How could I ever trust myself again? What if the sleepwalking didn't stop? What if I harmed someone else? My heart racing, I paced up and down the room. Perhaps I should give myself up after all. But that would put me in the mental hospital. My mind was going around in circles. It would be the end of me; I'd rather be dead. Why didn't I kill myself and get it over with?

I opened my wardrobe, fetched the plastic bag with my bloodstained jumper and jeans and put it at the bottom of my case. On top I packed the other clothes. There were trousers and dresses I had hardly worn, new expensive things I had brought with me from Carlisle. Drawing out the purple velvet jacket, I touched the soft material and put it against my face. It still smelled of the perfume I had worn at the meal with

Clara and Philip. How proud I had been when Clara had invited me – how exciting and promising everything had looked back then. I swallowed hard and moved around the room, picking up things, the stacks of papers beside the bed, various books and the toiletries that were on the windowsill.

I went to bed early. It was a cloudy night. My eyes wide open, I stared at the pitch-black ceiling. I could hear Amy outside, her heavy footsteps moving to the bathroom and then downstairs again, probably packing her case. The rumble of a heavy freight train sounded like far-off thunder. *I'm in her hands*, I thought. *She's the only one who can help me now.* I could hear her in the kitchen listening to music on the radio and eventually I must have drifted off.

I woke up with a start the next morning. Amy was banging on my door. Light was pouring through the window. My clock said it was half past eight.

"I'm making breakfast," Amy shouted. "I've just been to the shops and bought some bread and eggs."

Making my way downstairs, I could hear her in the kitchen. It smelled of coffee and toast. She was wearing jeans and a bright yellow blouse I hadn't seen on her before. There was a rosy, feverish tint to her cheeks.

"Coffee?" She plunged the cafetière and poured a mug without waiting for my reply. The table was set with butter, eggs and marmalade. We'd never had breakfast like that before.

"Lovely day," she said, her voice raised and exuberant. "There are a few car hire places – I'll have to see where I can get the cheapest deal."

"How long will it take?" I put two slices of bread in the toaster.

"Why? A couple of hours perhaps, maybe less. It depends

if I find what I'm looking for." She paused. "We should leave as soon as possible. It's quite a drive up there."

"I can share the driving with you." I felt a tightening in my throat. Two hours was quite a long time. Maybe the police would come for me when she was gone. Would they break in if I didn't open the door?

"We're late," she said, gobbling down her egg. It looked underdone; the egg white still runny. "My alarm was set for seven, but I slept right through it. I hope we can still get there this afternoon." I looked at her anxious face, wondering what she was worried about.

"Yes. We'd better not waste time," I agreed, "if we want to get there before it gets dark."

She got up. "I'd better get going. Can you get everything ready so that we can leave straight away?"

I could hear her in the hall, rummaging through the drawer, looking for something, probably her glasses, and then the front door clicked shut behind her and she was gone. I finished my toast and started clearing up. I washed the dirty dishes under running water and put the eggs, the bread and butter in a plastic bag for us to take along. Then I threw away the old food from the fridge, the yoghurt, a shrivelled cabbage and a piece of dried old cheddar.

I was just about to get my suitcase from upstairs when the telephone rang. The sudden high-pitched jangling made me swing around. The phone sat on a table in the hall, grey with a large dial and a curled-up cable. My parents had had a similar one at home. I stared at it, willing the horrible ringing to cease.

No one had our number, no one apart from Clara and Claudia and maybe Margaret. Had they given it to the police? Was I a suspect now – was that why they were trying to get hold of me? All of a sudden it stopped, but then it erupted again as soon as I turned away. This time I went upstairs to my room. When I came back they had given up. But the silence was eerie now. It lurked in the echoey rooms like a suspended moment, a foreboding of something terrible to come. My steps were too loud; I could hear my own breathing, erratic and strange.

To keep busy, I fetched the bin bag with the kitchen rubbish to throw it in the wheelie bin outside. It was a fine cold day. The sun was shining from a cloudless sky. As I stepped out of the front door, I saw a man in the garden next door. I had thought the house was empty. It was in a much better state than ours, but the curtains had always been drawn, and I'd never seen anyone go in or out.

"Hello there," he called out, seeing me at the bin. "Nice day for it." He looked to be in his late seventies, tall with a slight stoop. He was bald; there were age spots on his shining head and hands, but his small eyes looked sharp behind his metal-rimmed glasses.

"Hi," I replied feebly, keen to get away. But he didn't get the message and came over to the fence.

"Six months away and the garden has turned into a wilderness, completely overgrown. Nothing but brambles and stinging nettles," he said. "I was staying up north with my daughter. It was great to see the little ones, but there comes a time when you have to go home." He gave me a searching look. "Good to see that someone's moved into the house again. About time after all those years."

"I'm only the lodger," I said, about to go back inside. "Amy is the one who lives here. But she's been here all her life."

"Amy?" He stared at me. "Someone called Amy lived here thirty years ago. "Lovely little lass she was."

"But she's been here all her life," I repeated, wondering if he was *compos mentis* after all.

"No one has lived here for at least thirty years," he insisted. "The house was still empty when I went away in

May; the windows were boarded up." He shook his head. "We often wondered what had happened to her. Someone said she was in Whitchurch Hospital. The poor lass went to pieces. It was too much for her."

"What was too much?"

"The accident. Amy nearly died; it was touch and go for a while. She was in hospital for weeks, and then they had to tell her that her mother hadn't made it. She blamed herself, the poor little thing, said she'd distracted her from driving. She apparently asked for the sweets she always kept in her glove compartment. Said it was her fault that she had taken her eyes off the traffic."

"Had she been drinking?"

"Amy's mother?" He shook his head. "Of course not. She wouldn't have. Lovely lady she was, beautiful and so talented. They were both musical. Amy was only ten, but she played like an angel. Everyone thought she'd be a famous pianist one day. Her mother started teaching her when she was five. My wife and I often listened in the summer when she practised her pieces with the windows wide open."

"And her father?"

"He died long before that – some sort of cancer it was. It wasn't easy for them, but Rachel was stronger than she looked. She started teaching the piano, at first private lessons and then in school. The kids really liked her. She just got on with it – never complained. They all came to her funeral; the place was packed, people were standing outside – that's how popular she was. Amy was just like her: slender with red hair, freckles and that lovely smile."

I thought about Amy, her broad shoulders, the pallid complexion.

"Are you sure that the house was empty for so many years?"

"Yes, the accident was in the eighties, mid-eighties as far

as I remember. As I said: windows all boarded up. Amy never showed her face. You never saw anyone in there. We always wondered why she didn't sell up if she didn't want to move back herself." He cleared his throat. "And then my wife died last year. That's how it goes." He glanced at his watch, as if embarrassed for talking so much. "Tell her that the old neighbour still lives next door – if it is her after all that time..." He shook his head, turned around and went back inside.

I just stood there and watched him disappear, unable to move, the bin bag still in my hand. Had Amy been lying about her mother's excessive drinking? What had happened to her in the mental hospital? Why had she made up all those things?

From where I stood I could see her window; the curtains were drawn. I had never been inside her room and she had always made sure that her door was closed. Once or twice I had caught a brief glimpse of the chaos inside. I'd always assumed it was the reason she didn't want me to come in. I had to know what was going on, and maybe there was something in her room to provide some sort of explanation. It would be risky looking through her things, but I could hardly ask her directly. There was no other way to find out what was going on.

I had at least an hour until she came back. I ran up the stairs and pressed the handle down. The door was locked. I had always respected her privacy. But things were different now. How could I go away with her, not knowing who she was? I went to my room, opened the empty cupboard and got a wire hanger out. I pulled it and bent it straight, like I had seen in the movies, then I returned to Amy's door. There was a little hole in the knob. I inserted the wire and moved it about – but it didn't budge. The palms of my hands were moist with sweat. I tried again, holding it straighter this time;

now I could feel the lock on the other side. When I applied more pressure, it popped and the door was open.

I gagged at the stuffy, sour smell. When had she last opened the windows in here? The thin curtains let in enough light to see that the room was a mess. The bed was unmade, and there were books and clothes strewn all over the floor. Her old typewriter was nowhere to be seen, but on the table were some typed sheets of paper.

Every surface was littered with dirty cups – some with mouldy remnants of coffee or tea. On the floor next to her bed was a bowl with dried-up soup. She had obviously been packing too: there was a big black suitcase on her duvet with the lid already zipped shut. In the corner near the wardrobe was a pile of clothes. I made my way to the table, treading on discarded wrappings and picked up the printed paper. The writing was double-spaced. My eyes flew over the words:

When I go back, I see that Mummy is drunk: her head down on the kitchen table, a burning cigarette in hand. She has been sick again, and the table is soiled with her vomit. I know her Silk Cut will drop any second and could set the table alight. Let the house go up in flames, I think. Why should I save her? I would have killed her at that moment if I'd had the guts.

A sudden clatter outside made me jump. I peered out through the gap in the curtains. It was only the neighbour dumping the garden rubbish in his bin. I thought about what he had told me about Amy's mother, how lovely she had been. It was obviously a page of the book she'd been working on, but who was she writing about? There was no time to carry on reading. She could be back any minute. I knew that she didn't have a passport, but maybe there were photos or some other evidence of what was going on.

I pulled open the upper drawer of her desk. There were more papers with parts of her memoir – different versions of the same chapter. The bottom drawer contained some letters and cards. I picked up a picture postcard from Rome, showing a view of St Peter's Basilica. It was addressed to Miss Frances Palmer, Whitchurch Hospital, Cardiff and written in the spidery hand of an older person.

We saw St Peter's yesterday. There was a guided tour and
a visit to the cupola. Beautiful frescos and mosaics! I went
to a church service today. You were in my prayers.
Best wishes, Aunty Pat.

There were other postcards and letters, all from the same woman – a couple unopened. Underneath were some loose photos. Looking through them, I came across a picture of two women sitting in a Victorian style garden summerhouse. One of them was obviously Amy. She wore a baggy T-shirt and jeans and had her arm around a friend who appeared quite fragile next to her. It struck me how much she looked like the woman in the picture I had found. Her face was covered with freckles, and she wore her red hair cut short.

Amongst the photos and letters were newspaper clippings. I held my breath as I looked through them, scanning the stories. Most of them were about Whitchurch Hospital. There was another one from the *Echo*, depicting the red-haired girl at the piano. It said:

Patient Amy Mary Brayfield playing on the ward. Musi-
cians entertain patients on the wards and perform in
concert in the main hospital foyer. The event is sponsored
by consultant psychiatrist Mark Bridgnorth and organised
by ABMU Arts in Health coordinator Huw Roberts.

I stared at the photo, trying to understand. Amy Mary Brayfield! If the woman at the piano was Amy, then who was the Amy I knew? What the neighbour had said was beginning to make sense. The house had been empty and boarded up when he had gone to live with his daughter, so she had obviously moved in afterwards. Was her friend still in that hospital? My stomach churned. I glanced around the room, wondering what to do.

My eyes rested on the suitcase. Maybe there was a clue to her identity inside. I walked over and opened the lid. Inside was the usual chaos. It looked as if she had randomly stuffed in some clothes, sweaty T-shirts, jeans and several pairs of socks and underwear. Was there anything else? I had to force myself to rummage amongst the unwashed clothes. Digging around, my fingers came across some packets underneath: bottles and boxes of tablets, dozens of them, all neatly stacked, filling the bottom of the case. Getting some out, I had a closer look. They seemed to be all prescription drugs: sleeping pills, antidepressants, tranquillisers and various medications I had never heard of before. None of them had a label; there were no names of the patient or pharmacy.

With trembling hands, I kept on looking. In one of the zipped-up side pockets was Amy's address book. I opened it. The entries weren't in alphabetical order. There was my mobile number and the password for my computer. How had she got hold of that? My mind went blank, and then it dawned on me. I had given it to her a while ago when she had to look for something on the Internet. Clara's details were listed and there was even Gemma Adams's name. A few pages on I saw Jack Turner's mobile number and home address.

I felt like I couldn't breathe for a moment and had to sit down on her office chair. Had she read my emails? Was she responsible for the fact that half of my essay was missing? My thoughts ran riot. The day of the party came to my mind. I'd been so tired all day. Had she given me those tranquillisers then? But if my mind had been completely numbed with drugs, I couldn't have got up that night.

I flicked through her address book again. What else had she done? Did she have something to do with Dr Turner's death? If I could only prove my innocence. The woman was obviously insane. She was just pretending to be Amy and for some reason had taken over her identity. The only way to shed some light on it would be to go to Whitchurch Hospital and talk to the real Amy. She was the only person who'd be able to help me now.

19

The sun was still shining. The air was clear and crisp – the sky an unbroken postcard blue. The light was too bright after the gloom inside and I paused a moment to adjust my eyes and bring the autumn day back into focus. The neighbour had gone inside. A curtain twitched as I passed his house. I could feel his eyes following me.

I was lucky to get a taxi on Inverness Place.

"To Whitchurch Hospital please."

The driver gave me a quick assessing look. He was in his early twenties and looked like a student to me.

"It's closing down next April," he said, as he pulled into Crwys Road. "I read about it in the paper."

"What will happen to the patients?" I glanced at his serious face.

"Care in the community," he said. "Ridiculous."

We drove in silence except for the tinny music coming from his radio.

"Visiting?" he said eventually.

"Yes, a friend of mine."

"My brother worked there," he said. "Spooky place. He fixed the electrics in the passageways below. Gave him the creeps. He could hear the footsteps from above: people shuffling about all day long, talking to themselves. Everyone was drugged to their eyeballs. He never went back."

As we passed the hospital gates the complex of red-brick buildings came into view. With its looming tower it looked intimidating and foreboding, like a Victorian workhouse or prison. The driver let me out in the car park.

"Have a nice day," he said, when I gave him the fare, and then he quickly drove off.

I walked down the path to the main building. A breeze had come up, blowing dead leaves about. They crunched and rustled underfoot. Tall chestnut trees lined the way, their naked branches gnarled and twisted. My breath rose in visible puffs in the chilly air.

Two steep steps led to the entrance. I pushed the heavy door open and entered a gloomy hallway. There was a wooden desk with an old-fashioned push bell. I hesitated, not sure if I should ring for attention. To my relief a middle-aged woman entered from the other side. With her light blue blouse and corduroy trousers she didn't look like a nurse, but I guessed from her brisk efficient gait that she was probably staff.

"Excuse me," I said as I went up to her. "I'm looking for Amy Brayfield. Would you know where I can find her?"

"Amy Brayfield?" She nervously glanced at the door as if hoping for someone to come to her help.

"Yes, I'm her cousin. I was abroad and haven't heard from her for quite some time. Someone told me that she was here."

"I'm sorry – what was your name again?"

"Kate. I'm Amy's cousin."

"Yes, you said." She shook her head. "I suppose you'd better talk to the staff nurse."

I followed her through the double-doors and down a narrow corridor. I had to fight the impulse to turn around and walk back into the late autumn sun outside. It smelled of cabbage and stale cigarette smoke. The windows were frosted – you couldn't see out. An old man came towards us. He didn't lift his head as he shuffled past, his lips moving as if immersed in some sort of inner dispute. We came into a stairwell and walked up the echoing stairs. After another short passage, we entered a large common room. There were a lot of chairs, a pool table and an old-fashioned television set. Some patients were sitting around it, watching, eyes glazed over or just staring into nothing. The air was stuffy. Light fell through the sash windows, which didn't look as if they could be opened.

"I'll fetch the staff nurse for you," the woman said, leading me into an office. "If you could wait a minute."

The room was shabby, the furniture ramshackle and old. There was a scratched wooden desk and a bookcase with reference books and box-files. The walls were painted an institutional green, and there were no pictures at all, no cards or photos on the mantelpiece.

As she left the room I went over to the high windows. The room overlooked a big untidy garden with many old trees, brambles and bushes. In the distance I could see the pointed green roof of a Chinese style summerhouse. It looked exactly like the one I'd seen in Amy's photo. Standing on my toes I glimpsed a few plastic chairs pushed against the wall, but no patients or staff.

When the door opened, I turned around. The staff nurse came straight towards me, armed with a resolute smile. She was stocky built with a short, grey bob.

"I'm sorry we kept you waiting." She shook my hand. "I heard you are Amy's cousin."

"Yes. I was wondering how she was. I haven't heard from her for quite a while. Is she still here?"

"Why don't you take a seat?" She gestured towards the upholstered chairs and then sat down opposite me, her grey eyes watching me sharply. "When did you last visit her?"

"It must be a while ago. I've been working abroad."

"Well," she held my gaze, "I'm very sorry, but I've got bad news. She died last April."

"That's terrible." I could feel my heart pounding in my chest. "How did it happen?"

"She took her own life – an overdose of barbiturates. A patient found her lying behind the summerhouse." A look of real sorrow crossed her face. "It was too late, she was already cold."

"Why did she do it?"

"We don't know." She shook her head. "She wasn't on suicide watch. No one expected it because she had seemed to be doing so much better. Her consultant had discharged her the day before, so she was free to go. Maybe she feared that she wouldn't be able to cope in the outside world. She'd been out before and came back. It happens a lot. The patients get used to being looked after. But we all thought she would make it this time. She had plans..." She trailed off.

"What sort of plans?"

"She was a musician. I think she wanted to go into teaching, to do a degree at music college."

"At music college?" I felt a shiver go down my spine.

"She was a very good pianist; she would have passed with flying colours."

"How did she get the sleeping pills?"

"I'm not sure." She shrugged. "She must have hoarded them. Some patients do get them every night. It can be noisy on the dormitory wards."

"Which ward was she in?"

"I think it was A3C."

"Did she have to sleep with others in a room?"

"No, she didn't actually." She smoothed down her grey skirt. "A3C has individual bedrooms, small, but quiet and clean."

"So she didn't need the pills to sleep?"

"I'm not sure." She frowned. "Well, it's not the only way she could have got them. Someone broke into the hospital pharmacy at night – the CCTV was switched off. Some patients are very shrewd. They sell the tablets on or swap them for cigarettes. We've improved the security now."

"Who found her?"

"A friend. It was terribly upsetting. They had been on the same ward together for years. When Amy didn't turn up for breakfast that day Frances got worried and started looking for her."

"Frances Palmer?"

"Yes, how do you know her name?"

"I knew they were friends," I said quickly. "How can you be sure that it was suicide? Why would she do it when she had things to look forward to? You just told me that she had plans."

"There was a post-mortem examination by our pathologist. He had no doubt. The overdose of barbiturates had caused a cardiac arrest."

"But why would she have done it?" I insisted. "She had no motive. It doesn't make sense. But perhaps someone else had a motive. Maybe someone wanted her dead."

"What are you trying to say?" She shook her head. "Amy was very well liked. She was a lovely girl, sweet-natured and friendly with everyone. No one wanted her dead."

"What about this friend of hers, Frances?"

"What about her?"

"Maybe she knows more." I watched her closely. "Maybe I should talk to her."

"That's not possible. She's not here anymore."

"Was she discharged?"

"Well, I must say..." Spots of colour had entered her cheeks. "I can't discuss other patients with you." She rose from her chair. "This is all I can tell you. The pathologist had no doubt that it was suicide – and that's good enough for me."

"He only said that the pills caused cardiac arrest. But that doesn't prove she took her own life. Someone else could have been responsible. Someone could have poisoned her."

"Well, I say." She stared at me, her mouth twitching. "What are you insinuating? Are you saying that we're trying to cover up something?"

"Of course not." I got up too. "It just doesn't make sense."

"I know, it's all very sad." She unclenched her fists, as if trying to compose herself. "We can't always understand the darkest depths of the human soul. I really am extremely sorry for your loss." She glanced at her watch. "But I've got to go. There's a staff meeting – and I'm late already. I'm sorry to cut you short. It's always difficult to accept the death of a loved one, especially if it's suicide. But I hope I've been of some help. Would you like to come along with me? I'll show you the way out."

I followed her back through the ward and down the stairs.

"The exit is that way," she said, gesturing down the corridor. "It was good to meet you. I wish I had had better news for you." She gave me a strained smile.

"Thanks for letting me know," I said. She obviously wanted to get rid of me. Life had to go on; her mind was already somewhere else, maybe at her meeting. She firmly shook my hand and rushed back up the stairs again. I waited until her footsteps had faded and then headed in the opposite direction.

They had been on Ward A3C. Maybe there would be someone who had known them and could tell me more about what had happened. Had she given Amy those pills? If I could only find a witness. The police had to know. It was the only chance I had to set things straight and clear my name.

It was cooler in the hallway than upstairs. I shuddered as I walked down the long narrow corridor. The green paint was flaking off the wall, revealing a grey undercoat or maybe concrete underneath. There would be no new decorating, now the hospital was about to close. From ahead I could hear footsteps, the clacking of high heels.

"Ward A3C?" I asked the girl who was coming towards me.

"Got a fag?" She had the small, thin figure of a teenage girl, but as she came closer, I saw she had to be about my age. Her pink fluffy jumper looked as if it belonged to someone much bigger than her; she was wearing the sleeves rolled up.

"Sorry, but I don't smoke." I looked into her gaunt face. It was tired and pale with jutting cheekbones and dark bluish circles under her eyes.

"You're new here?" she asked with a wry smile.

"No, just visiting. I'm looking for Ward A3C."

"Who are you visiting?"

"A friend."

"Who?" She paused, giving me a shrewd, assessing look. "I'm on A3C. But I'm not sick. I don't belong there."

"Frances. Do you know her?"

"Frances?" She stared at me, then nervously glanced up and down the corridor. "No, she's gone. She ran away a few months ago. She'd probably had enough. I don't blame her. It's a nuthouse here." She shrugged. "Anyway, I'm glad she's gone."

"Why? Didn't you get on?"

"No." Her face contorted with distaste. "They're all nuts

here – how can you get on with them? I hate it in here. They make us eat all the time, potatoes, pasta, sturdy meals to fatten you up and keep you quiet." She let out a heartfelt sigh. "I hate their horrible food. I don't eat it."

"Are you going to A3C now?" I asked casually as we walked side by side down the corridor.

"Yes, but I need a cigarette. Everyone smokes. It's the only thing you can do in here. I would leave straight away if I could, but where can you go without money?" She touched my arm. "Have you got some change? I need to buy fags."

I opened my purse and got out a fiver. I waited until she had shoved it into the pocket of her jeans. "What was Frances like?" I lowered my voice. "I bet she was a real pain."

"What do you want to know?" Her shoulders stiffened. "I thought she was your friend."

"No, she's not," I said, sensing that I had to be honest with her. "But we actually shared a house. She did some really weird things. I just want to understand."

"What things?"

"She got me into trouble. I need your help to figure out what happened."

"What if I say no?" She accelerated her gait.

"Don't worry," I said, trying to keep up with her. "Look, I've got more money. Maybe we can talk somewhere in private. I'll make it worth your while."

"How much?" She slowed down a bit. "I'm Paula. You can come up to my room. But first I'll have to get the fags."

She led the way through a metal door, then up another flight of stairs into a high-ceilinged room. The air was thick with smoke – all the windows were shut. There were chairs lined up against the walls and two men smoking. I waited in the open door and watched as she went up to the younger one. She exchanged the money for an open pack of cigarettes. The man was tall and scrawny, his fingers stained yellow.

"I'll get some more later," she said. He gave me a fleeting glance, his face sallow and without expression. Then he returned to his smoking again, his eyes fixed on the floor in front of him.

"Just follow me," she whispered as we entered the ward. Her room was on the other side, and we had to go past the big window of the nurses' station. I could see a couple of women at the table engrossed in paperwork, but I needn't have worried: no one looked up.

Paula's room was stuffy. She carefully closed the door and gestured for me to sit down on her unmade bed. She pulled a cigarette out of the pack and lit up.

"We're not allowed in here," she said, eagerly inhaling, "but who bloody cares?" She shoved aside some clothes and sat down next to me. "How much have you got?"

I opened my purse again and held up a twenty-pound note. "You can have it, but you'll have to tell me a few things."

"What do you want to know?" She exhaled smoke, watching it float upwards, twisting and distorting. Looking at her more closely now, I saw how skinny she was. Her legs were thin as twigs and she seemed awfully small and frail in spite of her oversized jumper.

"You said that you didn't like Frances. Why was that?"

"Because she was a lying cow. She was always twisting things. When she found out about a weakness or something embarrassing, she'd use it against you. Everyone was afraid of her."

"Amy as well?"

"Not at first. She wasn't scared of her like we were. Frances could be really charming when she wanted to. And Amy had no self-confidence. Frances properly sucked up to her, listened to her for hours and flattered her. She didn't like people much, but with Amy she was different. The fuss she made about her. It was all about herself of course – because

Amy was more classy, she played the piano and came from a posh family. Frances wanted that for herself."

"So they got on well?"

"You could say that." She shrugged. "They were together."

"Really?" I thought of the pictures I had seen of Amy. It was difficult to imagine the two being lovers. "For how long?"

"A few months? I don't know exactly. I told you Frances could be charming. She somehow managed to make Amy feel special, and Amy was grateful to have someone who cared. She even started playing the piano again."

"What happened then?"

"Amy was really popular. A lot of people liked her playing and some wanted to be friends with her. Frances didn't like it a bit. You could see it in her face when she was watching – she wanted Amy for herself. That's when she started to get more controlling. Once she was so angry she slammed down the lid of the piano when Amy was playing. Her fingers were all bruised and swollen. Amy never complained to the nurses – but I think she was a bit scared of her then."

"Did she talk about it?"

"No, but you could see it. She once said that she felt guilty. Frances always said she didn't care. That she was stuck up with her upbringing and piano playing. She always made out that she was the victim – she was good at that, always going on about how horrible her mother had been to her and what a terrible childhood she'd had. The mother sounded like a real nutter."

"What was she like?"

"She stayed in bed all day, drinking gin. It made her really sick and one day Frances found her dead. But she didn't tell anyone. She just closed the bedroom door and carried on – even went to school as if nothing had happened. And when she ran out of money she started selling stuff to her school-mates: her mother's phone, some of her own clothes, even the television in the end. Someone came to collect it and then they noticed the smell. I don't know how she could live in there all that time. Once she said it was her fault, that she had killed her mother – that she had suffocated her with a pillow. Another time she said that she had beaten her. But I'm not sure about that. She always tried to make herself more interesting."

"That's terrible." I took a deep breath. "What else did she do to Amy?"

"She lied and twisted things like she always did." Paula stubbed out her cigarette. "She started badmouthing Amy, telling people what she was really like. She was a good liar – really convincing. She said that Amy looked down on them all, that she thought she was better than everyone else. Some people believed it and stopped talking to her."

"Did Amy know about that?"

"She must have had a good idea, but she kept quiet. She just wanted out. Later she had piano lessons again. The nurses organised them for her. She thought about what she would do outside, that she wanted to become a teacher. She had to go to college, and she wanted to prepare for that."

"Frances must have been beside herself."

"You bet. She even tried to drug her. The nurses give out the drugs after mealtimes. Amy was on antidepressants, but she always seemed OK with it. She had never watched a lot of TV, but then she changed. She started watching everything, game shows, soaps, the lot – just sitting there with the others, staring or nodding off. I'm sure it was Frances. She had laced people's drinks before. She had a lot of drugs hidden away somewhere. The nurses became suspicious. Someone went up there and told them. They even searched our rooms. And then it suddenly stopped and Amy was back to normal again."

"Do you know what happened the day she died?"

"Not exactly. I didn't have breakfast and stayed in bed until late. Someone said she had been discharged the evening before. When I came out of my room, she was gone. I thought she'd left. I was a bit sad because I wanted to say goodbye. I never tried to be her friend. She was the sort of person who could really have had a good life outside. She was different, there was something nice about her – she wasn't like the other nutters. It was sad when they found her dead."

"Do you think Frances killed her?"

"Don't know." Her expression grew remote. "Maybe, maybe not. I'm not saying anymore."

"That's OK." I gave her the twenty-pound note. "I just needed to know what happened. I've got to go."

I glanced at my watch; it was nearly three. Frances would be back home by now and wondering where I was. I'd left my suitcase in the hall. She'd probably know that I'd been in her room and gone through her case. She would have been furious to find her door unlocked. There was a good chance she'd be looking for me. I'd have to report her to the police. Time was running out.

20

W hen I stepped out of the main entrance door, the sun had vanished behind the chestnut trees, and it was even colder than before. I had lost precious time. Once out of the ward, I had walked in the wrong direction and had to go all the way back again. The endless network of echoing corridors had given me the creeps – what if I never found my way out of there again? My heart was still racing. I could feel it beating in my throat.

I had to ring someone. Walking down the path towards the hospital gates, I got out my mobile. I had a missed call from Margaret. When I tried to ring back, her phone went to voicemail.

"Amy is..." My breath was short and rapid; I could hardly speak. "She's not who she says she is. I'm at Whitchurch Hospital. I've just found out how dangerous she is..."

I stopped as I noticed a large car, a dark brown people carrier, accelerating in my direction. My legs went weak. I couldn't move and in that frozen moment I saw Amy's face behind the windscreen. The car came to a screeching halt.

"Hi." She rolled down the window. "Thought I might find

you here." She stared at me with narrowed eyes. "You shouldn't have gone through my things. You think you're so clever…"

"I'm sorry…" My eyes darted around the car park, from the well-kept bowling green to the bell tower with its pale green dome, but the grounds were deserted – there were no patients, staff or visitors in sight. It would be pointless to cry for help. No one would come.

As she got out of the car, I smelled the stench of sweat on her – the smell of fear. I could see the perspiration underneath her arms soaking darkly into her baggy T-shirt. I had never seen her sweat like that before. She opened the back door and pushed me towards the passenger seat.

"Get in," she said. "I think we need to have a chat."

I started to tremble, my heart beating faster, but my legs were still numb and unable to move.

"Get in!" she was screaming now. She grabbed my arm and snatched the phone I was holding in my hand. She threw it on the ground and stomped on it with her boot. I tried to resist, but she opened the door and pushed me onto the back seat. I saw the baseball bat in her hand and felt a sudden sharp pain. I instinctively raised my arms to ward off a second blow. Touching my forehead I felt something wet. My tongue was soaked in the taste of blood.

"If that's the way you want it," she said, tying my hands with a light blue cord. She got out a cloth – its sweet cloying smell wafted over; I knew it had to be some sort of anaesthetic – chloroform maybe.

"Don't be silly," I said firmly. My head was aching from the blow. "I was only upset because you shouted at me. Of course I want to talk. I owe you an explanation."

"Yeah, right." She stared at me, suspiciously, as if debating her next move. "Yeah, maybe it's best if you stay awake. Just remember, I can still knock you unconscious if you don't do what I say." She wrapped a woollen scarf around my eyes and tied it behind my head. "Don't even think about escaping. The locks are childproof." She banged the door shut, climbed into the driver's seat and started the car.

We drove down the path and then turned, probably onto the main road. My head was throbbing. I let out a moan.

"It's all your own fault," she said crossly. "You shouldn't have lied to me. You left me no other option."

We stopped at what seemed to be a traffic light.

"I didn't lie to you."

"Yes, you did. You said that you'd go to Blackpool with me, and then you went through my stuff and sneaked away to Whitchurch. You thought you were clever, but I saw straight away that you'd been in my room. The suitcase wasn't even zipped up properly, and the photos in the drawer were all mixed up. You thought you'd sussed it all out, that I was untidy and I wouldn't notice you'd been there. But you were so wrong. I always find out about things."

"Where are we going?"

She didn't answer. We drove on in silence. The scarf had loosened a bit and slipped to the bridge of my nose. It was itchy and hot, and I still couldn't see properly, but there was some light coming in.

"Are we going to Blackpool?" I tried again.

"What's it to you?"

I suddenly felt nauseous. There was still that nasty taste of blood. Was it concussion, I wondered. Would I be losing consciousness soon?

"I still want to go."

"Yeah, right. And that's why you went to Whitchurch instead. I thought you were at home waiting for me, but you betrayed me. And now you have to pay for it." Her tone was matter of fact – as if she was telling me about the cleaning rota or an increase in rent.

"Don't be like that," I said. "You said you'd be a few hours, and I thought I'd be back in time. I just thought I should know about you – to understand what you've been through. I understand you better now that I know all those terrible things your mother did to you – and the other stuff."

"What other stuff?"

"The disappointment with Amy."

"What do you know about her?" There was a sharp rise in her voice.

"Only that she betrayed you. She wanted to walk out on you to start a new life, but then she chickened out and killed herself."

"Who told you that?"

"Paula."

"That silly cow," she sneered. "You can't believe a word she says. Always tries to make herself interesting. Did she tell you that she only eats white food? And then she sticks her finger down her throat to spit it all out again. I've never seen anything more disgusting."

I managed to fake a little giggle. "We didn't talk much, but it was terrible to see what it's like inside. What a dump. You must be so glad to be out of there."

"You bet."

There was less stopping and starting at lights. The car was going at a steady speed – we were obviously on a major road. Where on earth were we going?

"Look," I tried again, "I really want to go to Blackpool with you. We can go on the roller coaster and have drinks on the pier, but can't we drive up there tomorrow? We'll be so late if we go now. It takes at least four hours, and it'll be difficult to find somewhere to stay. Why don't we go home first and have something to eat? We could order a pizza. It'll be much more fun tomorrow."

She let out a dismissive laugh. Neither of us said anything for quite a while.

"What did that disgusting woman have to say about my mother?" she said suddenly, as if she had been brooding over it.

"Nothing much. Just that she'd stayed in bed all day, drinking her gin, and that you had to look after her. It really sounds like a terrible childhood. I'm not surprised you hated her."

"What would you know about it, Mrs Psychologist?" she said. "I was glad when she couldn't get up anymore. At least then I was safe."

"Did she hurt you? That's awful. Why didn't you tell someone?"

She didn't answer. We had come off the main road and were driving down a very bumpy path. After a few minutes she drew to the side and parked the car.

"What makes you think we're going to Blackpool?" She turned off the motor. "You must think I'm really stupid."

"I thought that was the plan."

"Yes, *WAS*. Until you told everyone. I saw you on the phone. Pity that you just can't keep things to yourself."

"No, I didn't say anything." I drew a long breath. "You've got it all wrong. I was really looking forward to it."

"Of course you were. That's why you were gone when I came back. That's why you nosed around in my room and tried to dig out stuff about me. You should have trusted me. Oh no, of course you wouldn't tell anyone. You wouldn't betray the only friend you've got left!"

I could hear her rummaging through her bag, looking for something or other. Then she opened her door and got out – a cold draft of air came in. "I won't be long," she said. "Don't even try to get out. There's no point."

She banged the door, and I heard the muffled buzz as she locked it with her key remote. Where was she going?

My head was throbbing as I reached past the front seat. With my tied hands I tried to pull the lock up, but it always went down again. I couldn't hold it up while opening the door. I briefly wondered if I should blow the horn, but there was probably no one around. It would only infuriate her more. I sank back on my seat again, panic gripping me. Had she driven into the woods? Was she going to kill me here? Maybe she was already digging a grave somewhere. Perhaps she wouldn't come back at all. I held my breath, listening for the grating sound of a spade sinking into the ground, but there was nothing but silence. The place seemed deserted – no cries of seagulls, not even the faintest rustling sound of a tree. It was as if nature was conspiring to keep me in the dark.

The pain had taken over my entire head. I felt light-headed and woozy and wondered whether my wound needed stitching up. It seemed an endless wait. After maybe half an hour I heard her hurried footsteps and then she was back.

"We're having a picnic," she said in a cheerful voice. "I've got us some stuff, crisps and some whisky for you. She put the shopping bag on the front seat; I could hear the clunk of the bottle inside. "Don't worry. I also got you something for the pain. Open your mouth."

I did as she told me and took the pills. They were small and bitter, not like painkillers at all. From the taste I guessed that they were tranquillisers. I managed to roll them under my tongue and keep them there as I swallowed the water she poured down my throat.

"Where are we?"

"You'll see soon enough," she said. "We're going for a nice walk later and then we'll have something to eat. You must be starving. Maybe I'll even take off that scarf if you promise to behave."

"Of course. I'll do everything you say."

"Yeah, of course," she said in a sarcastic tone. "We're going to have a good time." She closed the door again from outside.

The pills had mingled with my saliva, and I was beginning to feel a bit drowsy. I rolled over into a foetal position and hid my face behind my tied-up hands. I spat what was left of the pills on the floor, praying that she wouldn't notice. Then I must have nodded off. It didn't feel like much time had passed before she came back.

"Wake up," she said, shaking my shoulders. "I thought you were hungry. It's time for our picnic now."

I tried to get up, but the sudden movement made me feel dizzy, and I fell back on my seat. She opened the back door, grabbed my tied-up wrists and fiercely pulled me outside into the cool air. I staggered against the car.

"For crying out loud," she complained. "What's the matter with you?"

"I can't see."

"Fair enough. We don't want people to get the wrong idea anyway." I could feel her cold hands fiddle with the knot. She chuckled. "Not that there's anyone around so late."

She pulled off the scarf. I blinked to clear my vision, glancing around to see where I was. It was already dark, a bit misty, but the stars and a pale crescent moon gave just enough light. We were on a big patch of land – a car park by the look of it; but there were no other vehicles and no one else about. Turning around, I saw a disused harbour – dark water and a few abandoned boats.

"Let's go." She linked her arm through mine to steady my gait. "Pull yourself together," she growled. "I can't drag you all the way up."

I half-leaned into her as we walked on. We passed

through a gateway with the words *Welcome to Whitmore Bay* and onto a path leading through the woods. The trees were tall and black, blocking out all natural light. There were a lot of leaves on the ground, rotting and slippery underneath our feet. I breathed in the sweet smell of decay.

We were stumbling along in the dark when Frances slipped and nearly fell over. She let go of me, and for a couple of seconds I wondered if I could give her a push and escape. But how could I get away with my hands tied? Images flashed through my mind as I weighed my options. I saw myself tumbling over, unable to get up again – and then the moment was gone.

"For Christ's sake," she screamed, fumbling for my arm.

After a while the trees became sparse, and I caught a glimpse of the black seawater below. There was a breeze and the sound of waves lapping onto the sea rocks.

"Where are we going?"

"The cliffs. I told you we're having a picnic. We'll have a good view from up there."

I glanced at her, but her face gave nothing away. Did she really think I was so drowsy and befuddled that I believed her silly picnic story? She was obviously planning to get rid of me. My breathing sounded heavy and loud in my ears.

Soon, the woods opened onto a concrete path that meandered up through the grass toward the end of the cliffs. The weather had changed. The sky had clouded over and a light drizzle was falling; the fine droplets settled on every surface and dampened my hair. A chilly breeze came towards us; my teeth were chattering with the cold.

"Let's go over there." Frances directed me to the right. "The view is better on the other side."

Her arm still linked with mine, she led me to a bench and made me sit. The descent of the cliffs looked steeper here, not as gently sloping as on the left. Sheets of solid rock charcoal grey shone in the pale light of the moon. The sea crashed violently against the black base. The wind had got stronger and the waves seemed bigger on this side.

"I bet you'd like a nice drop of whisky now," she said, rummaging through her plastic bag. She pulled out the bottle, opened the screw top and held it to my lips. "It's just what you need," she said with a chuckle. "It'll warm you up. Come on, it's good stuff. Have a little sip for me." The acid smell was revolting. I gagged and spluttered like a child. When she tried again, I turned my head and I felt it run down the side of my face.

"For God's sake, watch what you're doing," she growled. "The stuff was expensive."

"My head hurts. I feel sick. Just let me sleep." I closed my eyes and started breathing evenly as if asleep.

"OK, you do that then," she said more patiently. "But first, take a few more painkillers – they will help you with the headache." I heard her going through her bag again.

"Here you are." She grabbed my jaw and forced me to open my mouth. She crammed the pills past my lips, a much bigger dose this time. Again, I rolled them under my tongue.

"It's nice here," I said, slurring my words. "Where are we? Have you been here before?"

"Barry Island." She took a long sip of the whisky. "We used to come here every summer. Of course, it's much nicer when the sun is out. We always went on sunny days. Mother gave me money for the fairground, enough for the rides and candyfloss. I liked the dodgems and the roller coaster. The view from the top was really something. On a clear day you could see all the way to Weston-super-Mare. And the screams when we came down..." Her voice was soft and dreamy.

"Where was your mother?" The pills tasted bitter as the coating wore off – but the fear kept me awake.

"She was always waiting for me in the café on the beach.

She used to sit on the balcony, looking out onto the sea. She was still beautiful then: her eyes blue like the sky. I could keep the little cocktail umbrellas she got with her drinks. On Saturdays we went home at six o'clock. Sometimes her friends came over for a chat. She put bowls of nuts and crisps around the living room for everyone to eat. They sat around talking and drinking, and I could stay up as long as I liked."

"And what happened then?" I mumbled.

"What's it to you?" She unscrewed the bottle and took another slug. "Why aren't you asleep?

"It hurts." I stretched out my tied-up arms. "Can't you take it off?" I started breathing more deeply, my eyes still closed, my head slightly tilted to one side.

She just sat there, silently waiting. After what seemed like ages she got something out of her bag.

"I guess I'll have to do what you want. We don't want to create the wrong impression." She was speaking in a low hoarse voice. "What a shame it has to end like this. We could have been good together. Why did you have to ruin it?" I could feel the cool scissors on my wrists as she cut off the tape. "They all know how crazy you are. No one will be surprised that you killed yourself." She was whispering now. "My mummy was crazy like you. I'll tell you what happened. She couldn't stop drinking, that's what happened. She drank until she was sick everywhere. And when she ran out of booze she sent me to the shops to get more. I had to bring the bottles to her bed because she couldn't get up. She always fell over and hurt herself; there was blood everywhere. It was disgusting. She needed me for every bloody thing, always yelling my name: Frances, Frances!" She burst into an eerie cackle of laughter. "Don't tell me you wouldn't have done the same. Don't pretend! Like you wouldn't have killed that Dr Turner if you'd only had the guts. So I had to do it for you! Like I killed my mum before. I just wanted her to be quiet...

to shut up! That's why I put the pillow on her face. Is that what you wanted to know?" She shook my shoulders. "I tried to wake her up again, but she wouldn't open her eyes – just like you now." She let out a strange sob. "I always knew that you would leave me in the end. Let's get on with it. Get up!"

She rose from her seat and for a moment turned her back. It was my only chance to knock her out and make a run for the car. With a sudden movement I got up and lunged at her. I slammed my fist into her face and pushed her down. Blood poured out of her mouth as she grabbed for my ankles. I staggered and went down as well. We began to roll towards the edge of the cliffs. She managed to lift herself up and with a scream banged my head on the ground.

"You'll pay for that," she cried.

As the back of my head hit something hard everything went black for a few seconds, but a surge of adrenaline gave me a sudden new lease of strength. Blood roared in my ears as my survival instinct took over. I straightened my leg, and with all the force I could muster, kicked her stomach. With a cry of anguish and pain, she let go.

I tried to get up, but the grass was wet and slippery. Still on my hands and knees, I saw her reaching for the bottle. She was standing by the bench, breathing heavily. She stared at me, her eyes wild with hate, the pupils dilated.

"You'll pay for that!" she screamed again and then she started charging towards me, the bottle in her raised hand.

I somehow managed to haul myself up and jump aside. Just in time. I could hear her heavy breathing as she came past. It felt as if everything was in slow motion. Coming to stop at the edge, she slipped on the wet grass. She desperately tried to catch her balance, windmilling her arms, but with a hideous scream went over.

I stood for some moments, staring at the sea. The dim light of the crescent moon shone on the water. There was no sign of her – the sea was still rough. All I could see was the white foam on top of the waves. Sickness welled up in my stomach. I wondered if she could have survived the fall. I imagined her crawling back up any minute, bottle in hand, screaming, but there was nothing but the crashing of the waves against the rocks.

When I turned away at last, I found that her mobile had fallen out of her pocket during the fight. It felt as if my legs were giving way as I walked over to pick it up. I sat down on the bench, switched it on and clicked on her contacts. Scrolling down through her address book, I found a few familiar names: Gemma and Margaret, along with other students I had known at college. There were about fifteen missed calls from Clara. With trembling fingers I rang back.

"It's me, Kate."

"Oh my God! Where are you? Margaret was really worried about you. She said you sent a message. Where is Amy?"

"I'm at Barry Island – on the cliffs. I think she is dead," I choked. "She tried to kill me. I need your help."

EPILOGUE

The police launched a murder enquiry into Dr Turner's death. Clara had already told them what had happened. I was still in hospital when they questioned me. An officer in uniform stood at my bed, making notes. He was middle-aged, in his mid-fifties perhaps, with a protruding belly and a benevolent podgy face. I described how Frances had abducted and drugged me, how she had tried to kill me with the broken bottle and how she had fallen over the cliff.

"She said that she had murdered Dr Turner," I said, a sudden rush of adrenaline making my heart race again. "She probably thought she had done me a favour."

In spite of an extensive search around Whitmore Bay her body was still missing.

They had given me a single room because of the circumstances. My head hurt from the concussion and my mind was still fuzzy. I was very lucky to be alive. The hospital screening test had detected a high concentration of drugs in my blood: benzodiazepines, barbiturates and various other substances. The house was searched and forensics found the tablets stacked in Frances' case. They detected residues in the cups she had left in the sink – there was no doubt that she'd been drugging me with her sweet tea for weeks.

"No wonder you'd been feeling sick and tired all the time," the nurse said, shaking her head. "I'm surprised you were able to function at all."

No. 112 Chapel Road was all over the news. The house was cordoned off from the street and surrounded by police officers. Forensics moved around inside, looking for further evidence. I watched, horrified, from my hospital bed, half-expecting Frances to step out of the front door.

I had mentioned my bloodstained jumper to the police and expected them to arrest me. Maybe I had stabbed him after all. I had imagined it so often that it felt possible. Clara had tried to talk me out of it, but the images kept flashing through my mind: how I had rung his bell, how the knife had pierced his shirt and sunk into his flesh, how I had twisted it and pushed it deeper into his chest. Every night I woke up with a start, drenched in sweat, still imagining his guttural chokes as he lay dying on the ground. I could see his blood gushing out and soaking my jumper! Wasn't that proof enough? Maybe Frances had falsely confessed. What evidence was there that she had done it?

One afternoon the officers came back. My heart missed a beat when I saw their faces in the doorway.

"I hope you're feeling better," the podgy one said politely, but his voice deadly serious. "We need to have another chat."

I hadn't seen his colleague before. He had the build of a teenage boy, but his close-cropped ginger hair was thinning at the crown. He stared at me curiously but dropped his eyes when I glanced back.

"We found more evidence," the older one said. He crossed the room, his black shoes smacking the floor, and sat down in the visitor's chair next to my bed. He rummaged through the pockets of his coat and produced a notebook.

"What is it?" I took a deep breath.

"A pair of jeans with blood on them. We sent them to the lab for tests. Looks as if they belonged to your friend. And the jumper had her DNA on it as well. It was on the deceased too – enough evidence to charge her." He clasped his red hand, cracking his knuckles. "Well," he glanced over at his colleague who stood guard at the door. "You will be relieved that we no longer consider you a suspect. We've confirmed your story that she tried to kill you on the cliffs. You're lucky to have survived that blow with the baseball bat – and all those drugs. They turned out to all be from Whitchurch Hospital. She was certainly one mixed-up lady." He cleared his throat. "We went to Whitchurch and had a word with the staff. It looks as if she killed her friend, Amy, there too, the woman whose family owned the house on Chapel Road. There are witnesses. Frances drugged her as well."

He shook his jowly head. With his flattened features and skin folds around the eyes he looked like a sad old bulldog. "And then she murdered that lecturer of yours. God only knows why she killed the poor man. We suspect that she'd been wearing your jumper to make you look guilty. We've analysed the messages on his phone – it clearly wasn't you talking. His body will be released soon. His folks will be pleased to be able to bury him. They've been waiting nearly two weeks already."

"What about Amy... er, Frances, I mean?" I swallowed hard. "Is she still missing?"

"Yes." He nodded gravely. "But she's got to turn up somewhere."

My mind was swirling when they were gone, unable to take it all in. *It wasn't me*, I thought, my heart hammering wildly in my chest. *I didn't kill him. It was all her doing. I'm not crazy after all!*

I phoned Clara to tell her the news, and she promptly arrived with flowers and grapes. She had some news herself.

"Claudia sends her love," she said looking at me with her clear grey eyes. "She's going back to New York." She gave me an inscrutable smile. "She wants you to know that she's really sorry. She shouldn't have doubted you. I've stripped her bed and emptied her big old wardrobe. We'll store her things in the attic. You should have seen Philip's face when she told us. They got on better straight away. I've never seen them so chummy before. She wants to sort her life out over there. There's unfinished business, she said. Anyway, the room is ready and waiting for you to move in." She absently took one of the grapes, wiped it on her skirt and put it into her mouth. "Philip is already weighed down with guilt. Maybe we should all fly over and visit her in the summer. What do you think?"

DR TURNER'S funeral was held at St Teilo's the following week. It was a grey day with low hanging clouds – the air was heavy with moisture. By then, I was out of hospital and staying with Clara and Philip. We drove together in Clara's old Volvo and parked near the Music Department, a ten-minute walk from the church. The place was heaving. There were wooden folding chairs at the back to accommodate more people. For a moment we waited near the door, but then I saw Margaret in her dark blue trench coat gesturing for us to join her in the second row where she had kept some seats.

Only when I sat next to her did I see the music students in the choir stalls – a lot of familiar faces. Gemma, who was looking ahead, her face pale and serious in the half-light, hadn't seen me yet. Did anyone know that I had been under suspicion, I wondered.

"Everyone will be so glad to see you again," Margaret whispered, as if sensing my thoughts. She touched my arm. "They don't even know you lived with that woman. I'm glad you're out of hospital. I've been so worried. Thank God it's all over now."

I nodded. Earlier in the week a decomposed body had been recovered from the sea near Rhoose, and a nurse from Whitchurch Hospital had identified her as Frances. There was going to be an inquest, but the detectives had reassured me again that no case would be brought against me.

"We miss you in the library. I don't know how we ever managed before you joined," Margaret said. "And don't even think about dropping out. You'll make an excellent teacher."

I glanced at the coffin they had positioned near the altar. The polished mahogany wood gleamed in the light that streamed through the stained-glass window. Sudden tears rose to my eyes. *Oh my God, he's really lying in there*, I thought. *It can't be true!* It was a Wednesday, half past eleven, exactly the time of his class.

The organist began to play and the choir sang *Wie lieblich sind deine Wohnungen* from Brahm's Requiem. The music echoed around the masonry and up to the vaulted ceiling.

"He loved that requiem," Clara whispered next to me. "We sang it with him last year."

The priest had based his sermon on Psalm 23. "Though I walk through the valley of the shadow of death, I will fear no evil: for thou art with me; thy rod and thy staff they comfort me."

Then his daughter came to the front, a teenager still, maybe thirteen or fourteen years of age, with a pale face and soft brown eyes. Dr Turner's eyes, I thought. She described what a wonderful dad he had been and how she would miss him every single day. She spoke of an event from her child-hood, but I could hardly understand through her desolate sobs.

There were other speakers after her, friends and colleagues – and finally Philip. He said what a generous friend Dr Turner had been to him, how he had let him sleep on his sofa for months in London when he had had nowhere to go.

I tried to focus, but my mind was fogged up and I found it increasingly difficult to follow. Post-traumatic stress disorder they had told me at the hospital. The fog was apparently nature's way to numb the pain. And there were other symptoms too: terrible nightmares and flashbacks of Frances, running towards me on the cliffs, trying to kill me with the broken bottle in her hand.

By the end of the service, my heart was racing, and it felt as if the walls were closing in on me.

"I need to get out of here," I whispered, pushing my way past Clara. "I need to clear my head."

THE MIST OUTSIDE had turned into drizzle, but I didn't open my umbrella. The cold rain in my face felt redeeming – as if it could wash away my thoughts. I began walking down Crwys Road and stopped on the railway bridge. Leaning over the iron railing, I watched a freight train thunder past. When it was gone I kept looking, my eyes fixed on the rails. Then, slowly, as if in a trance, I made my way down the old stone stairs.

The house was no longer cordoned off. There it was, dirty and bleak, with the same old weeds growing through the cracks. It was as if nothing had changed: the bowed stone wall at the front, the shabby and uncared for garden, the dirty lace curtains downstairs.

It was almost exactly three months since I had stood there on a rainy day, looking at its gloomy front, wondering what the woman inside would be like. Only twelve weeks – but everything had changed. Would I ever be my normal self again, without the dreadful nightmares and panic attacks? Would I be able to forget and keep those images out of my mind? Would I be able to trust?

There had to be a better future – a future without the urge to run, to escape and hide away. Clara and Philip were very supportive and patient with me. The doctor said that it would get better with time. Maybe I could be a teacher one day after all. *I just have to carry on trying*, I thought as I turned and walked away. *I just have to keep on – one step at a time.*

THANK YOU FOR READING

Did you enjoy reading *The Tenant*? Please consider leaving a review on Amazon. Your review will help other readers to discover the novel.

ABOUT THE AUTHOR

Angela Lester loves writing psychological suspense that explores the dark side of human nature.

A philosophy graduate, she came over from Germany in 1991 and has lived in Cardiff ever since. She plays the piano, sings in a choir and loves walking in the great Welsh countryside. She has worked as bookseller and translator, but her real passion is writing. She has written short stories and novels in German and English. *The Tenant* is her first published thriller.